Northwest of Boston
Stories

To Mark

Best wishes for Christmas
and a great 2023.

Stuh Olm
12/22

NORTHWEST OF BOSTON

STORIES

STEPHEN O'CONNOR

LP

Loom Press
Amesbury, Massachusetts
2023

Book design: Keith Finch
Cover art: Brian O'Connor
Author photograph: Kevin Cavanaugh
Printing: Versa Press, Illinois
Typeface: Bobbin, Bebas Neue and Adobe Caslon Pro

Loom Press
15 Atlantic View, Amesbury, MA 01913
www.loompress.com
info@loompress.com

Stephen O'Connor: oconnorsteve41@gmail.com
Instagram: @briman_draws

The stories in *Northwest of Boston* are works of fiction. All incidents and dialogue, and all characters with the exception of some well-known or historical figures, are products of the author's imagination and not to be construed as real. Where real life or historical figures appear, the situations and dialogues concerning those persons are fictional and are not intended to depict actual events or to change the fictional nature of the stories.

It is true that we shall never reach the goal; it is even more than probable that there is no such place. And if we lived for centuries and were endowed with the powers of a god, we should find ourselves not much nearer what we wanted at the end. O toiling hands of mortals! O unwearied feet, traveling we know not whither! Soon, soon, it seems to you, you must come forth on some conspicuous hilltop, and but a little further away, against the setting sun, descry the spires of El Dorado. Little do ye know your own blessedness; for to travel hopefully is better than to arrive, and the true success is to labor.

—Robert Louis Stevenson, "El Dorado"

For the laboring men and women of Lowell and everywhere: the immigrants, including my Irish grandparents and my Colombian wife and her family; the roofers and accountants, the refugees struggling for a foothold, the diner waitresses and car mechanics; the factory workers, the drywallers and nurses, the teachers, the plumbers, the cops on patrol and the weary bartender who extends last call for the soldier come home.

Contents

Continued

July 19th, 1969

Saturday night. Jack Sheils stopped at the corner of Westford and Coral and leaned against a telephone pole. "Outa shape," he muttered. He should never have taken the desk job at the post office. Up until five years ago, and for the previous nineteen years he'd been on his dogs, walking the South Lowell route every day. And before that, he was drilling with the 5th Infantry in Northern Ireland and then marching around Normandy and into the Rhineland. The Red Diamond Division under General Stafford Leroy Irwin. Their motto: *We will*.

He clasped his short-sleeved shirt between a thumb and index finger and gave it several tugs to feel something like a breeze on his chest. Gazing upward, he saw that a few stars were visible through clouds, yellowed somewhat by the city lights. He recalled as he walked on into Cupples Square that it had been named after Lorne Cupples, a WWI soldier who suffered severe stomach wounds near

Verdun. After visiting him, the chaplain wrote to his family, "He will die like a soldier, and that is the greatest thing to do."

Jack set off through the square along Westford Street, some part of his mind, as ever, wandering the old paths of war and remembering some of those faces that would not be seen again. But his mind also kept turning to the Americans out there in space, beyond help, hopefully not beyond prayers, relying on machines to get them to the goddamn moon and back. Machines break down, which was why he was on foot. He had bought a 1964 Ford from a guy in Pawtucketville. "Runs like new," the guy said. It had, for a while. But engines malfunction. Parts give out. Joey Geoffroy was putting in a new water pump for him on Monday, so Jack had to hoof it for the weekend. The car was a Galaxie Sunliner. Joey pulled a water pump out of a wrecked Galaxie Victoria, but he said it'd be compatible, and Joey knew.

He wondered if the Apollo craft had a water pump. Ah, but a dried-out seal, a loose belt, an oil leak; any of the thousand glitches in a complicated machine could spell doom for those spacemen. They must have great faith in the engineers and in the men and women who put the rocket and the capsule together. Great courage, too. Courage to spare. There were always those who would say, "*We will.*" Even after the last crew was burned alive on the launch pad. He told himself that NASA had learned from that tragedy, and, after all, it was no Ford Galaxie they were taking out to the galaxy.

A couple of drunks were hollering incoherent accusations at each other outside the Highland Tap. A gaggle of co-drunkards had issued from the bar and were trying to separate them and calm them down. How quiet it must be on the moon. Jack had even heard birds in the Ardennes, and you wouldn't believe they would stay in those cratered forests where trees fell like so many matchsticks under a rain of German artillery. But on the moon, there were no birds, no crickets, no Harleys thundering past, no howling drunks. The silence must be terrifying. Only the sound of your own breath—inhale and exhale—

inside that claustrophobic helmet. Terrifying. To be stranded alive on the moon if the engine failed—a lonely death in silence—sympathetic radio voices. But then, they knew that well, and as Shakespeare said, *the readiness is all.* Sometimes, during the siege of Metz, at the Bulge, or later, smashing through the Siegfried Line, Jack had envied the dead. The torn limbs and the thousand-mile stares, the screaming missiles, the frantic digging at the frozen earth—it was all over for them.

He supposed that the idea of safety was an illusion down here. After all, as they say, the earth is just a big spaceship. But the illusion is comforting. Our tether to life seems more secure on solid familiar ground, though many are happy and healthy tonight who'll be dead before the astronauts are scheduled to return. Mary Jo Kopechne was a carefree young girl when the astronauts set off on their mission, and she had already drowned in a car.

And look at poor Finny Doyle. Jack hadn't seen him in years; then today when he was driving with Joey G. down Parker Street to go to the scrap car lots on Tanner Street, he saw him getting out of a car with a woman Jack didn't know. "Slow down a minute, Joey. I know this guy." He rolled down the window and said, "Hey Finny!"

Haltingly, he turned and said, "Hi, Jack," in a soulless voice while the woman kept walking.

"How the hell are you?" Jack asked, pretending he didn't notice that his old friend looked bad.

"I'm dying," he said and followed the woman.

Poor Finny. Jack called Charlie Samis later and found out that Finny's liver was shot. Kidneys too. He was on borrowed time. Charlie said that on Finny's last visit, the doctor had said, "I can't believe you're still alive." What a thing to say to a person. Jack thought he'd like to find out who that doctor was and give him a good shot in the kisser. And so, later in the afternoon, he had walked down to Molloy's Bar, because sitting at home Jack kept thinking of his old friend's yellow face, and the words: "I'm dying." And he had drunk too many beers, not to mention the shots of Jamie, but at least there was a ball game on the radio in the bar, and a few guys to talk to about whether Ted Kennedy was all done, and about whether they would like to go to the moon if they had the chance. Dick Guthrie said he'd go in a heartbeat, but everyone knows brave words in a barroom don't amount to much.

Jack quickened his wavering pace because he had to piss. He walked up the front steps of 832 Westford Street but was having trouble getting the key into the door. He heard a screen rising in a window above him. The landlady, Mrs. Powers, leaned out.

"Mr. Sheils?"

"Yes, Mrs. Powers?"

"I thought that was you."

"Yes, Mrs. Powers. My key . . . ."

"Mr. Sheils, you don't live here anymore."

The thought clouds that had hovered over his brain began to thin, and he recalled that yes, he had moved out of this place. "Jesus Christ!" he said. "Excuse me, Mrs. Powers."

"That's all right, Mr. Sheils."

He turned about and descended the steps but paused at the bottom and looked back up, where the old woman could still be seen in the window frame. He was all fuddled. He could recall the look of the new place, but for the moment couldn't remember the best direction to get there. "Mrs. Powers?"

"Yes?"

He was feeling a bit light-headed. "Where . . . where is it I live now?"

"It's 82 Harris Avenue, behind..."

"Oh, yes, of course. Thank you. Behind the church."

"Would you like a cup of coffee, Mr. Sheils? I think you need a cup of coffee."

"That's very kind of you, Mrs. Powers. You know, I think I would like a cup of coffee, and if I could use your bathroom?"

"Of course."

The old woman went into the kitchen to make coffee while Jack found the bathroom. He recalled the last time he had been in this apartment. He had heard a thud above him and came upstairs to discover that her husband Tom had fallen. He helped Mrs. Powers get him onto the couch, where Tom normally sat all day in his housecoat smoking Raleigh cigarettes and speaking in a jumbled way that only his wife could understand. He had returned to her from the Great War a shadow of the man she had married. Jack couldn't recall if it had been gas or shell shock or what, but poor Tom was done. All done.

When Jack had taken a seat in the small living room, Mrs. Powers called from the kitchen, "How do you take it, Mr. Sheils?"

"No sugar, thank you. Dash of milk if you have it." He looked around the room. The walls were papered with a botanical design, lush ferns and hanging leaves in muted colors. A bit Victorian, Jack thought, but reassuringly homey. A bowl of plastic apples sat atop a Magnavox television set. Neat writing desk with mail sorted into slots. Bookcase beside his chair. He leaned sideways to read the titles: *Longfellow's Poems. The Conquest of Mexico. Little Women. Emerson's Essays. Forty Easy Meals You'll Be Proud to Serve.* There was a photo of her late husband in his military uniform on a side table, and above the couch where her husband used to sit, a painting of a ship that appeared to be struggling in a storm. Oval braided rug. All order and peace here, and it made Jack feel calm. The smell of old Tom's cigarettes still lingered under the smell of furniture polish, giving his ghostly presence substance.

When she came in with the coffee on a tray, he rose instinctively, but she told him to sit down, she had everything in hand. "Now drink that," she said. "And shall I make you a ham and cheese sandwich?"

"Oh, no thank you, Mrs. Powers. This is an awful lot of trouble for you."

"Well, as my old mother used to say, it's not very Irish to offer a guest something to drink and nothing to eat." Before she went back to the kitchen, though, she went to a hall closet and came back with a fan. She moved her husband's picture and put the fan on the table directed at him. "Very warm tonight," she said and went off to the kitchen while he sat placidly sipping his coffee and listening to the sounds of a dish retrieved from a cupboard, the jangle of silverware in a drawer, a jar of mayonnaise set down and meat unwrapped. The sounds and his position brought him back to the day when he first returned from the war and his mother hugged him and cried, pushed him into his father's stuffed chair and ran off to the kitchen to get him food.

"You're too kind, Mrs. Powers," he said when she set the sandwich on the hassock in front of him. Only then did he realize that he was hungry and began to eat.

"Well, I do miss you, Mr. Sheils. You were a fine tenant. Up every morning and out to work. Lights out at ten o'clock. Kept the front walk shoveled in winter. Helped me with Tom that time." She shook her gray head. "And thank you for coming to his funeral."

"Not at all. You were very good to him. And he sacrificed a lot for his country."

"Yes, he did. We all did. I often recall the words of Milton: *They also serve who only stand and wait.*"

He nodded and swallowed. "Yes."

She sat up then and smiled indulgently, "Now I never knew you to be a big drinker, Mr. Sheils, except at Christmas, maybe. I hope nothing is troubling you."

"You needn't worry. It's just . . . did you ever feel a sense of foreboding?"

"A premonition?"

"Not a premonition of anything in particular. Not like, you know, I'm afraid to get on this airplane. It's just . . . I don't know. It's the country. It's a bad time. Ted Kennedy drove off a bridge with that young girl. She went under, and he didn't call the police. He just left. Why would he do that? They say sometimes there's an air pocket in the cab of the car. What if she was alive for some time? Why didn't he wake up everyone and get help? Get the divers down there."

Mrs. Powers sighed. "He says he was confused."

"His brother wasn't confused after an enemy destroyer cut his PT boat in half in the middle of the night, and the oil burned in the sea all around them. He took command and saved lives. A leader has to keep his head and do what he can do." He shook his head. "It's a bad time. About two, three weeks ago, *Life* magazine published photographs of 242 young kids killed in Vietnam in one week. *One week.* And nobody is sure what we're supposed to accomplish over there. And then today, I saw an old friend and it seems his liver is gone, and he told me he was dying. That's all he said. I said, 'How are you?' And he said, 'I'm dying.' And he walked away. What do you say to that?"

"Oh dear," she said. "My, my."

"And I find myself wondering, or worrying really, about these guys up in that little capsule hurtling through space. How far is the moon, Mrs. Powers, do you know?"

"Yes, as a matter of fact, I looked it up in my encyclopedia today. It's 240,000 miles away."

"And sometimes it looks so close. But think of that. It's what . . . three thousand miles from Lowell to the Pacific Ocean? Think of all the cities and plains and rivers and mountain ranges and trackless rolling forests and vast deserts between here and there. That's just three thousand miles. They're going two hundred and forty thousand miles away from every other human. No one has ever been that alone. America needs heroes badly right now, Mrs. Powers. And I'm so proud of them, you know, but I find myself very tense lately. Worrying about them."

"Yes. I can understand that Mr. Sheils."

"That's why I overdid it a bit tonight. All of that."

"Yes."

He took another bite of his sandwich and sipped his coffee. The old woman watched him. The fan blew his graying hair. Her husband had never been fit to have children with her, and how could she have raised a child with him anyway? She thought that if she had had a son, he might be around this man's age.

"It's none of my business, Mr. Sheils, but did you never think to get married? You would have made some girl a fine husband."

"I became a cynic, Mrs. Powers. Would my parents have brought me into this world if they could have known that in my prime of youth I'd be sent off to war? I don't think so. Not if they knew what that meant." He paused and looked down at the braided rug. His brow furrowed as if he were trying to solve a problem. "In May of '45, just a few days after the surrender, I accompanied medics of the 5th to Czechoslovakia. *Helmbrecht*. It had been a concentration camp for women. I won't describe it, Mrs. Powers. I can't describe it. You lose, or I lost, the will to bring children into a world with so much evil in it. And suppose I had come home and married a nice young woman and had a son. It's the same thing all over again. Two hundred and forty-two boys in a week, Mrs. Powers. Maybe my son would be one of them. Or like this poor Callery boy they renamed Highland Park for just a few years ago. Or, forgive me, your husband who suffered so much from the First World War. It goes on and on. People never learn."

The old woman looked at her hands as if she could find some answer there and then clasped them together, twisting the gold band of an old promise on her finger. "I can certainly understand your feelings, Mr. Sheils."

He finished his sandwich and rose. "I feel so much better. I guess I hadn't really eaten today. Thank you, Mrs. Powers. Sorry to trouble you like this. What a dope, standing at the door with the wrong key."

"We are creatures of habit. It's no trouble at all. Do take care of yourself, Mr. Sheils."

"I will. By the way, I was happy living here. It's just, there's no yard here, you see, and I wanted to have a bird feeder, and you know, be able to watch the birds. I want to sit in the yard and watch the sparrows, the blue jays, the cardinals. It relaxes me. Read the paper out there. I like being outside."

"You don't need to explain anything to me. They say a change is as good as a rest."

"I just wanted you to know."

He took her hand in his and held it warmly, thanking her once again. She reminded him that they were going to show the moon landing on the television the next evening—she didn't know what time. "I'll be praying along with you, Mr. Sheils," she said. "They say they plan to land on a part of the moon called the Sea of Tranquility."

"Beautiful name," Jack said.

"Lovely name, isn't it? Poetic. Like 'the infinite meadows of heaven.' That's Longfellow."

On the way home, Jack stopped at Highland Park—Callery Park now. He said a brief prayer for Billy Callery at the stone memorial. PFC Callery had joined that endless column of ghostly infantry. Jack didn't know if it made any sense, or whether it was a good war, or if there was such a thing. But he had nothing but respect for those dead; all the young soldiers who once stood shoulder to shoulder under a rain of fire and wore on their shoulders the insignias of their units, the Big Red One, the Lucky 13th, the Pathfinders.

So many had never known old age, but by God, they had known brotherhood.

Jack wandered farther into the park and sat on one of the old swings that had rocked him through the air as a boy. The clouds had moved on. Gripping the cool chains in his hands, he leaned back and saw above the belfry of St. Margaret's Church, a half-moon like a glowing cup in the sky. Tears gathered in his eyes, as he whispered to the infinite meadows of heaven. "Come on, Apollo! Fly right! Do it, men! Christ Almighty, we need some good news down here."

Jailbird

December 22nd. Two men sat at a bar in Lowell, Massachusetts. It should have been snowing gently outside the plate glass windows that overlooked Middle and Central Streets, but it was pissing rain. One of the men, Emmet Burke, was gazing out the window, watching the rainfall through the yellow halo of a street lamp and thinking it was another example of how the real never measured up to the ideal, which of course was the White Christmas that Bing Crosby had made famous; Irving Berlin's nostalgic ode to some wonderful days we used to know, a perfect holiday that never really existed—the Christmas in the ads where everyone is wearing warm socks and drinking hot chocolate by the fire and harmony reigns. A beautiful lie. Like people who die in the movies. The sun is setting, and their loved ones are around, and they say some touching and memorable thing or pass on some beautiful secret and expire in the radiance of grace. The truth is, people often die crazy, in some nursing home that smells like dirty diapers, howling at the staff to fuck off and wheezing and gasping for that last breath. But not Bing Crosby.

"You know how Bing Crosby died?" Emmet asked his friend. "You know what his last words were?"

Tony Dos Santos turned away from the TV news, where a professor was explaining that mistletoe was an invitation to sexual harassment. "I made a lot of crappy movies?"

"He should have said that. He said, 'That was a great round of golf,' and he died. Right there on the golf course. He was a hell of a golfer. Better golfer than an actor."

"I hate golf, but that's a good death. Clean."

"Damned right. 'That was a great round.' Boom! I dream about dying sometimes. I'm always in a crash—an airplane or a car crash. And I survive the wreck, but then I know I'm dying. Hope that's not an omen, a foreshadowing."

"I have the same dream over and over—what do they call it?"

"A recurring dream."

"Right. Yeah, I have a recurring dream that I'm back in the slammer. The guard comes by and I ask him, 'When is my release date? Isn't it soon?' And the guard says, 'No, they added a few years, Tony.' And I'm there screaming, 'Why? What did I do?' I wake myself up yelling at the guard."

"That's a shitty dream."

"Awful. Sometimes I jump up with my heart pounding like crazy."

Emmet watched Tony gulp his Michelob Ultra. There were fewer calories, he'd told him, but Christ, that battle was lost. With the extra weight he'd put on after his release and his bad knees, Tony lumbered a bit now, especially after his eight-hour shift in the kitchen of the Falstaff Club. He was a shadow, a fat shadow, of the tough bastard he'd been before he spent two decades in the can for armed robbery.

In jail, he was recruited by gangsters who may have heard of him or seen him box in the Golden Gloves or watched him pound the shit out of the heavy bag in the gym, but somehow, he'd managed to steer clear of any affiliation. Work out and study and do his job in the kitchen; that was his life for twenty years. Got his GED in there, and then his associate degree in culinary arts. A woman who came in to teach a literature class got him into reading; he had plenty of time, and he started to read a lot. He told Emmet he read Jack London, Hemingway, Jack Kerouac, Kurt Vonnegut, Ursula LeGuin—a lot of books—even poetry. If you thought Tony was dumb just because he was a jailbird, you were mistaken. That's why Emmet liked him. He had originally been friends with his younger brother. He'd met Tony through him, though of course, he had heard the stories. Tony Dos Santos was a local legend, or had been. The legend was old now. The young guys didn't even know him. People forget when you're away for twenty years.

He noticed that Tony's beer was empty. He finished his draft and ordered another round. There was a Christmas tree set up at the far end of the bar. When the aging ex-con turned toward him, Emmet saw that the lenses of his glasses were spangled with the reflected blues, greens, and reds of its bulbs. But he also saw, or felt, that the eyes beneath that shower of joyful color were anxious. Jerry, the bartender, brought their beers and asked if they thought the Patriots had a shot at the Super Bowl this year. They both shook their heads and agreed they didn't have the horses. "Father Time is catching up with Brady," Tony said. "And he's undefeated."

"And this fella here knows about time!" Jerry said.

Tony nodded gravely. "Seconds, hours, and years," he said. He spoke the words as if they were a malediction or awoke the memory of pain.

Emmet pushed some bills across the bar and said, "That's good." Jerry nodded and rang the tip bell as he opened the register. Emmet reached for his draft and slid the Michelob toward Tony. To cheer him up, he said, "Dreams aside, you're out, and you'll never be back in the Big House. You're a law-abiding citizen now."

Tony didn't respond. He swigged his beer and looked at the Christmas tree. Finally, he said, "Let's take our beers over to the booth in the corner. I need your advice."

"Sure," Emmet said, and with his cell phone and damp coat in one hand and his beer in the other, he led the way. When they were installed at the table, the older man leaned forward and said, "I want to tell you something. I have to warn you that by telling you, I may be putting you in great danger. So, if you'd rather not hear it, I understand."

"Will I be able to protect myself?"

"Yeah, you just need to keep your mouth shut."

"I can do that."

"This information is dangerous to know because it's deadly to repeat. That's why I'm warning you."

"I get it, Tony. All you need to say is don't tell anyone. I take that very seriously."

Tony nodded and seemed to relax as if he were breathing freely at last. "Good. Good. I do know that. That's why I'm talking to you." He loosened his scarf. "Warm in here," he said and took a slug of his beer.

Someone at the bar yelled, "Who gives a shit about the news? Put the Bruins on!" A cacophony of voices arose. Emmet heard none of it, only the low voice of his companion—the quiet voice of experience, of dues paid, of a life redeemed.

"There's a guy," Tony began. "His name is one you would have heard. A street soldier from a particular gang of criminals. I won't repeat names here because that knowledge can only hurt you. He would kill you if his bosses told him to, or for a fee, or just because he doesn't like you. He'd kill you and think no more of it than you would of slapping a mosquito on your arm. I know him from the old days when I was doing drugs and robbing banks, and he knows me. Now there's another guy. He comes into the club most days, most weekdays, for lunch. And this killer—he wants him dead."

"Why?" Emmet asked.

"Hold off on that for now."

"Okay."

"So, this person, this street soldier, approaches me as I'm leaving the club the other night. I was not happy to see him. Like I said, he's a very bad person. He doesn't live in Lowell anymore, I don't think, so I was nervous. He slaps me on the back like he wants to talk about old times. 'Let's have a beer at the Worthen,' he says. You don't say no, Emmet. So, we cross the street and walk over to the Worthen, get a beer, and sit down, and finally, he says, 'I hear you're a cook at the Falstaff. That's where'—and he mentions this other guy's name—'comes in for lunch quite a bit.'

'Yeah,' I say, 'he's a regular.'"

The door near the two men opened, and they turned to see a couple coming in, lowering a shared umbrella. Emmet had been half expecting to see some scowling street soldier of an unnamed gang. A cheer rose from the bar, and he glanced over at the TV. Krejci had scored and was gliding over the ice, his stick raised in triumph. He squinted to see the score. Two-zip, Bruins. He turned back to Tony, who was thumbing the label off his beer bottle. "So, he asks you about this other guy . . . ."

"Right. And he asks me what the guy orders. I say, 'You know, soup and a sandwich, usually. That's what he likes.'

'Listen, Tony,' he says, 'I need a favor. I'm going to give you something, and I want you to put it in his soup. He won't taste it, and people will think he had a heart attack. Happens all the time. He's in a high-stress occupation anyway. And if they ever found it in him, anyone could have put it in his soup when he went to the men's room or whatever. There's a crowd at lunch, right? You will have cleared off his table and put the rest of the soup down the drain and cleaned the bowl. The poison will come in a small paper container. You burn it at the gas stove flame, or flush it, put it in the garbage disposal. There's no evidence. None. Someone could have poisoned him before he ever got to the club.'"

"Jesus H. Christ," Emmet said. "What did you say?"

"I said, 'Listen, I can't—I can't do that. I'm sorry. I'd like to help you out, but I can't do that.' I told him about my recurring dream, that I'd rather die than go back, that I follow the rules now 'cause I can't do any more time. I'm too fuckin' old.' I tell him all that because he can understand it, you see? I don't say, 'I'm not a killer. I never was.' I was a bank robber, Emmet. Yes. But I never shot a teller. I never would have, really. Like that old song says, 'I walked in a lot of places I never shoulda been.' That's true, but a killer I never was."

"How did he take it?"

"He listened, and he stared at me—right into me. I'm telling you when you look into the eyes of a guy like that, you can feel the cold. They have no feelings, Emmet, no sympathy, no conscience. Then he says, 'Five grand now and ten grand after? Would that change your mind? You know, the price is negotiable.' I told him it wasn't a question of money. I just couldn't do it. Finally, he says, 'I understand. People will be disappointed, but I'll explain the situation. You don't have to worry, Tony. I always liked you. When you went down, you kept your mouth shut and did your time. I respect that, and we'll do right by you. Only one thing I'm sure you already know. If it ever gets back to me that you told anyone what we discussed here tonight, *I will* kill you.' I told him I wouldn't blame him, and he got up and left."

After he had heard the story, Emmet said, "What's the problem? My advice is to shut up. Mafiosos kill each other all the time. You're not going to change that. You're off the hook."

"This guy they want to kill is not a mafioso. He's law enforcement."

"Not my brother! Is that why you're telling me?"

"Not your brother. Your brother would know him. This guy is a prosecutor in the city."

"Shit."

"I told you I wanted your advice, Emmet. That's not true. I guess I want your approval. Like I said, I did a lot of reading in jail, a lot of thinking. Who am I? Who do I want to be? It's almost Christmas, and I thought, how am I going to feel when this guy's family celebrates Christmas without him because some piece of shit doesn't like the way he does his job, and me, I just let it happen."

"You already told the cops."

He nodded. "I ain't gonna die like Bing Crosby, Emmet. But I'm at peace with that. I taped a deposition this morning."

Emmet's brother told him, a month later, that the cops had arrested Greaser DeCola, Mule Murray, and Garret Buckley and charged them with conspiracy to commit murder and a string of other crimes.

"Who were they planning to murder?"

"Tom Benchley, works for the DA. There was an informant. Then they got a wiretap that confirmed the contract these guys were planning to put out. The cops offered the informant witness protection, but he says he's going to stay in the city."

"Well, maybe when they're locked up . . . ."

His brother let out a skeptical chuckle. "Yeah. Good luck with that."

Emmet called Tony and pleaded with him to take the offer of protection. There was resignation in Tony's voice. "Come on, Emmet," he said. "I'm old and fat and worn out. Too tired to go count the days in some strange place. That's just another kind of jail. I never wore a mask when I robbed banks. Never liked to hide. Maybe that was stupid. But I won't start hiding now. I did what I did."

A month later, Tony disappeared. His body was discovered shortly after near the Pawtucket Gatehouse, tangled among the debris that gathered at the flashboards above the falls. There were two bullets in his head and the word "RAT" scrawled in marker across his shattered face. Emmet found that he was crying as he read the account in *The Lowell Sun*. He let the newspaper fall, and his head sank into his hands.

What a crazy world, he thought. We have priests who say they devote their lives to Christ and end up raping children. Respected lawyers whose job it is to help killers go free. Politicians who swear they just want to serve us, and no one can understand how they got so rich. And then you have a convict who dies for a stranger because he doesn't want to think of his kids facing Christmas without Dad.

He looked toward the ceiling and spoke to the spirit of his friend, or to his image in memory: *This whole stinking ship is full of rats. But Tony Dos Santos, you were not one of them.*

Cast a Cold Eye

I'll call him—well—considering the nature of the story—I'll call him Marley. And then I can say, along with old Boz, "Marley was dead." That is, he was dead to me. I believed him to be dead. Was I certain? Well, I didn't see the body. How do we know that most people are dead? We hear it. I don't get the local paper, so I'm not likely to read an obituary. Usually, what happens is I get gabbing with some high school chum about the old days and a name comes up, and I ask, "Is he still around?" And the chum says, "No, he died in the late nineties," and adds the cause of death if he knows it. Or, for instance, last Saturday morning, down at the coffee shop, I hear someone say, "Jeez, I saw Kate Ross just the other day at Brook Farm. She was walking out there with her dog, the Australian collie or whatever they call them with the blue eyes. She was a big hiker. She used to post a lot of pictures of sailing on the Merrimack."

"Kate Ross died?" I ask.

And everyone nods, and the same someone says, "Never sick a day in her life. Just told her daughter she was tired and wanted to lie down and—boom! Just like that."

This news requires that I readjust my mental picture of the world. Kate Ross—dead. No more to walk with the blue-eyed dog, nor wander fields where the moorcock calls, nor glide under a billowing canvas over the back of the Merrimack, nor tweet, nor post, nor like. Nor nothing. Alas, we could not entice her a while to stay. *In nomine Patris et Filii et Spiritus Sancti.*

How did I hear that Marley was dead? It began more gently. I heard he was sick. Then I heard he was in a coma. Weeks later, I heard that his stomach was full of some strange bacteria—ripe with it—and that these bacteria were multiplying and could not be killed by any intravenous antibiotic. Poor guy was nothing more than a comatose bio-hazard bomb. I understood he would never come out of it, that they had told his wife to prepare herself and to make the arrangements. I heard she went and picked out a coffin. And then I didn't hear anything for a couple of days, but when I asked, I heard—I clearly heard someone say: "Marley is dead." I had no reason to disbelieve it. Consequently, I made the mental adjustment. Marley and his bacteria—gone. I hung his image, the affable pock-marked face topped with wispy hair, in the "Gallery of the Dead," that hall of portraits in our minds that grows longer with time.

I didn't think it odd that I heard nothing of the funeral because Marley was not a close friend. I taught an English class for blockheads in summer school for a few years, while he was teaching an Algebra class, but we worked at different schools during the year. I'd see him around the building during the summer session, coming or going, maybe exchange a bit of Red Sox chat in the lounge area, and then, the five weeks were up. I wouldn't see him again until the next summer if I worked. But I would run into George or Linda, or other people connected with the program who knew him better than I, and it was they who had informed me of his lapse into a coma, of his impending demise, and one of them, I forget whom, of his passing. I said a brief prayer, after my agnostic but literary fashion:

O man! hold thee on in courage of soul
Through the stormy shades of thy wordly way,
And the billows of clouds that around thee roll
Shall sleep in the light of a wondrous day,
Where hell and heaven shall leave thee free
To the universe of destiny.

That evening, out on the deck, I raised a glass of vino to him. "You were a good sort, Marley," I said to the moony night. "Farewell!" I thought little more of Marley, to be honest. I had my own death to think about, which could not be far off, relatively.

Dead. Toasted. Hopefully not roasted. Picture in the gallery. Gone. Mental Adjustment complete. Bacteria victorious. Man defeated. Life goes on sans Marley.

Six months later, I found myself in an old mill building which had been converted for modern use, and where on the sixth floor, my doctor bustles about in his white coat. After my checkup, I was descending on the elevator with four or five other people, thinking about my slightly high cholesterol, my climbing PSA, and the doctor's admonition to cut the drinking down to two glasses a week. A week! Barbarous. I was lost in these sullen reflections, examining my reflection in the polished silver doors in front of me, when the car jolted to a stop with a jarring ding and the doors slid open. And there, directly in front of me, a foot away, on two living legs, looking a bit pale but not ghostly, was a living Marley with his pock-marked face and wispy hair. "Jeeeeesus Christ!" I cried, (unwittingly invoking the name of an earlier resurrectee). I staggered backward into the citizens who, in their efforts to exit, were pushing me toward the dead man.

There were expressions of bewilderment from those who had traveled down the shaft with me as I resisted their propulsion. The reason for my odd behavior was instantly made clear to them by my tactless, tasteless, and utterly spontaneous cry, "I thought you were dead!"

Marley stopped there in front of the elevator and responded casually, "Everyone thought I was dead." The crowd sauntered on, looking over their shoulders, while an elderly couple shuffled onto the elevator, which left without my now living friend.

I resisted the temptation to test his substantiality with a poke. "What the hell happened, Marley?"

"No one really knows. After they had given me up for a goner, I suddenly woke up, and I recovered."

"I apologize for my outburst," I said. He shrugged it off. I was still puzzled. "So—now—I don't know how to say this, but didn't they tell your wife to make the funeral arrangements?"

"Yup. She bought the very cheapest coffin they had, by the way. Not that I would have noticed . . . ."

"No. I suppose not."

"Still . . . ." he said, looking somewhat wounded. He asked if I would be doing the summer school that year and we spoke about that. The ding sounded, the elevator doors opened again, and I realized I must be holding him up from some appointment. "Well, I'm very glad to find you so... not dead."

"Thanks."

As I said, we were not close friends, and we had exhausted the momentous topics of summer school and his not being dead. "Let's get together for coffee sometime," I said in parting.

"Sure. Great," he said, but I didn't even have his number, and as my grandfather used to say, "Sometime is no time."

The final act of this little drama came a few months after the elevator encounter. I ran into George at Market Basket. "Hey, hey, hey," he said. That was his customary greeting.

"Have you seen Marley?" I asked.

"Poor Marley's dead," he said.

"No! He isn't! I ran into him downtown. Let me see, it was . . . ."

"He died on Friday."

Now I had just removed the image of Marley from the Gallery of the Dead and replaced the old familiar image triumphantly upright on the plane of the living. With us. And here was George telling me to lay poor Marley low once more. "Are you sure he's dead?" I asked.

"I ran into Dick Mulligan at the Worthen. He mentioned it."

"Dick Mulligan mentioned it, eh? That's the same Mulligan who once told us he was having a sexual relationship with a female demon spirit, an incubus?"

"I think it was a succubus. The difference is . . . ."

"I don't care what the difference is! Mulligan is *non-compos mentis*. I'm not going to be surprised by a living Marley again based on Mulligan's word. I'm going to investigate."

Investigate I did. I cut my food shopping short and drove home to search online through the obits in *The Lowell Sun*. Well, there was no question. There, among the photos of the recently dead, was the pockmarked face, the wispy hair, and the placid eyes taking a last peek at the living public. "Passed away suddenly at his home." It turned out that the wake was that afternoon, and I thought I should go.

There wasn't much of a crowd, just a few of the teachers who had worked with him at the high school and a gaggle of cousins. His wife, I have to say, looked well in black; she was taller than he had been, and I apologized mentally to old Marley if I gave her physique an approving gaze. I'm sure he would have understood. I'm not dead, yet. I took her proffered hand and told her that Marley was a good guy, that I had always enjoyed working with him, and that I was sorry to see him go. I didn't say, "for a second time." I was glad I had come because she looked touched. She was very sweet. I was hoping they had refunded her money for the first coffin and maybe given her a break on the second, which by the way, did not look cheap to me, but I confess I'm no connoisseur of coffins. I moved on and knelt in front of Marley and said a prayer from Tennyson:

Behold, we know not anything;
I can but trust that good shall fall
At last—far off—at last, to all,
And every winter change to spring.

I don't know if I would have been entirely shocked if, like Finnegan, Marley roused himself and sat up, saying, "I'm feeling a lot better." The whole series of events left me with an odd feeling. You're alive. You're dead. You're alive. You're dead again. There didn't seem to be a lot of difference in the grand scheme of things. No noticeable vibrations in the fabric of our reality. Physicists now believe our past and our future is forever being lived and relived somewhere in space-time, or so a professor told me down at the coffee shop. Behold, we know not anything. Shakespeare probably had it right, though. We are all players with our entrances and our exits, and unlike Marley, no re-entrances. For when we exit this brightly lit stage, it's damnably dark and cheerless in the wings, and you will never hear your cue unless it's for the last great curtain call.

Down to the Crossroads

Lee Van Dinter woke up early, with the beginning of a song he'd heard in a dream running through his head. The others, "my associates," as he referred to them, were still lying on the rows of cots around him, like so many piles of ragged wheezing laundry—stinking shapeless lumps, from which protruded bony arms and wiry beards. He sat up and tried to remember the lines that were left as the dream dissipated.

Those Charleston Manville bells don't ring . . . those Charleston Manville bells don't ring.

Been here two years I know one thing
Charleston Manville bells don't ring.

Where the hell did the dream come up with Charleston Manville? Was there such a place? He didn't know. He slipped his feet into his shoes. You sure as hell didn't want to walk barefoot in this place. He pulled his "old kit bag" from under the bed, took his toothbrush and toothpaste from the side pocket, and wended his way through the maze of cots to the bathroom. Goddamit, in the old days—the old days, shit, two years ago, he would have taken his guitar, his coffee, and a pad of music paper out on the deck, sat there in the sun, and written the song. "Ain't got nobody else to blame, asshole," he said to himself. He pissed and brushed his teeth—took off his flannel shirt and tee-shirt and washed up as best he could, wet down his hair and shook his dripping head, staring hard at the grizzled figure in the mirror. "Somewhat leaden and moth-eaten this morning, Van Dinter."

He'd shared a bottle of Old Ezra with some guys at a campfire in the woods along the tracks beside the overpass. They said it was 101 proof, if that was possible. He wondered if it might be better, in the long run, to go back down to the tracks, wait for a train to come by, and jump in front of the sucker. Oh yeah—*fear no more the heat o' the sun, nor the furious winter*—something. He decided against that because it would be messy as hell, and he didn't think he was ready to cash in his chips just yet. Anyway, he had a song to figure out, and that's a reason to live.

Janey was reading the paper in the kitchen, and another bum was sitting at a table drinking a coffee and looking out the grimy window at the dirt parking lot. She looked up and saw Lee. Janey had the hard Lowell accent, the kind that used to reassure him that he was home when he came back to the city after a stint on the road. "Ya want sum toast?" she asked.

"Just a coffee, Janey. Little milk, no sugar."

"Go ovah thea then an' gedit chaself."

"OK. And would you get my guitar? Frank lets me leave it in the office."

"Shoor Lee, but don' play it in hea yet."

"Can I play it softly?"

"Notch yet."

Once again, he remembered the deck at his home, the forfeited home, where he used to write songs. "I had a house in the Highlands here in Lowell, you know," he said as he poured his coffee. "Jesus, I lost it all for the bottle."

"Yup. The boddle bites back. *Hahd.*"

"No shit." He drank some coffee and said, "I had a wife. I guess I have a wife still. But—"

Janey was reading her horoscope and he could see she didn't really give a shit about his wife, or his life. Why should she? He finished his coffee quickly because he remembered his wallet was in the bag under his cot, not that there was much to steal in it. He asked Janey again to get his guitar, and she tore herself away from the funnies. When he had the instrument, he thanked her for the coffee and went and folded his blanket. He put on the flannel-lined dungaree jacket that lay at the end of the bed; he pulled his wallet and a Case pocket knife out of his bag and left the shelter, snatching a pencil and a junk mail envelope off the front desk on the way out.

It was a brisk and sunny morning in late March, something like Joni Mitchell once sang about in that song about Morgantown. Even the faded green and half-rusted struts of the overpass looked fine, and the smokestacks of the old mills were works of art, towering industrial monuments to a long-vanished working class. He recalled Jack Dacey, the house philosopher down at McCullough's Bar saying, "It's amazing how those smokestacks were all built in a perfect circular curve, even though the bricks themselves are not curved. And," he said, "the whole structure tapers as it rises."

By way of demonstration, his hands had risen and converged as if he would join them in prayer. They had agreed that those dudes were bad-ass engineers, not to mention the balls on the masons that climbed up there in 1890 or something to lay the bricks. Christ, you wouldn't want to be *up there* with a hangover.

He laid the guitar case down on a bench on Jackson Street by the stone-walled canal, lit a cigarette, and sat down beside the instrument – two old pals, he thought. He flicked the five snaps open and picked up the guitar by the neck. Addressing himself to an invisible audience seated over the canal, he said, "She's a 1947 Martin, 00-17, mahogany body with a tortoise pickguard. Yes indeed, she's a beauty folks, and like the song says, she's all that I got left."

He tucked the cigarette between his lips and strummed a few chords. He pulled a two-pronged tuning fork out of a compartment in the case and rapped it on his knee, placing the end against the soundboard; a perfect A tone rang out like a bell, and he tuned the A string to it, then twisted the other tuning pegs until he was satisfied. Most players nowadays used a Snark tuner that clipped on the head of the guitar and tuned by colored light bars, or they used some kind of cell phone app, but Lee had faith in time-honored methods. Robert Johnson sure didn't need no colored light bars. Lee didn't have a phone, but if he did, he wouldn't use it to tune the damned guitar. He laid the smoking butt on the bench and began.

Been here two years an' I know one thing
Those Charleston Manville bells don't ring.

He sang the couplet over three or four times, picked up his cigarette, took another couple of drags, and laid it down again. He looked across the canal and up at the old cotton mills—the endless rows of windows suffused with pink in the rising sun. He thought of the men and women who for so many years had answered the bells that now sat dumb and rusting in their worn cupolas and of the workers who climbed the great winding staircases to stand for years on end at the clanging looms—weave and spin, weave and spin. He remembered Nick, the old Greek communist, who asked him, "In what three places you hear bells?" Lee said he didn't know what the hell he was talking about, but the Greek said, "In prison, in school, and in church, you see? The prison is the prison of the body, the school is the prison of the mind, and the church is the prison of the spirit." Crazy old

Greek almost made sense sometimes.

Been here two years an' I know one thing
Those Charleston Manville bells don't ring
Three men killed in the miners' riot
But Charleston Manville bells are quiet.

Yes, the bells are quiet 'cause they don't give a fuck when workers die; they just call 'em to the factory, to the mine, to the church. Like his great Aunt Clara—she answered the bell for thirty years in the Lawrence Mills, and on the day she retired, the goddamn boss couldn't even bother to come down to the floor to shake her hand. Lee's head bowed over the instrument and a mournful sound rose, blues licks in the key of A minor. He bent the strings as he played, the way old Josh White and T-Bone Walker taught us all. He listened for and found the chords, A minor 7th, D minor 7th, F, and E7th. He wanted that 'St. James Infirmary' feel. That song knocked him out when he first heard it, like so much of the blues he loved, on a Josh White record. White was a dignified-sounding bluesman and a great acoustic player.

He took the pencil and the envelope out of his pocket and began to jot down notes to himself. He knew the chords, but he was working out the verses, singing softly, humming, trying variant lines. He cut Charleston Manville down to Manville. It wasn't a riot—it was a mining disaster, and the whole piece was morphing from a bluesy number into a more traditional ballad, like "Little Musgrave." Within fifteen minutes he had worked out the first two verses, and sang them over a few times to fit them to the melody:

Been here two years an' I know one thing
For us, those Manville bells don't ring
Twenty men buried down in the ground
But for the wailin', it was quiet in the shantytown

The men volunteered they must have been insane
To shore up the tunnel in the southwest vein
All the way to the cavern where the water did run
Like that river in Hades far from the sun

Lee craned his neck backward and squinted at the real sun that was climbing the blue now. He got up and headed back to the shelter to help Frank fold the cots and to use the toilet, maybe have some of Janey's toast. He was crossing an alley that ran between Jackson and Middlesex Streets when a big guy in a filthy Patriots sweatshirt stepped out from behind a dumpster and bore down on him, "You got any change?"

"Do I look like I got any fuckin' change?"

"Izat a guitah?"

"No, it's a fuckin' grand piano."

"Lemme see it, guy."

"No."

"Whattaya mean, no?"

"No means no. Piss off."

With his left hand, Lee felt in his pocket for the jigged bone handle of his knife and kept walking, listening for footsteps behind him. He would die in the alley before he'd let anyone rip him off for the Martin; hell, even for his tattered jacket. He took a deep breath when he got out onto the wider canyon of Middlesex Street, the bricks of its walls and smokestacks standing in rosy counterpoint to a cerulean sky.

After he'd used the toilet and was leaving the bathroom, he saw Frank, the manager of the center, coming up to him; thin dark hair neatly combed and the only carefully trimmed beard in the place.

"You have to take your guitar to the bathroom?"

"I'm afraid one of my associates might want to run off with it and join a combo."

Frank smiled and beckoned Lee to follow him. He turned a key and they walked into his office, a windowless room with a sports car calendar tacked onto the otherwise bare wall. The calendar was still stuck on February's red 57 Thunderbird. "I don't get it, Van Dinter," Frank was saying. "You don't belong with these guys."

"Oh, they have accepted me, Frank. We are a merry band. Once you lose your pride, it's easy to be merry." His head turned quickly for a second, the way a bird's head turns, because the line had caught his fancy. May be a song in that. There was a Dunkin Donuts box on Frank's desk and two cups of joe with the lids on. "Help yourself," Frank said. Lee thanked him and took a blueberry muffin, and one of the coffees. It was black and lukewarm, but that was fine. "How are you doin', Lee, really? You don't look merry."

"Well, you know, there's a tide in the affairs of men and all that. I'm at low tide, as you may have guessed. At the moment."

Frank nodded, and Lee bit into his muffin. Lee helped in the kitchen sometimes; he'd worked as a short-order cook, and he was handy with a spatula. Eddie, the kitchen manager, had told him that Frank had a degree in Chemistry from WPI. He couldn't be making much scratch in this place. What made a guy with a science degree want to work in a place like this? Religion? Or just something inside. You had to admire a guy like that because dealing with the crew out there couldn't be easy.

"Your brother called here looking for you."

"When?"

"Today. This morning."

Lee nodded and braced himself for a sucker punch to the gut. He put the half-eaten muffin back in the box. "Is my mother all right?"

"She's been askin' for you, he says. You know she's got dementia, but he says she keeps asking for you, and he thought . . . ."

"Ah, Christ."

"You think it's time to pull it together, Lee?"

"I always figured I would when I hit rock bottom."

"You can't feel the granite under your ass?"

Lee didn't say anything. He was thinking of too many things to say any one thing. Pictures of his mother, of his wife, smiling at him while he made her scrambled eggs, of the people he met on this road he was on, echoes of the life he was living—*Zat a guitah?* Snatches of old songs—bury me in my high-top Stetson hat.

Frank gave him a minute and then his voice broke the stillness. "Go see your mother, Lee."

He sniffed and nodded. "Yeah, I'm gonna go see her."

"It's time." He produced a twenty-dollar bill and stretched his arm across the desk. "Take that for cab fare. And if you drink it at Melanson's, I'll smash that guitar over your head."

"El Kabong rides again."

He wagged the bill a couple of times in front of Lee. "Come on. Take it."

"No, thanks."

"Come on."

"Nah, I'm all set. I got a plan."

"Nobody here is all set and damned few have a plan. You'll need the cab fare to get to Methuen. And nobody here has ever turned down a double sawbuck."

Lee took the bill, singing, "If I ever get my hands on another dollar bill...." "He stuck it in his pocket and said, "Thanks. When I get back on my feet... I suppose you've heard that before."

"Yeah, but when you say it, I almost believe it."

"I'll help you fold up the cots."

By nine o'clock, Lee was seated at the bar at Melanson's. The door was propped open and a guy with a hand truck was wheeling in boxes of bar supplies. Lee watched the sunlight streaming in through the door in one great holy shower of gold across the dim interior of the bar. He was thinking of a chorus for the miners that inhabited his song; he saw a band of gritty men with lamps on their hard hats rolling coal cars full of bodies up from the dark shafts to the realms of light, and on to some makeshift graveyard hard by the shantytown, while in the city above, life went on without a visible vibration in the fabric of society, and he felt the anger that might turn them into something like Molly Maguires.

Up on the hill, the church choir sings
Sunday morning and the big bells ring
But their cold steel throats didn't make a sound
On the sad Good Friday when the mine fell down.

He pulled the envelope out and scrawled more lines. He needed names for the miners, and in his mind, he ran over the names of men he'd known or names he'd heard.

Duggan and Clarke and eighteen more
Were down in the mine when we heard the roar.

He scratched out the second line and wrote:

Were in the underground station when we heard the roar.

He bit the pencil and squeezed his eyes shut, imagining men shouting and running toward the billowing mouth of the mine. He opened his eyes and continued writing.

We shifted rock, we tried a hundred ways,
But we didn't reach those men for sixty days.

Lee watched Walter, the bartender, look over the boxes and sign for the order and the delivery guy went out, closing the door; the shaft of light disappeared just like that—it was like God left, and Lee recalled the day when he was a kid, maybe just five, and his mother's father, Jack Shanahan from County Cork, retired Lowell cop, brought him into the Parkway Lounge. The old men rubbed their leathery paws over the crew cut on his fair head and laughed—what they said was long lost, but all these years later they lingered in his memory in some indistinct way, a crowd of shades, and he remembered wondering why on earth anyone would want to come into a dark place on a sunny day, to breathe air spoiled with cigar smoke, and drink stuff that made their breath stink. He left his grandfather knocking back a drink with his cronies and went and sat outside on the curb. Wasn't he smarter then than he was now? Paradoxically, it was in his innocence that he had seen things as they really are.

Walter came over and stood in front of Lee, his hairy arms leaning on the beer cooler. "Whaddaya want?"

"Good morning, barkeep. Pleased to see you looking so well."

"Come on, whaddaya want? I gotta put that shit away." He nodded toward the boxes.

"You know bartenders are supposed to be friendly? Apparently, it's good for business."

The door opened and a bleached blonde limped in on one high heel. She was carrying the other in her hand. "Waltah, you owe me a new paira shoes! My fuckin heel broke on your crappy sidewalk!" She took a seat at the bar and began to tell the story of her mishap in an angry voice.

Walter ignored her. "Whattaya want?" he asked again.

A nauseating feeling was growing in Lee's gut; revulsion was replacing thirst. What did he want? He was feeling as he had in the Parkway Lounge long ago. The day had lost its color in this place. *Like the river in Hades far from the sun.* Along with the smell of stale beer, he seemed to smell the ignorance and feel the hopelessness that hung in a cloud so thick it was choking him. He wanted to be in the light, awake, composing, and not here, in the dark, forgetting, losing.

His hands were sweating. "You think people can change?" he asked the bartender.

Maybe if he had reassured him, Lee might still have stayed, and tried to put down his feelings with a few quick shots and a beer. *Drink the bar dry of rum and rye.* But Walter, prick that he was, was honest, and not given to idle reassurances. "Once a fuckin' drunk, always a fuckin' drunk. Whaddaya want?"

"These fuckin shoes cost twenny dolliz at Payless!" the woman cried.

"You know what, Walter?" Lee said. "I don't want anything from you. Go fuck yourself."

He stood up.

The bartender snickered. "You'll be back."

Lee slammed the bar hard with an open hand, and the bartender, who had begun to turn away, shot a backward glance at him. "Look at my eyes. I'll *never* be back." Lee grabbed his guitar and slung his bag over his shoulder. He approached the blonde and slapped the twenty- dollar bill on the bar in front of her. "Put it toward the new shoes. Or drink it, as you like."

Her jaw dropped. "Dijoo see that Waltah? What a fuckin' gentleman! Thank you, guy—what's ya name?"

"I'm the Hoochie Coochie man," he called over his shoulder. "I got the black cat bone."

She laughed. "Heh heh heh! Thas' a fucked-up name."

"Then it's fitting."

"Anyways, you're a real fuckin' gentleman!" She pointed an accusing finger at the bartender. "Not like this asshole!"

"Shut up," he replied, tiredly, as he went off to stow the boxes.

Lee banged the door open and took a deep breath like a diver come up from the depths. Outside, he slumped down onto the curb like the little boy he had been, and maybe still was in some part of his mind. He was trembling. Something was overwhelming him. Without knowing quite why, he began to cry. How do you like that, folks? The freewheelin' Van Dinter sitting on the curb, crying. Looks like Good Time Charlie's got the blues.

What was he trying to do? To live the blues, like those old-timers—like Lighnin' Hopkins? He couldn't do it. There was too much losing here on every side. The bad luck, the hard times, the sad tales, the addictions, the psychoses, the disappointments, the betrayals, the unsatisfied needs—it was a hell-river of losing that rushed down Middlesex Street and swirled through the bars and alleys and shelters and he was sinking in it, drowning in it, falling through it into a darkness from which he could never to rise. Frank's words came back to him, breaking upon the confusion like a sudden wave that breaks over a jetty and sprays you with a cold shock. *You think it's time to pull it together, Lee? Go see your mother.*

Lee looked down the street and saw a knot of his associates, his former associates, goddammit, standing in front of the shelter, smoking. They waved at him and yelled something he couldn't make out. Sherman and Gordon and Diego Ruiz, Big Vickie V. and Alice Boney-Ass. Sad losers, all. Born under a bad sign. Rising, he set off in the other direction, composing as he walked, stopping at the bridge to watch the water of the Pawtucket Canal run under Central Street and to copy down the verses in his head.

We shook our fists at that city on the hill
Where the houses are white, and the bells are still
They won't shed no tears and the bells won't sound
For no Irish miners in a shantytown

Now we're drinkin' em up, boys, we're on a tear
Why call men like us to prayer?
No bell's gonna sound out our death knell
When we're standin' in the smoke at the gates of hell

He was feeling better. He stuck the paper in his pocket and slid the pencil behind his ear and continued down Central Street to Merrimack, passing two Cambodian monks in saffron robes staring at a brass Buddha before whom sticks of incense were smoldering in the window of the Battambang Restaurant. Maybe they got the answers. He stopped at a shop whose sign read: Silva Gold and Jewel Pawn Brokers. He stepped inside and called out to the thin man behind the counter, "Silva Gold, eh? No pawn intended! Get it?"

The guy didn't get it.

A half-hour later, he was in a D&D cab heading toward Methuen. Manny Silva, known as the Azorean, had offered him 500 bucks for the guitar. "Just sign here," he'd said.

"Look, in this compartment, I got the bill of sale from 1992. See that?" Lee shook it in front of him. "Twenty-five hundred dollars! And it's in better condition now than when I bought it. I had the neck removed and reset five years ago! I didn't just plane down the bridge like some guys do!"

"Is a nice guitar," the Azorean said.

"You bet your ass it's a nice guitar. Check on your computer there what it's worth—go ahead."

"I know what is worth. Is a nice guitar. Look, I give you 600."

"You can sell it any day for 1500!"

"You can sell it right now for 600."

Finally, Lee had taken 500 and a Yamaha guitar that had a 400-dollar bullshit price tag on it. He figured he'd done about as well as you can hope to do in a pawn shop, but as he signed the receipt, he told the Azorean, "'Some men rob you with a six-gun, and some with a fountain pen.'" He pushed the receipt across the counter. "Woody Guthrie said that."

"I don't know him," the Azorean said, and Lee took a last look at his guitar as its new owner put it in the case, and he sent across the space between himself and the instrument some kind of blessing or prayer or something, a respectful thank you—he didn't know what— just a feeling.

The Yamaha sounded okay. It wasn't a Martin classic, but what the hell. Lee took the pencil and pulled out the envelope still folded in his pocket, revisiting the scene of the mining disaster that he could now see played out in his imagination. By the time the cab crossed the Hunts Falls Bridge, he'd jotted down another couple of verses, and had a melody in his head, doleful, in A Minor.

Duggan, and Clarke and eighteen more
Were in the underground station when we heard the roar
We shifted rock—we tried a hundred ways
But we didn't reach those men for sixty days.

Duggan's wife—it was a terrible sight
Clawed away at the rock with all her might
Till her hands were bleeding for all to see
Crying Tommy Duggan come back to me.

He lost his train of thought because the cabbie, a young Black guy, put on some rap or hip-hop, or hopscotch or whatever they called it, and by the time they got to the Dracut line, Lee was giving him an earful on one of his favorite themes. "You can have your Snoop Dogg," he said.

The cabbie smiled. "He's Snoop Lion now," he said.

"He could be Snoop Bullfrog for all I care. Like I tell the young guys, the young Black guys, 'You don't want Magic Slim and Muddy Waters and Junior Wells and Howlin' Wolf and B.B. King? You don't want to hear Ethel Waters singing 'Stormy Weather'? I tell you what, I'll take that music. Oh yeah, this Dutch Irish boy will take the blues.' And the jazz heritage? God Almighty! Louis Armstrong and Duke Ellington? Dizzy Gillespie, Cannonball Adderley, Thelonious, and Miles and Charlie Parker? Are you kiddin' me, man? That's a pantheon right there, and that's just a beginning. Think about how many greats—"

The cabbie shrugged and Lee said, "You don't even know what I'm talkin' about. None of you young guys do! Now how the hell did that happen? An' now you got what, Kanye West? Give me a break. He's a dwarf next to Buddy Guy."

"Kanye can rap. And he can lay down a beat."

Lee raised his open hands. "Lay down a . . . . I don't even know what that means. Can he sing? Does he write songs? Does he play?"

"He samples stuff, and he produces it."

"'Samples stuff.'" He snorted. "Yeah, I've sampled a lot of whiskey. So, he's not a musician?"

"Shit man, you don't got to play a guitar or a piano to be no musician—we got technology to do that."

Lee's laugh turned into a cough. When he recovered, he said, "I guess I don't know what a musician is anymore. Maybe the computers can write our songs for us, too. Technology—shit."

"This here I'm playing is Kid Cudi. He's a dope rapper." He turned it up a notch.

"Does he rap about bitches and hoes?"

"A little," he admitted, "but the music's poppin', right?"

"Yeah, sorry. I ain't buyin' it."

"Well, you're old school, no doubt. But you got a right to your opinion."

"Why, thank you, sir! Not everyone believes that these days, you know. A cabbie tossed me out of his car about a year ago because I expressed an opinion about his so-called music."

"You best be careful! People are touchy about their music. And the truth is, you don't know shit about hip hop, anyway," he said, but Lee saw that he was smiling.

Lee smiled too. "I know I don't like it. Anyway, as Jack Kerouac said, 'If you can't say what you think, what's the sense of talking?' Somethin' like that. Anyway, I've gotten my ass kicked more than once, and I still haven't learned to shut up. But you could be right. I doubt it, but I may be missing something. We're all products of our time, our background."

The sun shone through the trees along the river and their shadows fell like a strobe on his closed eyes as the cab moved down Rt. 110. Lee sighed, and said, "I'm going to see my mother. It's been a while."

The cabbie said that was a good thing, and he turned the music down again. As they passed into Methuen, Lee said, "Let me ask you this—what's your name?"

"Eugene."

"Good name. Means 'well-born.' Let me ask you this, Eugene. You think people can change?"

"What kinda people you talkin' about? Like criminals?"

"Drunks. Bums. Losers. People that always have to fuck things up."

"I got an uncle was a drunk for years. Then one day he jus' quit. He woke up one mornin' and he said, 'I'm done with all that.' And he ain't had a drink in like twenty years. He drinks ginger ale, or that fizzy water with lime."

"Really?"

"Yeah, really."

Lee watched the old familiar landmarks pass by—the great brick archways of the Nevins Library, Marston's Forge, and the Clock Tower, and directed the cabbie to the stolid colonial where he'd lived some part of an earlier life. He paid his fare and threw in a ten-dollar tip, remembering old Stack O'Lee. *Lose your money, learn to lose.*

"Thank you, sir," Eugene said. "And you give Kid Cudi a lissen'!"

"Ah, any man calls women bitches and ho's, I just can't listen. Like you said, I'm old school. But I love you man, 'cause you know what you are?"

"A cabbie?"

"Shit, you're a *workin' man*! You're the salt of the earth, Eugene! You're the backbone of this whole damn country! Lemme give you a kiss!"

Eugene laughed and waved a hand said, "No. No thank you, Sir!"

Lee laughed too, and said, "Well then, lemme shake your hand!"

They shook hands, and whether Eugene smiled in his soul as he pulled away, or just shook his head and chalked it up to another crazy fare, Lee did not know, but he hoped he ran into him again sometime down the line because old Eugene was good people.

He still had a key in his bag somewhere, but as he approached the front door, Benita opened it. She was a Puerto Rican woman who cared for his mother. He hadn't seen her much for a while. She gave him a sad sort of smile and a hug. She looked worn out. He knew that her son had died about a year before. Then, while the poor woman was having Easter Dinner with what remained of her family, the asshole from the crematorium stopped by to deliver her son's ashes. "I was in the neighborhood," he said. Imagine that? Why thank you—Death! On Easter Sunday! No resurrection for you—just your boy's ashes in a box. What the hell was wrong with people?

"How's Margaret?" Lee asked.

"She's confuse, but she ask for you a lot."

"I'll go see her."

"I make you a plate—*arroz con gandules* and *tostones*."

"That'd be great. I feel weak."

"You want coffee?"

"If it's not too much trouble."

Nothing was ever too much trouble for Benita.

His mother's bed had been moved into the dining room. Well, it wasn't really her bed—it was an adjustable hospital bed with rails and an overbed table. She was sitting up in it, staring at some Hallmark movie. She turned to him as he approached, watching him, but there was no light of recognition. He picked up the remote from the bed and muted the movie.

"Hi, Ma."

Her eyes were vacant, inscrutable. "Where's mother?"

"Your mother?"

"Of course my mother. I keep asking and they say, 'Oh, she's gone.' I know she's gone! I'm not a fool! But where is she?"

"Ma, Gram died in 1991."

"I know. I know, she's dead and buried, but on Sundays, they go out for a drive, don't you see? And I'm trying to find out—I want to know, where did they go?"

Lee was alarmed, nearly frightened, to be in the presence of a mind that could hold these two ideas together: his grandmother, her mother, in the grave and out for a drive. He stammered, "I—I don't know."

"Oh, nobody knows anything."

He thought that was the truest thing she had said but wanted to change the direction of the conversation if it could be called a conversation. "How are you feeling?"

"Well, I didn't like the thunder. That was a terrible storm."

"When?"

"About an hour ago," she said. It had been sunny all day. She continued, "It was something awful. I had to move over in bed to let the children in with me."

He cleared his throat and nodded, silent for lack of words.

"I hope Lee wasn't out in the storm," she said, "I worry about him."

"I'm Lee, Ma. I'm fine. I wasn't out . . . ."

"I'm not talkin' about you. I'm talkin' about my son, Lee."

"I am Lee. I'm your son, Lee."

"You're not my son."

The words hurt in the way that his wife's words had hurt when she asked him to leave their house because she was tired of trying, and he was tired of failing, of holding her back.

"I am," he told her. "I'm your son, Lee. I've come home to see you."

"Oh, never mind about you! My son Lee is only fourteen!" She was getting agitated.

Benita appeared in the doorway, shaking her head. "Don't argue with her," she said softly. "Your plate is ready."

He unmuted the TV and went out to the kitchen and sat at the table in front of the plate Benita had put together. She poured him a coffee. "I been praying hard for you," she said. Hearing the earnestness in her voice, the compassion, he felt his eyes well once more with tears. He covered his face with his hands and cried, while Benita continued, "Yes, I pray for my son, and I pray for you. I pray that you stop hurting yourself, yes, that you get better."

By "get better," he knew what she meant. It was a phrase that took the responsibility away from him, but he was responsible. "I'm done with all that," he said, with a resolve he had never known, in his core, in his bones, in his soul.

"Yes, I know. I can see."

"I'm tired of losing, Benita. So tired. Yeah. I'm done with all that."

"Yes."

For the first time in years, as he sat there in his mother's kitchen, he allowed himself to imagine a future. Buy some new clothes. Get a job as a short-order cook at the Sunnyside Diner or the Country Kitchen until he could get his license back. Call Jim Rooney, and once he proved to him that he had his shit together, they could start gigging. And after he'd been straight for a year—who knows?

When he had eaten, he got the Yamaha out of its case. He sat for a few minutes on the bench by the radiator in the kitchen and wrote some notes and hummed to himself while Benita got his mother up to use the commode. He knew how the song had to end—there had to be some hope—some light at the end of that mining shaft—a chance. He played the whole ballad through with the final stanzas he'd just composed.

Gonna throw down my pick and throw down my shovel
Gonna leave this town and its miners' hovels
Wash off the dirt, lose the company collar
Try my luck in Seattle on a fishing trawler.

Or jump aboard the west-bound hundred and nine
Find a life on the earth and not down in a mine
No more breathin' the black damp, crawlin' through the drift
Just tryin' to stay alive to the end of my shift.

"You play the guitar?" his mother asked when he went back into her room.

"Yes."

"My son plays the guitar."

"I hear he's pretty good."

She nodded. "Yes, Lee is very good. Everyone says so." There was a basket tied to the railing of her bed, and out of it she extracted the old rosary Lee's father had given her, with beads of pale green Connemara marble. She drew them between her gnarled fingers and said, "I just hope he's all right, wherever he is."

He placed a hand over hers and said, "He's all right, Margaret. He's all right."

What He Lived For

When I was a high school freshman and my brother Conall was a junior, he was required to compose a paper on an American writer. He chose Henry Thoreau. The internet was undreamed of in those days, and so he had spent several days at the Pollard Library, covering index cards with quotations from *Walden*, *A Week on the Concord and Merrimack Rivers*, and various essays. I began to read the index cards that lay on the desk we shared, and thought, as I read, here is wisdom: "Live in each season as it passes; breathe the air, drink the drink, taste the fruit, and resign yourself to the influence of the earth."

With all the intellectual ardor of youth, I studied Conall's copy of *Walden*. I was even captivated by the cover. A rustic-looking figure in a broad-brimmed hat, hands in the pockets of a dungaree coat, head bowed as if lost in thought, traversed a field bordered by towering pines. My imagination was drawn into the green, nearly liquid depths of the wood's shade, illuminated here and there by misty columns of light that rose through the gaps in the fragrant boughs.

Some things speak to us so deeply, that years later, we wonder who we would have become if we had not fallen under their influence. For my father, it was Benny Goodman's clarinet. For my mother, it was the cult of the Blessed Virgin. For my brother Conall, eventually, it was the romance of the sea and his determination to earn his living on its back. And for me, it was Henry David Thoreau's New England-born, earth-grown, finely chiseled prose. "How many a man has dated a new era in his life from the reading of a book?" he asked, and I knew that for me, a new era had begun.

With the gravitas of an Old Testament prophet, he spoke not of God's law, but of man's conscience; not of how we should live our lives, but of the need to examine the lives we do live.

When Conall had finished his report, he gave me his copy of *Walden*. His encounter with Thoreau had changed him, too, but as he was already marching to his own rather spontaneous drummer, the effect may have been more difficult to detect. In any case, it was 1969, and we were all trying to "get back to the garden."

I carried *Walden* with me as a religious devotee carries his sacred text, and like such a zealot, I made converts—not many, but a few. I never brought them to Walden Pond, though, for I had learned through my mentor to cultivate a pensive solitude.

I am no more lonely than the loon in the pond that laughs so loud, or than Walden Pond itself. What company has that lonely lake, I pray? I am no more lonely than the Mill Brook, or a weathercock, or the north star, or the south wind, or an April shower, or a January thaw, or the first spider in a new house.

Before I was old enough to get a driver's license, I pedaled my Schwinn three-speed from Lowell to Concord once a week in the summer. It was my last trip of that summer that I recall most vividly. I locked my bike to the sidewalk side of a guard rail on Route 126.

After a ten-minute hike through the woods, I arrived at the site of Thoreau's cabin, where I paid my homage and meditated for a while in silent reverence.

Down at the water, I pulled a mask and flippers from my sweat-drenched backpack. I had read in HDT's journals that a couple of young women once knocked on his cabin door and asked him for a glass of water. He handed them a ladle and instructed them to drink from Walden Pond. They never returned the ladle. Thoreau decried their frivolous behavior, the giggling he detected as they walked away, and concluded that they had no doubt thrown his ladle into the pond.

Out in the middle, the pond was deep, about a hundred feet, (Thoreau had plumbed it). Wearing my mask, I had swum out from the western shore and seen the bottom drop off like a cliff some forty feet out. But Thoreau had constructed his cabin beside a shallow inlet, around nine feet deep. After I had spread my towel on the shore, I put on my mask and flippers and began to scour the pond bed. I had this crazy idea that I would find Thoreau's ladle there, poking out of the silt where it had settled after having flown from a young woman's hand in 1845, a twirling blot on the bright air for three or four seconds, swallowed in a silver splash.

All I found were some typically curious bluegills of various sizes who scouted me out, a couple of empty Schlitz cans, and an old New Hampshire license plate. Who brings a license plate through the woods to chuck into Walden Pond? "Live free or die"—right—he should have died, I thought.

I was annoyed that there were, near me, three boys about my age, climbing on each other's shoulders, splashing about and generally making a racket that I felt was disrespectful in this sanctuary. Their shouting faded as I swam across the inlet. Once on the far side, I walked along the water's edge, sometimes on the gravelly shore, sometimes ankle-deep in water, taking in this scene that had been so familiar to Henry. About a quarter mile along, I came upon a Black man sitting on a rock with his fishing line in the water. He was wearing a camouflage Boonie hat, Aussie style, with his fishing license displayed on the side that was pinned up. His vest was equipped with several bulging pockets. I used to like to go fishing with my father, either in the Merrimack River or Black Brook or deep-sea, with Eastman's out of Seabrook Harbor.

"What are you using for bait?" I asked.

"Nightcrawlers."

"Catch anything?"

He leaned to his side and slid back the cover of a cooler. Three trout lay on ice. "I'll see if I get one more pretty soon, then I'll pack up."

"Pretty good lunch."

He laughed. "That there's breakfast! I been out here since 6:30."

"Are the fish picky?"

"I tell you what—you walk along the edge of the water, you see like a rotten log sittin' there in the water—you turn it over, you probably see a crawdaddy under it. You catch one of those, the bigger the better, you gonna get a fish with that. You get a good size trout or a bass. Bass love them crawdads. Jus' don't hook 'em through the belly, though, you kill him. You hook him through the tail."

"Good advice."

"Yeah, they love them crawdads."

"How long do you spend here?"

"I fish the morning. Then I go spend some time with the family. Yeah, family's important, too. Then I be back to work tomorrow," he added, with cheerful resignation.

"You know how to enjoy your free time."

"Time is but the stream I go a-fishing in," he said.

I felt an instant kinship. "You've read Thoreau."

"Oh yeah. Sometimes I hear him playin' his flute out there in a rowboat."

"He died in 1862."

"Well, you don't hear with just your ears, you know." He gave me a knowing look and laughed softly just as his rod bent, and he began to reel in a trout. It was too small, though. He extracted the hook with practiced hands and set it in the water, where it shot in a speckled flash into the emerald depths.

"Thoreau is why I come out here from Lowell." I was thinking that I had stumbled upon the keeper of Walden wisdom, of the lore of the lake and the secrets of Nature. A philosopher fisherman, who could still hear, in the "undiscovered regions of his mind," Thoreau's flute on the Walden breezes.

"Yeah, I read his books." He stood and stretched. He locked his reel and hooked his lure onto one of the ring guides on his pole and leaned it against the bank as he began to pack up his gear. "He was strong against slavery; I'll give him that. He was a free thinker—we need more of those. An' he wrote wonderful stuff about this place, you know, in every season, but in the end . . . ." His nose crinkled, and he gave his head a curt shake. "His philosophy didn't make sense for me."

"Why not?"

"Well, you're kinda young, an' so I don't know how to explain it exactly, but, well, I like women, you see. Always have. I love everything about 'em. Now, this is beautiful . . . ." He stood tall, like Moses on the Mount, and stretched an arm out over the water as if he would bless it. I gazed at the vast liquid mirror, reflecting, at its edge, the shadowy pines, and beyond that the azure sky with its sailing clouds. "Beautiful!" he repeated. "But you know what? It ain't as beautiful as a woman! No sir! Now listen! Suppose I find me an honest, good-lookin' woman—with a big heart, too—an' I fall hard for her, see? Then suppose I tell her, 'Hey, you marry me, an' I'll take you out to a little cabin in the woods and we'll grow some beans, an' we will live really simple, 'cause we ain't gonna have no money. We are just gonna be Nature's children, an' live out there like the lilies of the field. Now, what is my fine woman gonna say to that? Hmmm?"

I defended my mentor. "I don't think he was saying that you have to live in the woods."

Having gathered his rod and tackle box in one hand and his cooler in the other, he began to ascend a makeshift stone stairway to the main path that encircled Walden. I followed, listening. "No, but you have to, if you follow that philosophy, you have to live simply, see. That means you have to get your ass out of the old rat race, am I right?"

"I suppose, yes."

"Uh uh. Won't work. 'Cause my wife, an' the woman you're gonna want to marry someday, too, she wants a house! Not a one-room cabin! A house is damned expensive, son. You need a mortgage! She wants some nice things. An' she wants a man who's gonna be a worker. I mean my wife works, too, but she doesn't want some guy who wants to walk in the woods all day an' write down his deep thoughts about it! Wonderful though they may be! Hell, no! You gotta bring home the bacon!"

I was sure there must be an answer to his objections, but I couldn't think what they were.

"And then!" he said, "I ain't even got into kids yet! Once you got kids, oh ho, then everybody gets their claws into you—clothes and tuition and piano lessons and birthday parties and Christmas and summer vacations and car insurance! Oh, yeah. An' they eat like hungry lions! And you're gonna be so damned busy workin', you won't have no time to philosophize, except, if you're lucky, you get up early on Sunday and come out here and catch some fish."

He gave me a moment to respond, and when, after we had walked along in silence for a moment, I had come up with nothing, he concluded. "I tell you what, young man. If you wanna get yourself neutered like a little puppy, an' forget about women forever, why then you go off an' do whatever you want. Live in a hut. Dress like a monk and read that Buddhist philosophy. Grow your beans and enjoy your companions—the birds. But if you're a man like me, you're gonna want a woman even more than you want peace of mind or enlightenment, see? Then you're gonna have to jump into the rat race. Yes sir, you're gonna earn your bread by the sweat of your brow. It's a hard life, but you know what? If I had to do it all over again, I'd make the same mistakes. Thoreau, he never had a woman, and that means he never had a family. An' like I said, family's important." We had come to a fork. One path led up through the woods, past the site of Thoreau's cabin to the main road. The other continued around the lake.

"Which way you going?" he asked.

I pointed across the inlet. "My stuff is over there."

"All right, I cut through the woods here. You enjoy the day, now." I watched his laden figure pass into the shadow of the woods. I never asked him his name, nor what work he did, nor where he lived. I continued to enjoy Thoreau's rich descriptions of the natural world, to ponder some of the questions he posited long ago, and to see the truth of much of what he recognized; chiefly, one's responsibility to one's conscience and the recognition of the miracle of all that is around us. And because of Thoreau, I never shared the desire that my friends seemed to have to drive a sleek new car. My daughter calls me a "minimalist," and it was no doubt Henry Thoreau who bent the twig of my youth in that direction.

But after that brief conversation with the Walden fisherman, I could never read the sage of Concord with quite the same blind devotion I'd once felt. I was never anyone's disciple after that. I found an "honest, good-lookin' woman" and married her. I have a mortgage, two kids, and a dog, and I've been working my ass off for a quarter of a century. I know I've had my days of quiet desperation, but when those days are done, my wife is in my arms, saying, "I love you so much," and I feel lucky. And there are those beautiful Sundays when I walk in the woods or cast a line in a running stream. It's all a mystery, deeper than Walden Pond, but I know if I had to do it all over again, I'd make the same mistakes.

Eschatology

The dream is vivid. I'm wandering the streets of Paris, trying to find the way back to my lodgings, but unable, after so many years, to recall the route. Eventually, I forget that idea altogether as I lose myself in the life of the city. I see no familiar face as I tour bars with polished countertops, shops where stylish women call "*Bonjour!*" to customers, and quiet chapels of glass-stained light. I trace the Seine, browsing as I go among the yellowing pages of old volumes at the stalls of the *bouquinistes*. The imposing bell towers of Notre Dame rise out of the Île de la Cité.

There is a Metro station. I descend the broad stairway and follow a tiled tunnel past advertisements that promise luxuriant hair, exciting films, seductive perfumes. I pass through a turnstile. When a subway car comes into view, it strikes me as odd that it is empty, and I become aware that I am alone on the platform. I retreat up the tunnel and stand before a grand map—a colorful network of intersecting subway lines. I do not recognize the name of any stop or terminal, and I ascend the stairs, returning to the world of men and women hurrying about their business. They hail taxis, wait in gathering groups for crossing lights, buy newspapers from a garrulous old man with a soiled change apron. They move with a sense of purpose that reminds me of my purposelessness. I walk among them, looking for a clue.

And then I see her.

She is sitting at a small table on the terrace of a café reading a *Classique Larousse*. Before her, a *demi-tasse* sits in a saucer and a cigarette burns in a triangular Ricard ashtray. She exudes intelligence, beauty, and of course, sexuality. *Thy hair soft-lifted by the winnowing wind.* She smiles in my direction, and I wonder, how old am I now? Who or what does she see halted on the sidewalk before her? An old coat flying about a frail creature under a halo of white? The young man who once shared her bed, or his ghost? Is her smile an invitation, or just benign recognition? It is neither. She is merely amused at something she has read and gazes skyward to laugh; she draws on her cigarette, taps ash into the ashtray, and turns her attention to her book. She has not even seen me, and if I call her, I know that she will not hear. I am no more to her than the wisp of smoke that flows from her fingers. And tears gather in my eyes, for I am afraid that she no longer inhabits the world to which I am awakening.

My notebooks are scattered, all but the few in the night table drawer, the ones I've filled since I came to this warehouse for the infirm on the sleepy outskirts of the old mill town. There is no storage space in this room I share with Mahoney, who will rise in a few hours, take tentative steps like a man on ice he doesn't trust, then put on his housecoat and shuffle off to the Dayroom to watch *Good Morning America*. Two narrow beds, two shallow closets, and a window that looks onto a parking lot. My world, once *le monde entier*, is now shrunk to half of a room.

But where are my notebooks and what good can they do me now? Stacked in several boxes, they lie moldering in my nephew's basement or withering to sere leaves in his attic. The pages recounting the brief months I spent with Celine would be in the box marked 1970-71. They would contain, in detail that it might pain me to read now, our first meeting, the frenzied days of that youthful spring in Paris, the summer and fall when we were lovers, and the Christmas season when the world celebrated a new beginning, and I began to ponder the end. I could ask him to find the box and bring me its contents. But why? To feel even more keenly the loss that I feel in my dreams? To recriminate myself once more for my failure?

I tell myself it is to pay homage to what I know after all these years must have been *un grand amour*, but which I considered at the time *un amour de jeunesse*. To write our story. To bring the woman she was to life between the covers of a book. That's what writers do, even old writers. But what does that mean, really? To haul a corpse from the sea of oblivion into a sinking boat?

No, it would be to create something lasting out of something ephemeral. That's the voice of creative desire. Disillusioned artists will recognize it by its hollow timbre. The voice of reason counters: *Lay not that flattering unction to thy soul*, old man. It's an illusion to think that you can keep anything alive, through notebooks, through memory, through art. "Who are a little wise?" the poet asked. "The best fools be." We writers are the very best of fools. We have a story. Oh, but it's more than that. It's a moment, recalled or invented, or both, that belongs to the ages; an incident or series of incidents that reveal character, a transcendent truth that we will make the reader—the great public of sympathetic souls—*see*. It's profound, significant, and immortal. Yes, darling, I'll immortalize you through my omnipotent arsenal of words. *Thy eternal beauty shall not fade, nor lose possession of that fair thou owest.* What hubris, even for Shakespeare, and none of us, darling, is Shakespeare.

Oh, I could keep Celine alive for a while, in some way, as my boat, as all our boats, founder. My recreation of who she was and what she felt—it's better than nothing, surely, even given the fading powers of a second-rate writer. There is a graveyard a mile past the nursing home. In the oldest part are the graves of some of the last of the Pennacook Indians who once inhabited this land. What they saw and felt, the color of their lives, has vanished; they had no writers, you see. Did they have a sense of humor? Recognize irony? Raise rebels who mocked their beliefs? A few sentences reported by a settler in an arcane history of the region is all that's left, a comment on some treaty, or an expression of faith in the white man's god recounted by a gratified white man. They left not one individual voice; at best some shadow of a collective view in a few folktales passed down and dimly recalled.

Place names: *Wamesit, Pawtucket, Massachusetts.* Their voices are as silent as their graves, and I can't help but wonder whether they were more than a little wise to live their stories and to carry them quietly there. They needed no Shelley to remind them of Ozymandias and the vanity of monuments of stone or intellect.

The stars above wheel in the heavens as I remember. From across the hall, I hear the young woman who was paralyzed in a crash cry out in her sleep, feeling once again the car careening off the road and seeing in the headlights, just for an instant, the tree looming there. Awakened, Mahoney rises and inches toward the bathroom. He says little to me, or little that I can make sense of. "Sully," he might say, "do you know there's not a stick of wood in this whole place?" Things like that. And you see, my name is not Sully. They'll be moving him upstairs soon, to the dementia ward, where memory, reverie, and reality are all one.

I have breakfast alone and sit by the window, seeing not the cars creeping in and out of the lot, the faithful visitors dragging the grandchildren to visit Grammy, but the stone bridges of Paris, the crenelated turrets of La Conciergerie, the august windows of Le Boulevard du Palais, the intricate spiderwork of Le Tour Eiffel. And I fill another notebook. Such is the shadow cast over me by the recurring dream and by memory.

Jenny, the day nurse, comes in and doles out my meds, quinapril for blood pressure, and digoxin for my heart, which sometimes flutters and seems to beat in my throat, making my breath thin, and my heart's blood flow like shallow water over a bed of stones. "Writing away!" she says. "I admire you, Patrick!" And she adds in that North of Boston accent, "You're so *smaht!*" She tries to coax from me some cheery sounds, and I know she means well. Jenny is a good person. "You're not gonna recite any poetry for me today?" I can oblige but curtly, with one verse that will not scatter the dream-cloud that engulfs me:

> *Love, faithful love, recalled thee to my mind*
> *But how could I forget thee? Through what power,*
> *Even for the least division of an hour,*
> *Have I been so beguiled as to be blind*
> *To my most grievous loss?*

She rubs my back encouragingly, says something, and is gone. Ah, why speak of immortality, when the sun itself will burn out and the universe collapse upon itself? They say there is a volcano in Yosemite Park that is wont to erupt every 70,000 years. It's seething below as I write. When it blows, the United States will be subsumed for centuries in an ash cloud that will make the entire country, maybe the world, uninhabitable. *Eschatology,* from the Greek, *eschatos,* the final things. There are a hundred ways it all might end, but end it will, and it was, I think, this fact that froze my pen, and made the effort seem absurd at times. The great artists believe they can achieve immortality. My agent used to call and ask when my next book would be ready. *The Unbroken Circle* sold 5000 copies, then *No Birds*

Sing sold 30,000. "The next one," he said, "will break out and make you a household name!"

He wondered at my lack of enthusiasm. But what difference did it make whether I sold thirty thousand or five hundred thousand? The work would still be less durable than the drawings of wild horses, lions, and mammoths, on the walls of the Chauvet Cave, discovered in 1994 by three locals in Ardèche, near the Pont d'Arc, not far from Celine's home. The drawings, and the imprints of human hands, have been carbon-dated at 32,000 years old. I know what you are thinking; it was laughable for me to put my books on some timeline with the sun, or even the cave drawings of Chauvet. And while I pondered my notebooks, the small years rolled on, very few really, but enough to quench my meager fire. My agent died, and the young agent the publishing house assigned to me declared, after reading sample chapters of a new novel, *The Satirical God*, that I didn't know what readers wanted anymore. So, my sun burned out long ago, no more to be renewed than the passport in my drawer, stamped with the dates and ports of my entry into, and exile from that other life.

Without hope, driven by whatever force it is that drives the creator of the unpublishable work, I begin the exposition:

It was the spring of 1971. Armed with a Ph.D. in Comparative Literature, and a high draft number (353), I responded to an advertisement in The Chronicle of Higher Education *for a job teaching "The American Novel" at Université Paris Ouest Nanterre La Défense, a new university that just a few years earlier had been the focal point of the student revolts against the government that escalated into a national strike. De Gaulle left office the following year and died in November of 1970, just before I arrived. My French was bookish, and I spent many nights at the Bar du Marche swept up in a tumult of animated discussions I couldn't quite follow.*

I pause and sip the watery lukewarm institutional coffee. *Sipping the Insipid* could be the title of a work about my life here. But that's not what readers want. An aide with the requisite perkiness comes in to take my blood pressure and asks if I want to "watch a little TV."

"No, thank you," I say, but the dream is departing before I have even begun to transfer to paper the smells and sounds of the Bar du Marche, the cloudy glasses of pastis, the wild conversations, or later, my visit to the Musée Jacquemart-André, where a blond woman sat with an open sketchpad opposite Van Dyck's *Time Clipping Cupid's Wings*. There is a distaste, nearly a revulsion, in her large brown eyes as she looks from her sketchpad to the painting and back, like a medical intern watching her first autopsy. Rugged, bare-chested Time, the grizzled general, with thin hair and a beard of wiry silver, winged not for frolicsome flights, but only for swiftness, holds the terrified Cupid over his knee. The cruel shears in his right hand are about to close on the boy's delicate feathery wing. On the ground before them, between Time's iron scythe and death skull, lies Cupid's quiver, in which a single arrow is left. Even wounded and wingless, Cupid will never be utterly powerless.

After all these years, I couldn't tell you exactly what Celine was wearing that day. I must consult my notebooks for that. I know that she wore a red silk scarf, though, because it was all she was wearing when, three hours after we met, we fell on her bed, and I sank between her legs. She made love with abandon, as if to escape the cold foreboding that the brutal curving scythe and the hollow skull had cast over her.

I have a thought, and in the margin of my notebook I pause to write: *Love's not Time's fool, though rosy lips and cheeks within his bending sickle's compass come.*

What do I remember of Celine most often through nights when, asleep or awake, I'm visited by her image? I remember waking in the dark when, in the slightly open bedroom door, I saw the flicker of candlelight and heard her crying softly. I found her there in its glow, sitting on the floor with her back against the couch, her blond hair mussed, an open sketchpad in her lap, and a cigarette burning in an ashtray beside her. "*Qu'est-ce qu'il y a?*"

She showed me the sketch: a little girl standing beside the sign for the Trocadéro Metro station. Her hair was unkempt; with one hand she held a plaid shawl together at her throat; with the other, she pointed to her mouth. At her feet was a can, and leaning against the Metro signpost, a placard bearing the words: *SVP J'ai faim.* Please. I'm hungry. "How can people leave a little girl to beg on the streets? I should have brought her home."

"You can't take a child off the street," I told her. "She's not your child to bring home."

She let the drawing fall as her quiet sobs burst forth in open weeping, her hands covering her face, the pencil still under the knuckle, jutting from her hand as if it had pierced her eye.

"Celine, what's wrong?"

"She *could be* my child!" she cried.

I was confused for a moment. I thought she might be speaking in terms of some Christian obligation to our fellow-creatures, but the depth of her emotion, the wrenching pain of her sobs convinced me otherwise. "You have a child?" I asked, and I saw her nod. The candle began to gut, the slender flame palpitating as my old heart sometimes does.

"Where is that little girl tonight? Where is she?" Her body began to rock like the old Irish women, keeners, I'd seen at a wake in my boyhood.

There was nothing I could do but hold her in my arms as the candle died and the long windows brightened from black to gray. In the somber dawn, she lit another cigarette and told me the story haltingly, like a shamed penitent to her confessor, how as a sixteen-year-old student at an *école privée* in Aubenas, she had become pregnant and had been pressured by everyone, her father, the boy's parents, the good sisters, and the priest, to give up her child for adoption. "I should have fought for my girl," she said. "How could I have let her go? I betrayed her." Of course, I told her that she had very probably done a good thing for the child, but I abandoned that tack when she turned away and said, "You sound like the priest." This was the hole at the core of Celine's being: the handing over of her newborn had left her heart raw.

She admitted that she felt "too much." *Paris Match* ran a series of photographs of the turmoil in Viet Nam; Celine became almost physically ill at the sight of South Vietnamese General Loan preparing to shoot his prisoner in the head, and of the self-immolating Buddhist monk, Quang Duc, sitting upright and perfectly still in the heart of a pillar of flame. It was as if she could smell the burning flesh and hear the shrieks of bystanders.

There was another incident a few weeks after her revelation. I stood idly by, watching her as she turned a carousel full of postcards at a newspaper kiosk, looking for one that might please her mother in Ardèche. A teenage girl sidled up to her, pretending to scan the post-cards, but I saw her hand slide into the bag Celine had slung over her shoulder. I stepped forward and grabbed the thief's arm and shouted at her to "*Foutez le camp!*" slang I'd picked up in Paris best translated by the English phrase, "Fuck off."

"Her hand was in your bag," I explained to Celine, but she looked at me as if I had wounded her. She ran after the girl as she slunk away and began to speak with her. I kept my distance, watching them. I winced as I saw Celine pull out her purse and hand the girl some money, fearing that I would soon be chasing the pickpocket through the allies of Paris to recover Celine's purse, but the street girl accepted the notes, nodding tearfully. They embraced right there in the Place Gambetta, and the pickpocket swiped at her eyes as though her heart were touched, though it's true that beggars and thieves are fine actors. Celine said nothing when she returned, and I asked her nothing because I understood.

Of course, when I write the story of Celine, I must include her joy, too, her wild laughter and radiant eyes as we watched two street clowns performing a mock ballet, or the endearing way she would try to suppress a smile as I mangled some French expression. I will include it all, her courage, her intelligence, and of course her art, which was an expression of her soul: a *clochard* sitting on the church steps, an old man with a wild mane of white, sitting in a wicker chair with a blanket over his legs, staring into the past as I do now, and of course the little girl at Trocadéro in her forlorn shawl. I will smile with the reader at her quaint jealousies of women who could never match her scope or charm. And I will cast the first stone at the man who left her because the hundred petty affairs that he thought constituted his life were waiting elsewhere.

The decision to return, when my time as visiting lecturer had concluded, was less than a decision. I simply adhered to the plan I had made before I'd come. My apartment, my real job, my library, my publisher, were all back in the States. And I had never said that I would stay forever. I was still too young to consider forever, which really is not a long time. And I will describe the silent pride that I admire so much from this distance in time. How would I phrase it in my novel? *She loved him, yes, but she would never beg him to stay.*

And yet I forgot Celine, never entirely, but I let her go for many years, for decades. I married Clare when we were both in our forties, and I suppose our marriage was like many others. But now, near the end of life, it is this woman I knew so long ago who emerges from whatever compartment of my brain has held her in thrall and whose image is the companion of my days. So, there she stands astride my past, ever-growing in significance. But how can I tell you her story? There was no grand conflict, no insurmountable obstacles that love surmounted, no bitter arguments, no letters from other lovers discovered in a false compartment, no horrible interventions by the strumpet Fortune, no terrible personified entity to clip the wings of love, only *me*.

The story must include another scene. There was a time as autumn gave way to winter when Celine's period was late. One day she told me that if she was pregnant, I need not worry about it, that she would be perfectly happy to raise the child herself in France, and I could go on with my life. She said this without irony or bitterness, but as a simple statement of fact. Fool that I was in other ways, I knew that I could never live with that, and I told her quite clearly that if she was pregnant, either I would stay in Paris, or she would come with me. I felt that in some way it would almost be a relief to have the situation resolved by a force beyond my control. I was incapable of taking the necessary leap without some push. But a child would decide the matter for me.

Then one morning she got up early and went to the bathroom. When she returned, she slipped under the covers and whispered, "*J'ai mon regle.*" I have my period.

I felt no relief, but unexpected disappointment. And I drifted back to the worn path.

The strange thing is, I don't have a specific memory of our parting. I don't remember whether I left her at her apartment, or the train station, or at some café with my single suitcase in hand. I do remember the steam rising around her as she poured a *tisane* on a bleak morning of December that must have been near my departure, and how I felt the great tenderness of love for her then, but somehow, for some inexplicable reason, I dominated that feeling. I'm sure our parting is recorded in my notebooks, but I don't think I could bear to read the account.

Of course, I know what readers want—the dramatic arc. They want conflict and resolution. That's the game. And so, shall I create a story around our affair? Shall I place the real Celine in a plot of my invention, the only authentic flower in an artificial bouquet? All the writer knows is that a memory so persistent deserves a tribute of words, a love elegy. But what is the tribute to a woman who felt too much, who loved too much, and who was not loved completely in return?

I suppose that is the story, that the young man could not love the real Celine as much as the old man could love her memory.

Unless . . . there might be another story. It has occurred to me that in my dream I see Celine sitting at the café smoking, but that really, she had quit before I left. Quite suddenly, the way a woman might who wants to protect a life within her. What if she sensed that I would stay, not out of love for her, but simply out of a sense of obligation to the child, and so she took that moral constraint off the table with four syllables whispered at dawn. It would not have been beyond her power to abort a plan based on anything but love and my desire. It's too late to matter now, except in some fictional world where a long-lost daughter would find me and hurl at me the curses that I deserve, or, who knows, as in some gentle fable, rain forgiving tears on my hoary head. I assure myself this is merely a storyteller's dream because there comes a point when remorse is a chasm too deep to contemplate.

The morning wanes and I can hear the aides wheeling the lunch cart farther down the hall; just then Mahoney peers around the edge of the doorway. Seeing no one about, he whispers, "Psst! Sully! I'm bustin' outa this place tonight! Are you in?"

I must clear my throat to respond because I have hardly spoken all day. "Yes. Yes, Mahoney. I'm in." He taps his nose with his forefinger like some con man in a 40's movie, gives me a foxy wink, and disappears.

I will not record here the "events" of my afternoon in the "home." Nothing happens here, except that from time to time a long hearse pulls into the driveway and glides around to the back entrance. The staff tries. They have bingo and even cocktail socials, but no reader wants to hear of those grim parodies of life. That's why we are here, and the rest of the world is out there. "Life is many days," James Joyce wrote. And one day, it is few. Enough of that. My notebook is nearly full, and I'll be leaving here tonight, not because Mahoney dreams of busting out; he does that every day, but because my calendar says that the moon will be full. Jenny comes before her shift ends to say goodnight and goodbye, and solid woman of Pawtucketville that she is, passes me a nip bottle of Bushmill's and places a finger over her lips. I pat her hand. "Thank you, dear."

"Can you quote me some poetry before I go?" she asks.

Without forethought, I recite the first lines that come to mind, words that must have been simmering below my consciousness:

Now my charms are all o'erthrown,
And what strength I have's mine own,
Which is most faint: now, 'tis true,
I must be here confined by you.

She smiles. "That's beautiful," she says, "but so sad!" She shakes her head in wonder and repeats what to her is a kindly blessing, "You're so *smaht!*" She blows a kiss and says, "See ya tomorrah!"

My alleged co-conspirator is asleep by seven o'clock. I put on my Aran sweater for warmth, recite Tennyson's "Ulysses" for strength, and grip the handle of my cane. There is a receptionist who watches the main door, where visitors sign in and out. The other doors are unguarded, but you need to punch in a code to unlock them. I know the code because writers observe, and when the corridor is empty, I tap the numbers that hardly deserve the name of code: 4-3-2-1 and open the door.

Not the bitter chill of Keats' St. Agnes' Eve, but the welcome chill of autumn; it is always too warm for me in the institution, where the air is redolent of urine and disinfectant. Outside, I smell burning wood and the great river that flows nearby from the mountains of New Hampshire. I pass a row of cars as if looking for my own and then slip across the street and head for the woods along the river, where I pause and listen to the dark, looking up to study for a moment the brilliant disc of the moon set in the naked branches. Step by step, ten fingers around the curving handle of my cane, I lower myself down the embankment to the water's edge. In my youth, I loved to run through the Indian woods, but now I am huffing like an old train engine as I descend.

The river flows onward to empty into the sea at Newburyport, and there, one could board a ship and hail, within a week, the rugged coast and lighthouses of Finistère; from Brest the train ride to Paris is a straight line, less than five hours. But you can never sail back to the days you spent there. Within his bending sickle's compass—all come. I think of Guglielmo Marconi at the beginning of the last century receiving through a kite in the air in Newfoundland the first wireless transmissions from old Europe, whispers rushing invisibly through "ether." And what other forces will man discover—inexplicable powers coursing along paths yet unknown? Perhaps I might send a message along this river and across the sea to one who is lost from me in time and place and perhaps life itself, but who still has more substance than the days I spend.

Quantum physicists say that nothing is lost, that there may still be a living time in which Indians roam this shore, where Cro-Magnon man, deep in the cavernous chambers of the stone mountains of Ardèche, is breathless before the horses he has created on walls of stone. They seem to move in the torchlight, a swirling herd of powerful nodding heads. *I am here*, he whispers into eternity, *and I left this thing of beauty, this image of power. This was my world as I saw it.* Then perhaps the old sages were right about the immortality of the soul. Yet a deeper certitude than faith or physics tells me that nothing of mine will remain. I pull my notebook from where I've tucked it into my belt and trusting more to invisible powers than to my feeble art, I hurl it over the dark water where it flutters like a wounded dove and falls into the river to run toward the sea. I say farewell to all my words, and to the single regret I will share with her to the end: *How could I have let her go?*

I ease myself onto a low stone overlooking the moving plain and reach into my pocket for the nip bottle. God bless you, Jenny. Out

in the moonlit river, I can see the notebook moving silently east-
ward. *I'll drown my book.* I raise the bottle in a trembling hand to the
same pale moon we watched from Montparnasse, and drink to my
Celine, whose approach, across the fathomless valley of time, I can
almost feel.

Blind in Darien

Twenty-one students sat in front of Thomas Quinn, waiting idly for the show, but not much caring what it contained. They were, for the most part, inner-city kids, second or third-generation Hispanics and Asians. Kids who could not afford to be distracted, but who were endlessly distracted—who walked into the class with phones in hand and wireless buds tucked in their ears.

He noticed an empty desk which Jenny Botero usually occupied when she came. He glanced at his attendance roster and added another "A," making it three for this week. Dynesty was missing, too. He kept calling her Destiny, which naturally annoyed her and caused her to ignore the lesson and stare at her fingernails for quarter-hours at a time. "It's Dynesty!" she would chide him.

"I'm sorry. I've had a lot of Destinies, but I've never had a Dynesty." He wanted to add, "And why the hell did your mother misspell the name? So you could correct people about it all your life?"

66

Sometimes it seemed to him that his teaching career had been one long desire to speak tamped down by the imperative to keep his mouth shut. He recalled the obnoxious girl who'd loudly proclaimed in the middle of class, "You have a big, long hair growing out of your neck!" This was followed by donkey-like braying from the back of the classroom. *The loud laugh that bespeaks the vacant mind.* As he smoldered, he swallowed the burning retort that stirred in his throat, "Thank you, and you know, you're *really fat!*"

In his own high school days, the brothers, or the rough, crew-cut Mr. Kowalski were never reluctant to shout, "Hey, knuckle-head! Cut the crap!" He and his classmates had expected rigorous discipline and they never had to run to a counselor about it. Quinn marked Dynesty absent and closed the rank book. "Cell phones away! Earbuds out!" There was sluggish compliance; a few kids desperately typed out their final texts or tweets or Instagram comments. Someone asked the old familiar question: "What are we doing today?"

"See the vocab packet on your desk? That's what is known in police circles as 'a clue.' Another clue might be that it's Monday, and I've given you fifteen words every Monday since September. It's now March. Eriana, put the phone *away!*"

"It's my mother—she's face-timing me and my phone is vibrating in my pocket!"

He strode down the aisle, hand outstretched. "Give me the phone. I'll explain to her that you're in class."

She shoved the phone into her back pocket. "All right, all right."

"God, you are totally addicted!"

"Well," she said, "I wouldn't check my phone so much if people didn't keep texting me!"

"That's really your logic? Right. And I wouldn't be an alcoholic if there were not so many liquor stores."

He walked, more slowly, back to the front. "Elias, David—lose the hoods. Guys, really, you have to rule the phone. You can't let the phone rule you. Don't be a slave." He felt as if he was at the bottom of a hill that he just didn't have the strength to climb. *Move on.* "All right, we'll do a bit of vocabulary, and we'll continue with *Of Mice and Men*."

Julian, a friendly enough kid generally, with a man-bun and earphone cords dangling over his ears, was looking over the packet. "Mister, nobody uses these words. I never heard these words."

"Like what?"

"De-but? What's that mean?"

"It's not pronounced 'de-but' it's *day-byoo*. If an actress is in her first movie, it's her screen debut."

"What?"

"Her movie debut. Her first movie."

"Why doncha jus' say 'It's her first movie.' You don't need these words."

Quinn sighed. Was it becoming harder every year to reach them, or was he just getting older? He remembered the article he'd seen in *Atlantic.* "Has the Smartphone Destroyed a Generation?" These kids had grown up with smartphones—connected from an early age, not to words, but to videos, to images, to 'face-time and 'Snapchat.' And because they never turned off their phones, they received texts and alerts throughout the night. Their brains, overstimulated by 'Fortnite' or 'Grand Theft Auto,' could not wind down in restful sleep. In thirty-two years, he had never seen so many tired kids.

Twenty years ago, even ten years ago, Julian's complaint would have been the catalyst for one of Quinn's urgent pleas for literacy. He might have told them how a good carpenter had a shed full of tools, some of which he used only rarely, that language was the greatest tool, and that you needed to stock your toolbox from the great shed of the English language. Words! Just to say, 'You know what I mean,' is not enough! Say what you mean! Say *exactly* what you mean.

I did not wish to live what was not life, living is so dear; nor did I wish to practice resignation, unless it was quite necessary. I wanted to live deep and suck out all the marrow of life, to live so sturdily and Spartan-like as

to put to rout all that was not life, to cut a broad swath and shave close, to
drive life into a corner, and reduce it to its lowest terms . . . .

Yes, he would have felt an obligation to try to elucidate all of this,
or some of it, in language they could understand. There is a reason
we're here. It's called education. Shaping and sharpening the tools
of the mind. But he knew from repeated demoralizing experience
that this sermon would be met with vacant stares and tired yawns.
Nothing he could say, no fine paragraph of Dickens or Dinesen or
Thoreau could compete with what was in their pocket—the viral video worth a thousand words. The photos of Kim Kardashian's pon-
derous wobbling ass. The endless pouting selfies, the twerking, the
big-breasted girls guzzling tequila at a roadhouse bar, the gang fights,
the skateboarder slamming into a tree—the uninterrupted stream of
attention-stealers—all the titillating and degrading spectacles rising
out of the witch's cauldron of the garbage culture and projected onto
impressionable minds. We don't need these words. This book is boring. I hate reading. Why do we need to write? Who's Billie Holiday?
Who's Emily Dickenson? Who's Jack Kerouac? Who cares?

His grandparents, immigrants with an eighth-grade education,
could recite large swaths of Thomas Moore from memory. They read
and wrote in a beautiful cursive script that looked like calligraphy.
These kids couldn't write or even read cursive; educators had given
up teaching it in elementary school. "Google and Apple stockholders
are rich," Quinn thought, "and our children are so damned poor."

The hard truth was that the battle was lost. Did anyone care
for finely expressed sentiments? To reach a greater understanding
through being forced to express it? Was it Hemingway who said,
"How do I know what I think about something until I write about
it?" Until I'm forced to hold it up in the light of language. These
students would never learn to express feelings and thoughts that are
difficult to communicate, difficult even to sound within themselves.
They would never appreciate words, understand the wisdom of prov-
erbs, the meaning of a sonnet, the truth of a metaphor. They would

never be aware of how a gullible public is manipulated by politicians and influenced by marketers. They would not learn this from him. They would not learn it from anyone. They didn't want to know. *You don't need these words.* It wasn't just the reluctant scholar of the past. There was something different here—a sea change in perspective, worldview, attitude and attention span.

He began to go over the weekly vocabulary on the Smartboard: *adequate, aspire, bias, blatant, candid, confront, debut, enroll, fluster, impunity, intensify, intimidate, lethal, redundant, status.*

"No one uses these words," Julian muttered again.

"They are common words!" he nearly shouted.

It was time to retire. The gulf between him and them grew wider every year. An old white man. That's what they saw. With a worldview that might as well have been derived on another planet. He thought he should hold on for one more year; his daughter would be done with college, and he could walk out of this window-less, cinder-block-walled room forever. "Look," he said, "I'm sorry, Julian. It's just that I'm too tired to explain once more why this is important. I've been over all that in this room with generations of kids before you were born. You'll just have to take my word . . . ."

"I'm jus' sayin' I never heard 'em," he mumbled sullenly.

When the introduction to the week's vocabulary was over and they had looked at some of the roots and done a brief reading that used the words in context, Quinn turned their attention to *Of Mice and Men.*

"Can't we jus' watch the movie?" someone asked.

"Reading books and watching movies are not the same thing. We read chapter four yesterday, in which we see the loneliest character in the book, Crooks, the stable-buck." A thought occurred to him. Someone could argue that Curley's wife might be the loneliest, but any such assertion was beyond the scope of the very limited interest they took in this or any book.

"Crooks is an outcast among the working men because he's crippled and African-American. He's bitter, naturally. He's also quite literate. You know what I mean by 'literate'?"

The class was silent. A few shook their heads.

"He could read. In fact, he reads a lot. Remember that at that time, the 1930's, it would not have been easy for an African-American to get a good education. Many couldn't read."

"Mister, that's racist." Alan Kheav was rarely serious, but he liked to stir the pot when he saw an opportunity.

"The society was racist, yes. Absolutely."

"You shouldn't say they couldn't read," he ventured.

"Oh, really? Is it also racist to say that slavery existed in this country until 1865? And that during that time it would have been illegal to teach a slave to read, making the achievement of someone like Frederick Douglass nearly miraculous—nearly a miracle?" He pointed to the poster of Frederick Douglass on the back of his door. *Knowledge makes a man unfit to be a slave.*

Alan shrugged and gave his disarming smile, as if to say, *I'm just busting your balls, Mister.* He really had no opinion worth asserting or defending. He had assimilated the idea, the fear, that any statement mentioning African Americans might be racist, but not why, or in this case, why not.

"Do you know what's racist?" Quinn asked them now. "Do you know what I think is racist? When society allows Apple and Google and Facebook to conduct large-scale tests on an entire generation of kids, a lot of them minorities like you, kids who may not have anyone at home to tell them to turn off the video games and the phone and take off the earphones and pick up a book or just go to bed. And these kids, some of you, are not developing the skills you need to succeed. Look, before we get back to the book, let me give you two pieces of advice. First, you need self-discipline if you want to be successful. You can't be entertained all the time. You have to force yourself to do some hard work, to learn things you may not want to learn, to read things that you don't quite get yet or that you think are boring. Keep doing it—it will get easier, and your tastes will develop. If you swim every day, swimming becomes like walking. If you read every day, it gets easier and more and more interesting. And you'll begin to think more clearly and understand the world in a deeper way. As my grandfather used to say, 'If you don't read, you don't *know*.'

My second piece of advice is to get *passionate* about something. Find something creative you can do as an outlet. Paint. Write a poem or a song. Pick up a musical instrument. If you cut out one hour a day out of YouTube and social media and spend it practicing the guitar, within a year or two you'll have a talent! Learn a new language. Make a study of something! Imagine if you really spent one hour a day learning math on your own? Push yourself! No one forced Frederick Douglass to learn to read and write so brilliantly—they tried to stop him! His body may have been in chains, but he freed his mind, and made himself unfit for slavery! You are responsible for your own growth as a human being! Don't be satisfied with just what I'm trying to teach you here!"

He searched their faces, hopefully, thinking that maybe, somehow, he was reaching them. "Does anyone have something that you do on your own . . . something that you're passionate about, something you're really interested in, that you want to learn about, or some skill you would like to develop and master? Anyone?"

Karina, a slim, quiet student slowly raised her hand.

"Karina! Yes! What is it?"

"Can I go to the bathroom?"

He noticed that the other students did not laugh. They had not been struck by the incongruity of the appeal and the response. All his life he had loved words, he had been moved by words; he had seen into the heart and soul of this world through the words of great literary minds, sometimes finding himself breathless. Keats had once likened his reverent wonder at reading Chapman's Homer to the awestruck emotion of Cortez's crew, gazing out for the first time over the endless waterway of the Pacific: *Silent, upon a peak in Darien.* A large part of his charge here as a teacher was to enable or even to prepare these students to experience that feeling. But he saw, once again, that his words carried no weight. "Fill out a pass," he said. "I'll sign it." His own voice sounded distant and hollow to him; the mundane words of school-speak that they understood so well.

He put them in groups and gave them some questions to work on. He overheard a few students discussing a girl fight in the cafeteria "... was putting her on blast. Posting mad shit about her." He could not do this for another year—not for another month. Karina gave him the pass to sign. She had left the time blank, because, he was sure, she could not read the analog clock that hung on the wall, a relic of a former age. Quinn wrote in the time and signed it and handed it to her. Something was pressing on his heart, or something deeper, maybe his soul, which he felt was fully awake to the fact of its horrible enclosure, turning in desperation from wall to cinderblock wall within the windowless room, while the clock that no one could read quietly traced the passing hours. There was only one exit. He sat at the desktop computer and began to type his letter of resignation to the superintendent.

The Goldfish

The goldfish lasted for a week or two. My five-year-old son Alex and his friend Joey probably killed it by continually bringing it outside to oversee their Wiffle Ball contests, and by overfeeding it or feeding it things that a goldfish had little use for. The fishbowl grew cloudy with decomposing Saltines and Chips Ahoy! and though I changed the water a couple of times, the whole situation was probably traumatic for the creature, and before long "Goldy" was floating atop the glass-bound watery world that had been its brief home.

Alex cried, and to alleviate his sorrow, I suggested we hold a funeral ceremony for Goldy. Together, we lined a little matchbox with felt and placed the dead fish in it. Alex led the solemn procession, followed by his three-year-old sister, Sandra, his buddy Joey, and Joey's little brother Zach. Jake, our retriever, brought up the rear, tongue lolling. I waited with my hand trowel by the tiny grave I'd dug in the yard. Alex knelt beside it and placed the box in the hole. Then we all stood around for a minute, staring down at the matchbox coffin. Jake looked from the hole to the humans, expectantly.

"Would you like to say a few words, Alex?" I asked.

The maple tree stirred in a breeze, and the speckled shadows moved over his blond head. "What words?"

"Just some parting words, about Goldy?"

He nodded and thought for a minute. "Goldy," he began, but he paused, and his upper lip began to quiver. "You were a good fish!" he cried and burst into tears as Joey sniffled and Sandra looked about, confused. I wondered if the ceremony had been such a good idea after all. I said a quick blessing and filled in the hole. "Very nice, boys," I said. "You did right by Goldy."

In the house, I put the ballgame on the radio while I continued some painting I was doing on the kitchen cabinets. A while later I looked out to see the children chasing each other around the yard. When my wife returned from shopping and asked how the funeral had gone, I said it was a sad occasion, but that Alex appeared to have gotten over it. We heard the children's shouts and Jake's barks from the yard. I concluded that Goldy had joined the forgotten dead.

After dinner that night, I read *Burglar Bill* to Alex while my wife finished reading *The Cat in the Hat* to Sandra in the next bedroom. Finally, I tucked him in, stopped to kiss Sandra goodnight, and joined my wife, who was reading a detective novel in our bedroom. She took off her reading glasses and smiled. One of the things she had purchased in her shopping that day was a black peignoir. She looked beautiful, and I kissed her and asked her the old question with my eyes. She feigned a sort of shocked expression, and whispered, "Wait. The kids are still awake."

We read our books for a while—I was four chapters into *To the Lighthouse* and struggling to find a plot. I went downstairs to brush my teeth and get the coffee ready for the morning. As I headed back upstairs, thinking to share some intimate moments with my wife, I stopped. At the top of the stairs, I heard muffled sobs coming from

Alex's room. I opened his door and stepped into the boy's room, dimly lit with a night light.

"What's wrong, Alex? Are you still sad about Goldy?"

"No," he said, but he was still crying.

"What is it? What's wrong?" I approached and sat on the edge of his bed.

He choked out the words. "Jake is going to die, too."

"Jake's only five. Dogs can live ten or fifteen years."

"But he's going to die. And Grammy is going to die, and you're going to die, and mom is going to die, and Sandra, and everyone is going to die. And I'm going to die, too."

I felt as if my whole body, or my soul, if there is such a thing, were a lake, and his words were stones that fell against me and sank into my core. Those were fears I could not allay with philosophy or dismiss as unreal. I knew my wife, under such circumstances, would speak of heaven, and God and angels, and how we would all be reunited in heaven, and Jake too, and even Goldy, swimming in a big eternal fishbowl. But I didn't want to say that, because I didn't believe in that kind of heaven, in any kind of heaven really, and I hate hypocrisy above all things.

What could I say? That life was beautiful, eternal in some way, but probably not for individuals? Should I tell him to enjoy the people and animals he loved and to be kind to them because it's all over so soon, an 'insubstantial pageant,' as the poet said. Would that comfort a five-year old? I thought of the old cemeteries of New England, so full of gravestones whose fading names, if shouted, roused no memory among the living. And of the weeping families and friends who'd seen them lowered there, all gone and forgotten, too, and beyond that, back to the first humans who emerged from the plains of Africa some two million years ago—all gone without a trace.

I felt the bed beneath me shake with Alex's sobs, as, for the first time, Death had shown his pale face amid the playthings of childhood and pointed a bony finger at everyone the boy loved, and he had understood. I sat there in the dim glow of the night light, stroking his head, and finally leaned over and kissed him and said, "No matter what happens, Alex, we'll all be together again someday in heaven."

His crying ceased, and I heard his dear voice in the darkness. "Will we, Dad? Do you promise?"

"Of course," I said. "You know I always tell you the truth."

"Dad, will you lie down with me?"

"Sure, Champ, move over."

By the time I got to bed, my wife was asleep; but my amorous thoughts had vanished. I heard a siren in the distance and wondered, as it faded, what trouble it meant for someone. Love is so terribly hard. With every ounce of your will, you want to protect the ones you love, and never let them be hurt by anything, but the reality is you can protect them from so very little. Maybe the best you can do is prepare them for the hard truth of pain and death, and I thought that maybe I should have tried to tell Alex about the circle of life and that we are part of something so big that we, individually, are insignificant, like shooting stars that streak across the sky and then are extinguished and consumed to dust. Maybe I should not have filled his head with angels and eternal joy, with visions of his parents and his sister and Grammy and Jake and Goldy reunited forever, but it hurt me too much to watch the little boy ponder these separations.

I promised myself that when he was a little older, I would not hide my mind from him. I would tell him that his mother could well be right—that there could be a heaven—I had no way of knowing, but that I believed in the good sense of what Henry Thoreau had said on his deathbed, "One world at a time." I would tell him I hadn't wanted to lie to him; that love is hard, and it makes the truth of loss even harder. I would tell him that we were here, now; maybe not forever, but nevertheless bound deeply in the miracle of life and love, and that was truer than anything.

September

Cody Mullane leaned against a goalpost that cast its forked shadow out toward midfield and picked the clotted turf from between his cleats. Around him, the haggard players of the varsity squad of Cardinal Powell Academy, (where boys became men), panted like tired dogs, hands on knees, or, clutching their face masks, raised gaping mouths toward the sky. It was the start of the season, and earlier that afternoon they'd lost a scrimmage against Central High, 6-0. Coach Gage hated losing, even a scrimmage, and so, long after the visiting team's bus had rolled out of the parking lot, the Powell Panthers continued running plays and doing wind sprints. The coach paced the five-yard line. "You're doggin' it!" he shouted. "Let's go! Line up on the goal!"

Cody took his place. The smell of grass, churned earth and sweat engulfed him. The whistle sounded like some inexorable summons and the line surged forward. Running backs and receivers led the charge, leaving a ragged rearguard of linemen. The coach harangued the stragglers, trotting alongside them. "Lewis, you tub of shit! Move your fat ass!"

Standing in the end zone, the faster players shaded their eyes against the lowering sun and watched the pathetic display. "What a total asshole," Hurley muttered, between breaths, to no one in particular. Cody nodded, "For sure."

Green, Allen, Peterson, and the heavier guys lumbered up, with Lewis trailing while the coach barked insults at him. Finally, Coach Gage stood before them in his tight shorts and Cardinal Powell Football tee shirt. He was in his late twenties, which to the high school boys made him a man, quite old. He wore a crew cut, except that the hair in front was a bit longer and dyed blond. Short, muscular, and pugnacious, he always looked as if someone had just said something outrageous to him. It was given out that he'd played slot receiver at Holy Cross. And now he was their coach. He decided who would start, at what position, and for how many minutes. He had a hot temper and there were only a few players who were so good that he would never bench them.

Cody had not been one of them last year, but he'd spent the summer practicing, running sprints out of a three-point stance, catching bullet passes that arrived just as he turned on a square-out, and long balls from whoever would throw them, rehearsing over and over the slight sideways adjustments to the ball, so that it flew over his right or left shoulder and fell into his outstretched hands. He was ready to show what he could do, which had not been much today.

Gage had put him in at tailback, a position he'd shared with Hudson last season, and cornerback on defense. At tailback, he had never really been able to break through the jumble of bodies on the line to get free and show his speed. He needed a little space to receive the ball in a position where he could beat an opponent one on one. His greatest wish was to have the coach give him a chance at receiver, where he'd have a shot at one day being able to tell his father he caught the winning touchdown pass in the Thanksgiving game.

Coach Gage bit on his whistle, looking them over. Then he spat the whistle disgustedly; it dangled on the lanyard across his emblazoned shirt. "You guys tell me you want to play football, and I don't believe you! Diaz! You lost the game for us! You were standing out there with your jockstrap down! DeSouza, you're on the bench until you prove to me you can hang on to the damned football! Every one of you disgraced this school today! You are *not* football players! You are *pussies!*"

He shook his head slowly and made a face as if he smelled something noxious. The sunlight bathed the whole scene in the golden clarity of a September afternoon, but none of them was thinking about the beauty of the day. "What's the matter?" the coach demanded, "Were they too *big* for you?"

They were trying to avoid his accusing stare when another voice broke the silence. "Yeah, they were."

Frank Hurley was slightly smaller than most of the other players but rugged, quick, wiry, hard to bring down on a punt return. Cody moved involuntarily to one side; the whole team parted as the coach approached. He strode up to the offender and slapped the side of his helmet hard. Hurley staggered. "What are you, a goddamn comedian?" he shouted. "Everyone else to the showers! Hurley, stay where you are! Lewis! Peterson! Allen! Collect the pinnies and the balls."

After the other boys had showered and gone out to the parking lot, they saw that Hurley was still running laps, and the bus driver said he couldn't wait. Hurley would have to walk home. As the bus growled out of the lot, they could see Coach Gage strutting about with his clipboard and hear his ardent cry from the shadowy field. "You're doggin' it, Hurley! Pick it up!"

Hurly had guts and Cody admired him. The coach *was* an asshole, and there was only one reason that Cody even wanted to be on the team. He'd only tried out last year because he'd started to play a lot of tag football at the park and thought varsity ball might be fun. It wasn't fun, but the coach had convinced them that quitters were candy-asses, and he decided to stick it out for the season just to show that bitch he could take it.

Then there was his father. He used to play football with the Walker Warriors, a local semi-pro team until Pearl Harbor made real warriors out of all of them. But once Cody had made the team, success on the gridiron became the first genuine ambition his father seemed to have for him, and when the old man told him that he would be going to see him play one Saturday night against Oak Hill under the lights at Tomach Stadium, Cody was determined to make him proud—but Gage screwed him.

Every day at practice, and in every game so far, he'd run tailback; he had memorized all the plays and run them hundreds of times. "Bootleg right on the first go," "Square out left on the third go;" he had every play down, whether he would take the ball that was slapped into his gut and follow a blocker or a pulling guard, block on a quarterback sweep, or hang back for a draw play or to protect the quarterback.

Coach Gage arrived late to that game, as Halloran and Collier, the co-captains were putting them through their warm-ups. He seemed angry and distracted, rifling through papers on his clipboard as he announced the starting line-up. Cody was not on it, but that was all right; he'd be subbing in for Hudson at tailback, and would probably get in at cornerback on defense, too.

Five minutes into the game, Lemay, the starting halfback, fumbled. The quarterback recovered it, but Gage was furious; he ran out onto the field, calling for Lemay to come off. The ref raised a finger, entwined with his whistle cord, and warned the coach to get off the playing field. Wildly, Gage looked about. His gaze rested on Cody. "Mullane! Get in there at halfback!" *Halfback?* He had never played halfback—he didn't know the plays! "Coach, I . . . ."

"Goddamit, do you wanna play or not? Lemay sit your ass down!" Cody ran out onto the field, hoping that Hudson knew the halfback plays and that they could swap positions; the crimson uniforms of the team were bright under the lights, and the silver helmets shone; the grass was so green, it was as if he was in a Technicolor movie, and he knew that somewhere in the blur of spectators in the stands, the old Walker Warrior was watching his son. The huddle was already formed, and Cody leaned in and heard Billy Mack, the quarterback, say, "Slant right on the first go. Break!"

They all clapped on break and moved to their positions. Cody was lost. "Can you play halfback?" he asked Hudson.

"McDonald can . . . ."

"Can *you* for Chrissake?" He was sure he remembered Hudson playing halfback in practice, but the other shook his head. "Don't know the plays," he said.

"Shit."

It was a pass play, so Cody lined up in front of Hudson in an I formation, thinking it best to just protect Billy Mack, but he saw the QB holding the ball out to his right as if he expected him to run through for a play-action fake. He bowed his head and ran forward as if to receive the ball, left elbow up and forearms parallel, but just then Billy rolled out and nearly collided with him.

Even before the pass was thrown, he heard Gage's bellow from the sideline, "Mullane! What the hell are you *doing*?" He knew that his father heard it, too, and he shivered with shame. He wished he could disappear. The next five minutes, until the offense came off and the punting unit came on, were terrible ones, as he tried to guess his assignment on each play. Finally, he saw McDonald running onto the field calling his number. When the coach got in his face to chew him out, he was sure he smelled liquor beneath the peppermint he'd no doubt used to mask it, and he hated him. "I've never played halfback," he tried to explain again, but it was no use trying to explain anything to Coach Gage. On defense, the coach put him in at safety—again, inexplicably. He had never played that position either, but it was not as difficult because the safety on the other side told him to just key the end. Still, he slipped on one play and his man got well behind him. He gave up a long third-down completion. Oak Hill scored three plays later. The Panthers lost 21-14, and Gage said, "You let the team down, Mullane." Even worse, at home, his father said, "You looked indecisive out there."

"Of course I was indecisive! I didn't know what I was doing! I never played those positions!"

"I don't know. I guess you'd better learn what everyone's doing on every play."

He was right, because Coach Gage didn't know what the hell he was doing, either. Prick.

By the time Cody had eaten dinner and finished his math homework at the kitchen table, he was worn out and said goodnight to his parents. He felt a sense of home as he looked at them there, his mother knitting an afghan on the couch and his father reading *Grant Takes Command* in his stuffed armchair with his feet up on the ottoman. Upstairs, he thumbed through the records in the milk crate at the foot of his bed and picked out *4 Way Street*, the new album by Crosby, Stills, Nash, and Young. He set it on the turntable, put the needle down on "Cowgirl in the Sand" and lay on his bed, imagining the lovely cowgirl, her sweet smile, the soft contours of her body, and the warmth of her embrace as he kissed her neck, and inhaled the delicate perfume of her golden hair. He was nearly asleep when another figure intruded on these reveries. The cowgirl drifted into the tenebrous shade under the metal bleachers of the football field and before him rose the livid face of Coach Gage, fingers entwined in the bars of Cody's facemask, so close that he could smell the liquor and peppermint on his breath as he bawled, "*When are you gonna get tough, Mullane?* You knock that linebacker on his *ass!*" In dreams he glided through a maze of defenders, dodging their lunging arms or knocking them backward with a stiff arm. When he woke before dawn the visions of glory had faded and it was Hurley he thought of, doing laps around a vacant field.

There was an assembly in the morning. Father Sorrel came in to say Mass in the gym and bless the new school year. Cody missed the Latin Mass of his Catholic boyhood with its air of medieval mystery; it had been replaced with an insipid and monotonous English; the beautiful hymns had been supplanted with folksy renditions of what were supposed to be upbeat expressions of a hipper faith. He found them corny and dreadful. Two unmusical students with guitars swiped at innocuous chords as the principal, Brother Skulosky, raised his arms for all to join together in what he, unbelievably, thought was music, or at least a jolly spiritual sing-along. The Allman Brothers played music but listening to this crap really brought you 'down to the whipping post.'

Allelu, allelu, everybody sing allelu
For the Lord has risen it is true
Everybody sing allelu

Skulosky was known to the students as Screwloosky, or simply, the Screw. Behind him, Cody heard a couple of the boys singing their alternate rendition, which others soon picked up:

Fuck the Screw, fuck the Screw,
Everbody sing fuck the Screw.

After the Mass, the "Fall Athletes" were asked to go to the front and stand with their coaches. Mr. Tyler, the cross-country coach, praised his boys and urged everyone to stay for their first meet on Friday to support them. There was cricket applause and then Coach Gage took the mike with his team behind him. He was more subdued in front of the brothers than he was on the practice field or in front of his Phys. Ed. class.

"Well, ah, we got some work to do to get ready for the opener," he began, "but I know these guys are going to give it their all. They are going to push themselves harder than any team in this state, and when a team pushes . . . ."

A loud fart ripped the worn fabric of sporting clichés. The coach whirled about, red-faced, and glared at the team while the students who had been within earshot, about the first ten rows, burst into laughter. Gage covered the mike with his fist and said, "I'll see you jokers on the field." Then he gave a curt *thank you* and handed the mike back to the Screw, who offered a few fuddled words about the sort of demeanor that was expected of Cardinal Powell boys.

That afternoon, the coach, who normally came out five or ten minutes late for practice, was waiting for them on the field. He blew his whistle. "Form a circle around me!" There were thirty-eight of them altogether, and they formed a big circle with Gage in the center. Cody stood between Hudson and McDonald

"There are players here today who do not respect the team, the coach, the school, or themselves. They think it's funny to humiliate the team in public. Well, that's over. We are gonna learn discipline, and we are gonna get rid of the deadwood." He paced a circle within the larger circle, squinting at the boys as if he were Clint Eastwood. "Billy Mac! You're number one! Now count off!"

"One!" Billy shouted, and the circle spoke, each boy crying out his number, the full thirty-eight, as the coach made notes on his clipboard.

Then, with military resonance, he announced, "Welcome to the bullring!" He shook his head, regretfully, as if he was sorry that it had come to this. He stopped his pacing and said, "I wonder sometimes, who is the toughest guy on this team?" The boys shifted uneasily, and a clamor of voices rose in response to the coach's challenge, but Gage was only interested in one voice, and Hurley gave him what he wanted when he stepped forward and shouted, "I am!"

"Oh, really? You, Hurley? If you are the toughest Panther on this field, well, we're in deep shit. But let's see how tough you are. Take up your position in the center of the bullring."

Hurley stepped forward, chomping on his mouth guard and buttoning his chin strap.

The coach spoke to the rest of the team. "When I call your number, come out and hit Hurley as hard as you can. Your object is to get him out of the ring by any means possible. If Hurley gets *you* out of the circle, you take his spot in the center. The only rule is that there are no rules. It's time to *get tough*, girls. When you're in the center and you hear another number, you get out and let someone else have a crack at Hurley, or whoever is in the center. It will remain one-on-one at all times. By the way, we are gonna do this every day until we learn discipline and respect, or until those who show disrespect offer an apology to the coach and the team."

He stepped back and blew his whistle. Hurley stood in the center of the ring, waiting. "Seven!" he shouted. Ron DeCola came charging in and the two clashed. Hurley was knocked back a few steps because DeCola was heavier, but then Hurley grabbed his facemask and flung him to the ground.

"Thirteen!"

Gorman, a guard with thirty pounds on Hurley, rushed in, but Hurley threw himself sideways at Gorman's knees and brought him down. He sprang to his feet before the larger boy could get up and hit him again with a forearm to the helmet. Gorman was dazed, and Hurley had started to roll his body out of the circle when the coach shouted "Nine!"

Hurley turned and saw Paiva charging—he barely had time to stand and brace himself as Paiva slammed him back down, and the coach cried out "Twenty-nine! Footsteps Hurley! Footsteps!"

Paiva turned away and Hurley rose and turned to absorb a hit from Hudson. They rammed each other three, four times, pads and helmets crashing. Hudson tried to step on his foot, but Hurley was too quick; he moved sideways, punched him in the gut and slapped his helmet hard with the palm of his hand.

Hudson took a knee, gasping, and Gage shouted, "Three! Footsteps

Hurley! Footsteps!"

It was Bob Halloran, co-captain. He was tough, broad-shouldered, normally a quiet kid. Breathing hard, Hurley scanned the circle, and Cody saw that his nose was bleeding. "To your left, Frank!" he called.

Halloran slowed his attack, giving Hurley a chance to get set, but when they collided hard, Hurley was knocked flat on his back and his helmet flew off. Halloran stopped.

"What the hell are you waiting for Number Three? Get him out of the bullring!"

"He lost his helmet!"

"Are you fucking *deaf*? Get him out of my bullring!"

"I think he's hurt, Coach!"

"Cry me a river! Out of the bullring! *Now!*"

Hurley was pulling himself to his feet unsteadily. The blood from his nose was flowing onto his white practice jersey. He bent to pick up his helmet and fell to his knees, and the coach screamed at Halloran, "Hit him, you pussy!" Halloran stood immobile, and Cody could see in the expression beyond the facemask that some great turmoil was going on within him while Hurley staggered to his feet. Cody hoped that Halloran would refuse to hit him again. He wanted to see him take off his helmet and say, "Fuck you, Coach," and walk off the field.

Years later, he still wondered if some of them would have followed Halloran. Probably not. They had been brought up to respect authority, to defer to the adult, to follow orders. The coach was always screaming at them to get tough when the only real toughness they lacked was the toughness to tell him to go fuck himself. They were all afraid of him, all except Hurley, and that was why Gage hated him. And when Cody recalled his brief football career, he didn't regret that he never hauled in the winning pass on Thanksgiving Day, that he never had his eighty-yard run on some glorious Saturday morning, or that he never hoisted the division trophy before a roaring crowd. He didn't care about any of those things. His only regret was that he stood by when Halloran blew Hurley clean out of the bullring, and practice continued while he lay there. Cody Mullane's only football fantasy was to go back and do what he should have done that day and give his father a real reason to be proud of his son.

Here to Stay

I hadn't been to visit Henry in months. I always thought about it when I passed anywhere near the nursing home, but it was a trying experience emotionally, and it wasn't difficult to find a reason to put it off. I knew that when he was gone, I'd reproach myself for my faithlessness, and I resolved nearly every day to go and see him until I began to despise myself. It was at such a point, on a Saturday afternoon, that I crossed the rusting metal bridge and drove out to the Lakeview Nursing Home.

When I first began to visit my old friend at the facility, I was sure that he knew me. He would say my name and give me a thumbs-up, and his wife, Agnes, who was always there, would rub his arm and encourage him. If I told him a joke back then, he'd smile. Sometimes he repeated the last few words of my sentence. "You want to go out, Henry? It's a nice day."

"Nice day . . . ."

On my last visit, though, I had not been certain that he knew me or that he understood what I was saying. I was told he had a rare form of a degenerative disease that affected the brain. I know the name, but I don't even like to repeat it. I hate it. As the word "degenerative" indicates, there was nowhere for him to go but down. That's sad for anyone, but all of us who knew him felt that somehow it was sadder because it was Henry; he had always been larger than life—a man of resounding opinions, opinions that often contradicted those of everyone else in the room. He was blessed with a great heart; he had made some money, but he cared little for it and donated a lot of it to charity. He showered an unpretentious and forthright affection on his friends and family. He loved us all, and he didn't care who knew it. He was the life of every party, and of the card game he hosted every Friday night in his finished basement—a fine evening of whiskey, cigars, and good cheer.

His earliest symptom was a loss of that easy conviviality, a diminishment in humor. An occasional introspection devolved into a more habitual vacant withdrawal. He must have been aware that something was wrong. He had trouble concentrating on his poker hand and lapsed into long silences, and sometimes Johnny G or I would have to push his hand back so that he would not reveal his cards. Within a matter of months, the game had changed. It was difficult to watch, and one Friday night I traitorously found a reason not to attend, and then more reasons as the weeks passed until I met Al Preston at the Windsor Shoppe. He said Henry was still playing cards with them. "How's he playing?" I asked.

"Not too good," he admitted.

My old mother drew her worldview from the Catholic Church. She divided people into canonical categories. It was usually a woman who deserved the rank of "a saint," or "a martyr," whereas the best a man could hope for was to be called "a good egg." Quite often, though, he was a "lost soul," or "a devil." She, no doubt, inherited these categorizations from her mother, a native of County Sligo, because she pronounced that last term as "divil."

I probably absorbed some of this worldview, and yet, even had I been brought up by atheists, I'm sure I would have had the same opinion of Agnes, Henry's wife. She was a saint. Henry's sickness was an unspeakable curse, but he was blessed in her. No one ever took the vows, "for better or worse, in sickness and in health," more faithfully. She fought to keep him home, though her children knew that the situation had become untenable. Henry was a big man, and when he began to lose his balance, Agnes, with her tiny frame, could not support him. He fell, and she could not get him up. The ambulance had to come several times. It was not a safe situation for either of them, and her children insisted, correctly, that he would have to go to Lakeview. Agnes felt that somehow she had betrayed him by not managing to keep him at home, a regret she expressed on more than one occasion, and one which friends and family tried to assuage with reason. But, as the French say, the heart has reasons that reason cannot understand.

I don't know which was more painful, watching Henry slip into oblivion or watching Agnes try to hold him above the dark rising water. She was with him every day. She fed him. She talked to him. She brought him milkshakes or little nips of Irish whiskey which he raised in a trembling hand and drank quietly. Eventually, he was unable to do that, or even to swallow without some risk of choking. He required—more horrible words, a "feeding tube." He was ever less responsive, but still, she sat with him for hours, holding his hand, talking to him. What she said, only she knows, but when I visited, she would be there, talking softly, and asking questions that she had to answer for him. "Are you comfortable? No, you need another pillow. Here, let me tuck this in by your side. Is that better? Yes, that's better."

I'm not trying to paint a picture of pathos or sentiment, nor trying to pander to your sympathetic feelings. I'm just reminding you what's real. Some people can't see the words "saint," or even "love," without thinking that there's some ironic implication. There is none. And I'm not talking about Catholic doctrine or what we learned about heaven as children. I'm just saying that to me, a godless, card-playing, gin-guzzling, horse-betting *bon vivant* without a rosary or a statue in his house, Agnes was a living saint, and her love was a force of inexhaustible power.

"George is here to see you," she said as I entered the room. Henry sat in a wheelchair by the window. I used to bring him coffee, but as I said, he had no use for such gifts anymore. I shook his hand, and, rather awkwardly, he would not let it go. He held it firmly in a great fist that was still strong. "Let his hand go, Henry," Agnes said, "Let George go." She coaxed him to loosen his grip. I sat on the edge of his bed and spoke, rather too loudly. Agnes and I chatted about the forecast—impending snow, of the family, local news. She always included Henry in the conversation. Sometimes she would touch his arm, "Did you hear that, Henry? George says that Peter Tremblay threw his hat in the ring for the city manager's job." Henry blinked. Was that a sign of comprehension?

What astounded me was how Agnes seemed to feel at ease in this awful situation. I'm sure she had done her share of crying, and of raging against the inevitable, but she must have done these things alone. Before Henry, she was staunch. Her pleasant and seemingly carefree demeanor was an act of defiance against the disease, or fate. She behaved as though she were having coffee with her husband in their kitchen at home, as they had done for decades; as if he was only unresponsive because he was reading an interesting story in *The Boston Globe*.

After fifteen or twenty minutes, I had run out of things to say and was feeling more and more depressed. It was too warm in the room. I made my excuses and said my goodbyes, casting a last glance over my shoulder at the scene, as if to impress it on my memory for future reference, filed under *saint* and *martyr*, or maybe just under *love*.

There was a piano in the lobby, and as I got out of the elevator on the ground floor, I heard jazzy, unhurried chords. Some residents had formed a semi-circle with their wheelchairs around the baby grand; visitors were seated on the couches and wing chairs nearby; more chairs ran along the broad windows that overlooked a courtyard. I suppose Lakeview was a nice place, as such places go, but these "homes" are always separate realities outside the eager rush of life beyond their walls.

I had a sort of imaginative hallucination as I stood there watching this scene. For a moment, in my mind, I saw the pianist and all the people around him as skeletons, their various attitudes collapsed into jumbles of bones, their clothes tattered ribbons of fading colors, crooked mandibles hanging on bleached chest bones. The building, our bodies, the city itself which we inhabited, trifling barricades—castles of sand on the shores of leveling time. I roused myself and tried to shake off the feeling that seeing my old friend had produced in me, chiding myself that I was so reduced by a single visit, while Agnes had the courage, loyalty, and devotion to spend every day there with him.

The pianist, an older Black gentleman in a tux, cried, "George Gershwin!" and began to sing "Our Love Is Here to Stay." I took a seat and closed my eyes. The music soothed me, and though I knew that nothing was really here to stay, somehow the melody and the lyrics began to transform the brief tragic moments I had just spent with Henry and Agnes until finally I was left with an impression of something beautiful and ennobling in the hopeless fight. I thought of Agnes and the power of love to stay.

St. Lucy's Day

Frank recognized, as he opened the door and crossed the threshold to the dim interior, that nothing much had changed at the old downtown watering hole. It had been a hangout of his youth before he'd married a quarter-century earlier. Back then, he'd stop here after work, or on a Saturday night to see who was about, chat up women, or watch a few innings of a Red Sox game. Marriage, children, work, and bills put an end to all that, and it had been years, decades now, since he'd been back.

The smell that greeted him as he loosened his scarf and unzipped his jacket was like a handshake from an old acquaintance—stale beer, wood polish, and more than a hint of the lunch menu, which relied heavily on the flat grill and the fryolator. Above him, the tin ceiling was still stained to sepia with over a century of tobacco smoke, though smoking in bars had been outlawed in the new century. The wobbly belt-driven fans he recalled churning the air on summer nights were still on this December afternoon. It was the oldest bar in the city, they said, dating back to the 1800s, when, according to legend, Edgar Allen Poe had drunk here and rented the room upstairs. He came to the city to give some lectures on poetry, back when people cared about such things. Later, though still a few years before Frank's time, Jack Kerouac had regaled the crowd gathered at the long mahogany bar with tales out of *Don Quixote*.

What had changed, he saw, as the faces along the bar turned toward the closing door and his eyes adjusted to the shadows, was the clientele. Mostly college kids. Arthur, the gruff, perennial bartender in the days that were gone, no longer held his beery outpost like some antiquated Dickensian sentinel, his blue bartenders' union button pinned proudly on his white apron. In his place was a young woman with six inches of cleavage and sleeves of tattoos, and Frank tried not to resent her amiable smile.

He wished he hadn't come early, because until his friends arrived, he was an outcast of time, drinking in a place that, though physically the same, held only the vapors of the world he'd known. Or so he thought, but as he meandered into the murky sanctuary, he noticed an arm waving at the end of the bar and recognized an old friend.

"Willy!"

"Howsa goin' my man?"

"Ah, you know. Jesus, I haven't been in here in twenty years, and I think the last time I was in you were sitting on the same stool."

"Shee-it, man, this is my stool."

"And you look like you haven't aged a day."

"Well, you know what they say, 'Black don't crack.'"

"Guess not. How's . . . . Jesus, I forget her name . . . you wife?"

"Oh man, Linda, we been divorced fourteen years now."

"Ah, that's too bad. I liked her."

"Yeah, she's a good woman. We're still friends. Our son Bradley is in goddamn Afghanistan."

"That's a worry."

"Sure is." He drained his beer mug and pushed the empty glass away. "It *sure* is."

Frank caught the bartender's eye and ordered a Sam Adams, and another draft for Willie. "Last time I saw Bradley, you were pushing him on a swing over at Hadley Park."

"That's how time goes. You know, I apologize, but I haven't talked to you in so long, I forget your name. Was it Gary?"

"Frank!"

"Oh yeah, Frank. Shit, it's been a long time. Yeah, I ain't seen you in here for a *long* time. Just decide to revisit the old haunt?"

"Yeah, but you're the only ghost I see." Frank saw their reflection in the enormous mirror behind the rows of bottles festooned with artificial pine garlands and strings of red and green lights. Old ghosts. He had a sudden recollection of looking into this mirror the night before he got married, wondering how it would all turn out. He remembered the image he'd seen there: young, bearded, dungaree jacket. That's how time goes. "Some of us are meeting down here for Blinkie McNamara's sixtieth birthday. You remember Blinkie?"

"Ah, I probably remember him if I see him."

The bartender brought their beers. "Thanks. Stella, this is Frank."

She smiled, gave him a bright hello, and took his money.

"Ah, Stella," Willie said softly as she walked away, "how *did* you get so pretty?"

"Better lookin' than poor old Arthur," Frank said. "I heard he died."

Willie nodded and gave a rueful chuckle, "Arthur. Man, that was an old-fashioned bartender right there." They drank their beer and traded Arthur stories for a while until Lenny came in saying that it was only quarter to five and almost dark out there. "Shortest day of the year," he said, and Frank introduced, or reintroduced the two and asked Willie if he wanted to join them at a table in the back, but he said he was going to play a little Keno and was going to meet someone at Fury's to shoot some pool.

Frank gathered the change that Stella had left, pushing two singles back. "Listen, I'll see you in another twenty years, Willie."

"If I ain't dead, I'll be here!"

The old crew was assembled, Frank, Lenny, Walter, and the "birthday boy," Blinkie. They had gravitated to the same backroom booth near the window where they had sat decades ago as if no time had intervened. They found their initials among many others, painted over, but still visible in the tall backs of the wooden benches. They spoke for a while of the old days, which were somewhat glorified from this snug perspective, and which Frank found vaguely depressing. The truth was that there was a reason he had stopped coming to this bar and the other bars of his youth—a reason beyond the responsibilities of fatherhood and marriage. He'd been ready to leave all that behind; he never missed it, and he could not quite understand Willie's dogged insistence on maintaining his post at the bar while time moved on and the names of old friends faded.

"Just don't fuckin' embarrass me with that stupid Happy Birthday song," Blinkie requested. They immediately sang "Happy Birthday," to scattered, polite applause from the bar. Stella had the good grace, a minute later, to bring him a shot of Jack.

Blinkie tossed it back and said, "Sixty, Jesus Christ. I know *that's* old."

"O anguish," Walter proclaimed, "how the tormented heart trembles!"

Collective groans. "Oh, Jesus, there he goes with Shakespeare."

Walter, undaunted, corrected them. "Bach's *Passion According to Saint Matthew*. If I had stayed in Lowell, you homeboys might have got some culture." He was the only one of the old gang who had moved away. Though he'd been an English major, he had somehow got into sales of medical supplies, married a doctor, and made more money than the others combined. He had no inflated sense of self, though; he still valued his old friends and had flown up from Miami to be with them this weekend—though it was convenient that the holiday was near, and he still had family in the Valley.

"I resent that remark, Waldo," Lenny protested. "I got plenty of culture. I've watched every season of *Downton Abbey*. Just last night I dreamed I was banging Lady Mary Crowley."

"*Crawley.*"

"Whatever. She was *lovin'* it."

"Well," the birthday boy said, out of his glum reverie, "I suppose the next thing that will happen is we'll start dying."

A chorus of disgust. Walter made as if to get up and leave. "It was fun seeing you guys again," he said. More patrons had entered the bar and a couple of them started shoving coins into the jukebox.

Frank shook his head resignedly. "Boys, just be thankful you were not born forty years later. Look at this poor kid at the bar trying to chat up the redhead. He's talking to her, and she keeps swiping her phone and texting."

"Thank God they didn't have fucking iPhones when I was out there," Blinkie agreed. "I mean just about anything would have been more interesting than a conversation with me when I was twenty."

"Oh yeah, you've gotten a lot more interesting since," Walter said. "Now you can tell us about your swollen prostate."

"Oh fuck you, Walter."

"Hey, come on, it's his birthday," Lenny said.

"All of a sudden we're supposed to be nice to him just 'cause he's a venereal, I mean a venerable sixty?"

"Ah, we'll all be there soon," Lenny said, "but Frank is right; it's a different world. Maybe it's better, I don't know. I mean my son is gay—it's definitely better for him than it would have been forty years ago."

Walter had not heard this news before. "Arty is gay? Have you always known it, Lenny?"

"No, not really. I mean, maybe I suspected. And then he told us about a year ago. It was tough. I mean, you know, I love my son, of course, no matter what, but it's tough. And Carol was like, 'What's wrong with you? It's no big deal. What, are you homophobic?' I don't think I'm homophobic, but I don't know, am I supposed to be *happy* about it? Am I supposed to be happy that he'll never have the life I imagined, that I won't have grandkids of my own, see a lovely young woman caring for my grandkid—and that maybe he'll still face problems. You know, it's just not what I hoped for, I'm sorry. Call me a bigot."

"I hear you," Walter said. "I understand exactly what you're saying. But I wonder, you know, we're all products of our time, and I think that among these young kids today—they grew up so differently than us. They're much more tolerant than we were."

"No doubt about that," Frank said.

"Look how fast it's changed. Imagine if I told my father that two guys could legally get married? That would have been . . . unthinkable. They considered it a mental illness. And once we die off, which Blinkie says is coming shortly, there just won't be anything to it. You know, you're a lefty, you're a righty, you're straight, you're gay. We're the last generation that thought it was strange or wrong."

The others considered this, and Frank said, "My kid was filling out a job application, and there were a whole lot of choices for 'gender.' Male, female, transsexual, transgender, genderqueer, intersex, gender expansive, and then one that said, 'gender-void.' What does that even mean?"

"I'll tell you what. It's a fuckin' bizarro world out there," Blinkie noted.

"I don't know," Frank said, "OK, I'm an old fart, I know. Soon to join my friend here as a sextegenarian, or sexagenarian, or whatever it is, but the world that's coming kind of scares me. You know Maralyn was reading this article to me off the internet. Brad Pitt and Angelina Jolie, they have a kid, a girl, but they want people to refer to her as 'they,' a 'gender neutral' pronoun until *they* decide what sex *they* want to choose. I read that already in some places, school authorities don't want teachers to refer to children as boys and girls—they want everything 'gender-neutral' until the kids like, *choose* a gender."

"Christ," Lenny said, "*they* is plural. The correct gender-neutral pronoun would be *it*."

"Is it me, or is that fucked-up?" Frank asked.

"No, that's fucked-up," Blinkie assured him, "and by the way, this music really *sucks*. What is this shit? I'm gonna go put some Stones on the jukebox."

"Good idea," they agreed, and he slid out of the booth.

"Just to play devil's advocate," Walter said, "maybe in twenty years, 'cause this stuff is changing fast, if people heard this conversation, it would be like us hearing a conversation among a bunch of guys in Alabama in 1950 saying, 'Yeah these fucked-up people wanna stick blacks and whites together in the same school,' and to *them*, it seemed just as crazy as the shit we're talking about."

"I don't know," Frank said, "maybe. It's just that discrimination against someone because of skin color is a clear-cut violation of human rights. But this seems to be fucking with Nature."

"Or finally recognizing people's natures?"

"Are there really that many people in the wrong bodies? When did that happen? Or are adults putting these ideas in the kids' brains? I mean I don't care if 'they' want to change genders, but I'm just thinking, when we were kids, if the adults refused to recognize any differences between the boys and the girls, or said it was a choice we had to make, we would have thought they had lost their minds, right?"

Walter nodded and looked into his beer thoughtfully. "Well, yeah, it is pretty strange I guess, but the truth is we just don't fit in the new world anymore and that's it. You got four-year-olds with Facebook pages . . . posting and downloading shit. Dreaming of being a social media influencer."

"Remember when we were kids," Lenny said, "if we found a *Playboy* somewhere, what a big deal it was? I used to get excited about the marble nymphs frolicking in a fountain in an art book in the school library! Now, kids have 24/7 access to hardcore porno in their pockets . . . not to mention 'sexting.'"

"Yeah," Frank added, "along with how to make a bomb, join a suicide club, cyber-bully some poor kid, and everything else you can imagine and some you can't." Once again, they contrasted all this with the pastimes of their youth, when they used to swap comic books, build tree houses, and play tag football on the street. "And when you were home," Frank said, "you were disconnected from friends and had time to think, read, and become the person you were going to become."

Blinkie came back and picked up the thread of the conversation. "All in all," he declared, "we were better off before the fuckin' internet. Now you got child molesters and terrorists hookin' up with each other, girls from Oklahoma who see jihad propaganda bullshit and wanna go join ISIS. It's a fuckin' Pandora's Box is what it is." Frank listened to him, studying the haggard face and bloodshot eyes, the gray, drooping mustache; he was trying to recall the young man he had known. God, he looked old, as did Lenny, and Walter with his mane of white, and Frank wondered if they all saw him in this way, a shrunken, dried, and feeble shadow of the man he'd been, railing against the new world of which he was less and less a part.

They all felt better when the jukebox blasted the Stones' "Honky Tonk Women," and the conversation turned from the fucked-up world to women. The room was crowded now, and another bartender had come on to help, a burly guy with a Fu Man Chu and a bow tie. Stella came over and smiled good-naturedly at Blinkie's innocuous flirting. She cleared their bottles and he called for shots all around and more beer. Frank headed for the men's room. Passing amid the college girls, he felt once more like a ghost. He had become invisible to them. It wasn't that he wanted to cheat on his wife or even capture the interest of some woman young enough to be his daughter. No, it was just the strangeness of it—of this slipping through time, walking the same sunken floorboards, edging once again through the crowded space between bar stools and wall to the same graffiti-blasted bathroom amid the clatter of glasses, the ringing of the tip bell, the shouts, the friendly challenges, the bursts of laughter, while above it all now Mick Jagger vaunted his reputation as a Street Fightin' Man. It could be 1977, only for that fact that he had shrunk somehow, so that not a single woman smiled as he passed, or tossed her hair, or raised a pair of eyes to meet his. He had become a dull vitiated shadow of himself, a passing darkness that momentarily blocked the view of brighter lands.

When he returned to the table and reported that he had become invisible to women, the others nodded, understanding immediately. A story occurred to him, and he said, "When I was in college, I worked one summer with Blinkie here on the garbage trucks."

"Ashes and Waste," Blinkie corrected him.

"Right. And one day, I was tossing barrels with this guy, an older guy, well at the time I thought he was old—he was probably forty or something. He points to a guy crossing Broadway, and he says to me, 'You see that guy right there? He's forty-five years old, and he's never had a decent piece of ass in his life.'"

The others considered this awful revelation. "What was wrong with him?" Lenny asked. "Christ, I remember the day I scored three times with three different women in one twenty-four-hour period. Have I told you that story?"

"Many times," Blinkie said.

"I don't know what was wrong with him," Frank continued, "or anything else about him. I just remember this guy telling me that, and I thought it was one of the saddest things I'd ever heard. So, my point is, yeah, we're invisible, but what the hell, we're old. We did have our day, though. No one is ever gonna say that about us. Let's drink to that."

They drank to that, and Frank added, "May I also say, at the risk of being, what's the word . . . ."

"Obscene?" Walter asked.

"No."

"Palaverous?"

"Stop! Impertinent. At the risk of being impertinent, that I would say that all of your wives and my own would qualify as, you know, a decent piece of ass."

The others were quiet for a moment, and Frank said, "Look, I'm not suggesting wife-swapping or anything like that. You know, I just mean, they are attractive women, and ... very good women."

"Are you drunk?" Lenny asked.

"I think so, but we made out all right, single and married. And none of our kids is a drug addict or in jail. Lenny may not be overjoyed that his kid is gay, but he'll tell you Arty is a great kid, right?"

Lenny nodded, "Fabulous kid."

"Absolutely. We're happy, right? Why is everyone looking at me like I'm suggesting—like I'm suggesting something crazy or something?"

"Nah, you're not crazy," Walter said. "I think we're happy, probably happier than a lot of people. It's just that, you know, when you get to be our age, you do wonder how things might have been."

"Might have been?" Blinkie nearly shouted. "You're one of the beautiful people, for Chrissake! Swimming pool, no doubt a stainless-steel kitchen, deck the size of my yard, a knockout doctor wife, and a damned beach house! You *might have been* stuck teaching English at Lowell High and married to Dolly Muldoon."

Walter, who had always been able to laugh at himself, slouched in the bench, leaning sideways against his bleary-eyed accuser. Finally, he sat up and as the laughter subsided, he said, "Like I said, I'm happy. I've had a good life. So far—you never know what's coming. But I mean, OK, for example, I like to ski, right? I always have—we always skied when we were younger ...."

"Until it got too goddamn expensive," Lenny said.

"It is expensive. Anyway, my wife doesn't want to ski. She doesn't want to go anywhere cold. That's how we ended up in goddamn Miami. I'd love to take a ski trip with my wife. Yeah, I got the money, but my wife doesn't want to do that."

"So, you want a woman who skis?"

"I know it sounds crazy. But there's this woman, a neighbor of mine, and she loves to ski—we talk about it—she and her husband go to Vail, up to Maine, even the Alps. Not that I don't get along with my wife, but I wonder how it would have been if I had married *her*, or a woman like her, an active, outdoorsy woman who wanted to go kayaking, mountain climbing, skiing . . . . I just think it would have been a lot of fun. It makes you wonder, that's all."

"Human nature," Lenny said. "To wonder like that. But you know, the woman on the skis could have turned out to drive you crazy in some other way."

"I know. I know."

"And you wouldn't have the kids you have. You might have had the drug addict jailbird we were talking about with the other one."

"I love my wife. I love my kids. You just wonder a little bit sometimes. Or maybe it's that you want to live more than one life."

Lenny got up to hit the head, and Blinkie said he was going to order another round. "We're gonna have to take a cab and get our cars tomorrow," he said.

Walter said, "That's all right," and handed him thirty bucks, "It's your birthday, man. Your money's no good."

When they were gone, Frank leaned across the table and said, "Let me ask you one thing. You travel around for business all the time. Strange cities. Hotel bars. You ever cheat on your wife? It's in the vault, of course."

"Senator, I have no recollection . . . ."

"It's just that I always wonder about the traveling businessman."

"OK, for the deep vault files. Once. But it wasn't on business."

"The woman with the skis?"

"No. Only in thought."

"There was a woman. Afsoon, her name was."

"Afsoon," Frank said speculatively.

"Persian name. Working as a rep for another company. She used to come by sometimes. We'd share leads because clients who bought her products might also want my stuff and vice versa. Her family was from Iran originally, rich people back under the Shah who fled when the ayatollahs took over. Stunning woman. Huge brown eyes. Short dark hair. Even her voice . . . ." He shook his head and blew a sort of sigh. "I was attracted to her, what can I say? So, she comes by late one Friday afternoon. We're discussing foreign films and writers, having a great conversation, and finally, I ask her if I can make a copy of a couple of pages of one of her catalogs for a client—anyway, my section of the building is empty by now, but when I take the catalog, I thought she would wait in my office. She follows me down to this little copy room at the end of the corridor, and as I said, there's *no one* around. I'm making the copies, and I'm aware that she is right next to me, and suddenly my heart is beating like mad, and I'm panicking, what am I gonna do? I'm at the edge of this precipice, you know? I don't know whether to run or kiss her."

Frank waited.

"Well, I almost ran. I almost bolted for the door, but I was still young, and I suppose full of hormones, not that that's an excuse, but when she moved her body against mine in that small space . . . I turned and she was looking up at me with those big brown eyes, I just . . . well I'd have to plead temporary insanity if it came to trial."

"Right there? You did it in the copy room?"

"Temporary insanity."

"No affair?"

"The charms of this woman faded, I mean *immediately*, as panic set in. Terror! I saw divorce, disgrace, my wife betrayed, my kids ashamed, the house for sale. I realized I didn't even know if she was on birth control. What if she was pregnant—or if she had some disease? What if she turned out to be a fatal attraction, started calling me at home and breaking into my house to boil rabbits on the stove?"

Frank laughed. "None of which happened."

"No, and when Afsoon saw my reaction—I couldn't hide it, she told me not to worry. I never saw her again as a matter of fact. What a cowardly heel she must have thought me. The ironic thing was that I felt closer than ever to Laura afterward. I felt as if I had brushed with losing her, and it made me realize how much I did love her."

"Interesting."

"Yes, I fell in love with her all over again." He paused and drank his beer, then leaning over the table toward Frank he added, "which still didn't prevent the odd fantasy about a sexual encounter with a snow bunny at an Alpine retreat."

"Ah, you're a terrible man."

Walter nodded, "Aren't we all? And what about you?"

Frank shook his head. "Never. Couldn't do it. Like you said, the fear of losing the respect of your wife—your kids."

"And you love your Maralyn, right?"

"I do. And I think it would be much easier for her to cheat on me. All a woman has to do is . . . ."

"Stand too close to a guy making copies."

He shrugged. "And I wouldn't be happy."

"Well, you kept your vows. That's a good thing, Frank."

Lenny and Blinkie emerged from the crowd, the latter clutching a round of barroom bottles by the long necks. "Hey," Blinkie said, "this chick over at the bar says I'm the sexiest, sixty-year-old she's ever fuckin' seen! I'm tellin' you, she's impressed. I told her I could still show a woman a good time. That's why they call me *Irish swag-alicious.*"

"Yeah, she's still laughing," Lenny said.

"Sixty, Jesus!" Blinkie said. He set the bottles on the table.

"Sixty is the new forty," Frank said.

"Yeah, right. Fuckin' death is the new power nap."

"Speaking of Jesus," Walter said.

"Ah, shit. Here's that awful fuckin' ghetto gangsta bullshit on the jukebox again. What say we chug these beers and then walk over to the Greek joint—the Athenian—watch the belly dancer?"

Frank saw that Lenny was already yawning. It was near midnight and no doubt past their normal bedtimes. Not like the old days. They finished their beers and put on their coats and passed invisibly through the crowd and out under the stars. They breathed the chill air, expelling fogs of breath. Walter spread his arms as if to embrace the night or his old hometown, and recited:

Study me then, you who shall lovers be
At the next world, that is, at the next spring.
For I am every dead thing,
In whom love wrought new alchemy

"Oh Christ, let's go, he's drunk and now he's gonna get fuckin' eloquent! We'll see you at the Greek bar!" Blinkie cried, pulling Lenny by the arm, and Frank watched that dark parade set off along the canal in what seemed to him a somber reenactment of pub crawls now four decades gone, while Walter, the scholar of their younger days, continued his recitation.

But I am none; nor will my sun renew.
You lovers, for whose sake the lesser sun
At this time to the Goat is run
To fetch new lust, and give it you,
Enjoy your summer, all . . . .

Frank leaned back against the warped clapboards of the old building and listened.

The Dog, the Wife, and the Friend

"I am I because my little dog knows me."
—Gertrude Stein

Captain was old. Twelve years old. People always ask, "How many *human years* is that?" I don't know how accurate those kinds of formulas are, but if you're a Labrador Retriever, you're running out of time after ten years above ground. One thing about time—it never slows down just because a dog or a man happens to be running out of it. Captain began to fade after his ten years in the sun. Two years beyond that, his muzzle, once sleek and sable, was grizzled, and a mask of white crept around his eyes. No more would he charge through the woods on the heels of a rabbit or plunge like an Olympian into Flint's Pond just to fetch some crazy stick. He was done with all that, and he lumbered after me in the thin light of morning, a sad ghost at my heels.

His spine sagged and his haunches trembled. He was nearly deaf, and he snored, and sometimes he would just look up at me with cloudy eyes, kind of bewildered, as if to say, "Jesus, Ozzie, what the hell happened to me?" A huge lump grew out of his neck; the vet cut it and drained it and Captain stumbled around with a lampshade over his head, banging into walls and suffering shame. Another baseball-sized lump blossomed out of his side, but I ignored this one since it didn't seem to bother him as much as the lampshade would.

I brought him to the vet again, though, when he started pissing in the house. The first thing she said was, "He's due for his rabies shot."

"How's he going to get rabies? He hardly goes out of the house except for a walk around the park on a leash."

"It's the law," she said and poked him with the needle. Captain never flinched.

I explained to her that the dog seemed unable to control his bladder. My amateur diagnosis was a urinary tract infection, and I hoped some antibiotics would help.

"I brought a urine sample," I said, setting on the table a bag which held a Paul Newman salsa jar full of Captain's piss. I had held it under him in the chill dawn, standing in my slippers on the frosty earth while the dog blinked at me, his mild eyes saying, "You're a strange man, Ozzie."

Two vertical lines between her eyebrows deepened as she peered into the bag. "When did you get the urine sample?"

"Yesterday morning."

"That's too old. We'll have to catheterize him."

Yeah, let's just torture the poor animal, I thought. "I can get another sample."

"Oh, the catheter won't bother him. It's tiny." She raised a hand, forefinger and thumb nearly touching.

"I hope it's tiny. I mean he's no John Holmes." Her assistant snickered, but the vet frowned and turned back to the dog. "We're going to need to run some blood tests, too." I stood there holding the leash while they pulled him by the collar into an adjoining room. He was looking back at me, like "Ozzie, come on, man. What the *hell*?" I felt bad. First, that he didn't understand why I was letting these people mess with him, and second, that I knew he'd forgive me anyway.

I called after him. "It's OK, Cap'n," and went to sit in the waiting room. They had about fifty back issues of *Bark Magazine*, and I started reading an article called "Wolf Pack Behavior." Some poor sucker was paying his bill. "Jesus," he confided to me, while they went to fetch his schnauzer, "six hundred and forty bucks!"

"What, did he get hit by an Escalade?"

"She. Daisy woke up with a swollen face. They had to pull some teeth."

"How old is she?"

"Thirteen."

He saw my skeptical look. "I know," he said, "it's crazy. But we love her."

Guy looked like a working stiff, too. And how can you fault someone for excess of love? As my old mother once said, "Life forces you to make some funny choices." You hit the nail on the head there, ma.

Captain's visit was a hundred and seventy dollars, and the vet called me the next day with the diagnosis: Cushing's Disease. She delineated the treatment. "Your dog needs further tests to determine what *kind* of Cushing's, so we know which medicine to use. You need to leave him here some morning for that. Then we have to try different doses of the medication, and he has to come back every two weeks for testing so we can *adjust* the dosage."

"How much is the Cushing's treatment, ballpark."

"It's not cheap. Around a thousand."

"I'll get back to you." That was my polite way of saying, forget about it, Doc. Aside from the price, it was pretty clear that Captain was near the end of his road, and I didn't fancy having him poked and prodded and tossed in a cage at the vet's, feeling abandoned and surrounded by the smell of fear.

You may have deduced that it was just me and Captain, and that's true, but that was a recent development. I'd had a wife. Mary was an English major from Smith. She walked in beauty, and when first we were married, she used to love me to read poetry to her in the lamp-lit evening. "She Dwelt Among the Untrodden Ways" was one of her favorites, but you might say she wound up closer to "La Belle Dame Sans Merci."

I worked at that time as a financial advisor for a private firm called Lambert Investments. Bill Greely was a colleague. I liked Bill all right. I had never met his wife, but the comments he made were not encouraging. He referred to sex as if it were an occurrence so infrequent as to warrant a special celebration. She thought that because he worked in the investment business, their stocks should always rise, and I got the impression that she blamed him personally for the crash of '08. It didn't surprise me when Bill told me that she was leaving him for some dude with real bucks, an old flame she'd reconnected with on Facebook, and I thought Bill would probably be better off, but he didn't see it that way. He was falling to pieces, to the sad extent that clients were complaining of missed appointments and unanswered calls, and John Lambert, the eponymous CEO, nearly Vulcan in his rationality, suggested Bill take a paid leave of absence for three weeks to "talk to someone," and sort out his domestic affairs.

I don't remember Bill's wife's name, because as I think back on it, he always just called her "she." *She* had a lawyer who said he wanted to make sure *she* got her due, which meant that Bill was fucked. The worst of it was he said he still loved her. They had three kids, and every time he talked about them, he started to cry. I felt sorry for him. Who wouldn't? Well, his wife, apparently. Once or twice a week he'd call me, and we'd meet at the Old Court for a drink or two while in tragic monotone he recounted the latest developments in the Tale of Woe. I listened. I couldn't say much. I mean what could I tell him? I did advise him to get a dog. "A dog will *never* run away and leave you for some other person. I just read a story in the paper about a dog somewhere who kept returning to the hospital where his master had died. Yeah, a dog's loyalty is just . . . *dogged.*"

When I found out that his kids would be with his wife and her family for Thanksgiving, and he intended to eat by himself at the Elks Club, I asked Mary if she'd mind having him over to eat with us. Of course, I had to relate the aforesaid Tale of Woe, the outline of which I'd already suggested as part of the rambling conversation on our after-dinner walks. "The poor guy! Yes, of course. Invite him over. You're so good, Ozzie."

Since I've already told you that "I had a wife," you may have guessed where all this is headed. If not, you haven't watched enough afternoon TV. Ever ask yourself why people repeat certain sayings over and over? It's because they're true. I'm thinking of the popular saw, "No good deed goes unpunished."

In short, Bill started coming by the house, all disheveled and bemoaning his outcast state. At some point grief becomes sniveling, and finally I told him, "Remember what Abraham Lincoln said, 'I walk slowly, but I never walk backward.' You need to stop whining. Be tough. Advance!"

I was getting exasperated. I'd go out to lead the grimly determined tongue-lolling Captain around the park, feeling guilty for leaving Mary to endure Bill's tears. Well, it turns out that Bill's tears were a source of intoxicating sexual excitement for my wife. She offered him comforting words, reassured him of his worth and attractiveness, I imagine, and the next thing you know they were screwing away the lunch hour at Motel 6. Bill was probably blubbering as he came, and Mary was ecstatic. I don't know, but I imagined it that way until I forced myself to stop imagining it.

So: Mary and Bill. If there was one thing I was resolute about, it was that I would bore no one with my Pathetic Story, because as Lou Holtz once said, ninety percent of the people don't care, and the other ten percent are glad. I would shed no tears and I would carry on like Winston Bloody Churchill under the *Blitzkreig*. I took my after-dinner walks alone, meditating on faithlessness as I traversed the long streets that seemed to lead me farther and farther away from my old life.

My emotions only got the best of me once. That was when Bill came back to work. "I'm sorry, Ozzie," he said, "it just happened."

"Oh really?" I rammed my fist into his face. He looked funny sprawled over the credenza in the lobby. "Sorry, Bill. It just happened." Wolf pack behavior is not confined to canines, though I confess I felt kind of cheesy. No one sucker punches people for infidelity anymore, except maybe some guy who wears a gold horseshoe ring and owns a gym.

John Lambert called me into his office and said that wouldn't do. "You're a representative of a reputable firm," he reminded me. I apologized and promised that it would not happen again. Two days later, a cop arrived at my door and served me with a Personal Protection Order—I was to stay away from William Greely except when we had to be in the same building at work. "That'll be easy," I told the cop.

Now you're up to date. Almost. I was still in our condo. Mary and Bill were at his home with his confused kids, and his wife was in a big house in Andover with her new old flame. I tended to get up early, 4:00 or 5:00 AM. I'd generally listen to some Bach, take notes on the performance of my stocks, and read the business pages. While the coffee brewed, and the French Suites filled my kitchen with the harmony and order that my life was lacking, I called Captain and stood by the back door, waiting for him to hobble out of bed. He struggled to his feet, and just stood there in a sort of crouch as if someone had kicked him in the balls, though the poor bastard had none. Then he started to piss all over the place, staggered and fell sideways onto the floor. I cleaned up the mess, lifted him onto his bed, and sat there beside him, patting his old head. His eyes told me, "It's over, Ozzie," and I cried for my dog, and maybe for Mary too.

I started to think about that Steinbeck novel about the farm laborers. There was a character named Candy who had an old dog that was deaf, lame, and nearly blind. One of the other men convinces Candy to let him shoot the old dog because he's useless and is stinking up the bunkhouse. Later, this Candy keeps saying. "I should have shot my dog. I shouldn't have let no stranger shoot my dog." That sounded true to me. I didn't have any guns, but I had a friend who did—Nicky Spanos, a well-known bookie in Lowell. Nicky had three pistols. I explained the situation to him, and he picked out a Walther P22 and showed me how to load and unload the clip and where the safety was; I'd handled weapons in the service, and it wasn't complicated.

"Now you get caught with the gun, you say you came over here to visit me and you stole it. That's what I'll say, and I'm a convincing liar."

"Don't worry Nicky," I said, "I'm just going to shoot the dog and bring it back."

"Why don't you let the vet do that shit?"

"Like the song says, 'I'll do it my way.'"

"Tough to shoot your dog though. Especially the Captain."

"Life forces you to make some funny choices."

I bought some of those liver treats that the dog loved, then I wrapped him in a blanket and set him down in the back of the car. We drove out to the woods where we used to walk, or where I'd walk, and Captain would run. Now I had to carry him off the paths deep into the woods, ever conscious of the gun in my waistband. I found the ruins of a foundation that lined a leaf-strewn cavity—what had been a cellar who knows how many years back when some settler had built the stone wall that ran nearby. It had once separated pastures, I imagine, but now it meandered into a dim forest.

Captain deserved a good death, sudden, amid some pleasant reverie. I laid him down on the blanket and stretched my aching muscles, breathing like an old dog myself. I held a liver treat under his nose, but he turned his head away and let out a low, disconsolate whine, so I just lay down beside him and patted him for a while, telling him what a good dog he was. I couldn't look him in the eyes because I had this feeling that he knew why we were there. I slipped the gun out, pushed in the clip, and cocked it. "You were a good dog, Captain. The best dog I had." Before any doubts or second thoughts could move me from my course, I put the gun to his head, turned away, and fired.

I stumbled to the stone wall as the single shot echoed and sat there crying for old Captain, feeling that I had never really been alone as long as he was alive, and aware that my first thought after firing the gun was that I wished it had been Bill and not my dog that I'd shot—someone who had it coming. But Bill, piece of shit that he was, had three kids counting on him, and I'm not a killer anyway, not a killer of men. She's not worth it, I told myself, but I did miss her. Of course I missed her; maybe she was a bit of a flake, but we were together for twenty years. The nights had gotten long and the bed wide and cold. Ah, fuck it.

From the old moss-covered stone wall, I built a cairn for Captain, a lordly monument to my fallen friend. I removed the clip from the gun and put it in the backpack and cleared the chamber before I stuck it in my waistband since I didn't fancy shooting my nuts off.

Long before I met my Mary, when I was still a student in high school, my English teacher, Brother Iverson, had us memorize parts of the old Anglo-Saxon poem, "The Wanderer." As I made my way out of the woods, I recited those lines as I had a thousand times before, the only prayer in which I still had faith:

I have learned truly the mark of a man
Is keeping his counsel and locking his lips,
Let him think what he will! For woe of heart
Withstandeth not Fate; a failing spirit
Earneth no help. Men eager for honor
Bury their sorrow deep in their breast.

The words steeled me as a good prayer should. So that when I got home and found Mary sitting at our—at *my* kitchen table sobbing, I was in no mood to embrace her and offer forgiveness for her prodigal fuckathon with my former friend. I was the Wanderer, with churning oar in the icy wave, hard and unbreakable, and my sorrow was buried safely, deep, deep in my breast under a stone cairn.

"What do *you* want?" I asked her.

"I'm sorry for the way things worked out," she said between sobs. "I never wanted to hurt you. You're a good person, you are. Can you find it in your heart to forgive me?"

"No," I said. I lifted my sweatshirt and took the gun out of my waistband, placing it on the table. I opened the refrigerator and pulled out a beer. Her eyes and her mouth opened wide, and her sobbing ceased so that the only sound was the second hand clicking across the face of the battery-powered clock on the wall.

"What's the gun for, Ozzie? Ozzie, what the hell are you going to do with that gun?"

I drank the beer, gazing absently at the empty bed where Captain had spent most of the last few years. How had she not even noticed his absence?

"My God, you wouldn't shoot me or Bill, would you?"

I figured that if after nearly a quarter-century sharing a bed with me, she still didn't know me, why should I reassure her? I ignored her and guzzled the beer, realizing that at that moment I didn't love her. I didn't even like her.

She lunged across the table for the gun and aimed it at me, the barrel shaking wildly in her unsteady hands. "I'm going to call the police," she said. "Don't move or I'll shoot." I stared at her for a moment; then I began to laugh, harder than I had in years, hardly able to catch my breath, tears of mirth nearly blinding me. It seemed we'd been cast into some ridiculous low-budget comedy, starring my wife as Calamity Jane. And there was the perfect metaphor for her love—an empty gun aimed at my heart. I took the pistol away from her and brought it back to Nicky, who said he couldn't understand what was so funny about shooting a good Labrador.

You Have Reached Your Destination

Because we'd been in adjoining cubicles for five years, Thomas Ashe and I had gotten to know each other pretty well. When the workday was over, we often leaned back in our chairs and talked about life, books, the job, or Irish history, (Thomas was descended from some IRB battalion commander, his namesake, who had died on a hunger strike in a British jail in 1917).

When I'd mention an article I'd read, or a snippet of information I'd picked up from a magazine or from some guy at a bar, Thomas's eyes would widen, his jaw gape; he seemed to suspend his breath for a moment before giving vent to some earnest affirmation such as, "That's so cool!" Few at the company shared my interests, (history, old books and classic films), but Thomas was interested in everything and wanted to know about everything.

He was one of those people you come across in life who are so decent that you sometimes feel mean or narrow beside them. When

I told him an off-color joke, he would almost blush, and though he laughed indulgently, I knew he would never repeat it. He went to Mass every Sunday with his wife. He'd been a track star in high school, and when he wasn't with his family, he was training for road races, kayaking, or climbing mountains. He liked to quote John Muir, that a week in the woods could "wash your spirit clean."

Thomas was a friend. The proof was that even though he wasn't much of a drinker, and was somewhat out of place in a pub, he would spend a Friday after work sitting with me at the bar at Boomer's, consoling me after my wife told me, after just sixteen months of marriage, that "the whole thing was a mistake." She moved in with another guy two days later. What really bothered me was that this guy had a tattoo of Elvis on his arm—not the Heartbreak Hotel Elvis, but the character on the New England Patriots' helmets who has become known as "Flying Elvis." I was ashamed to admit that she thought a lamebrain with a football team logo permanently plastered on his body would be a better life partner and father for her prospective children than I would have been. And I was disappointed in myself for having fallen for a woman who had so quickly proven unfaithful and trite.

Thomas had made no such mistake in choosing a woman. He loved the hell out of his wife, Dolores, and their kids, and though I'd never met her, I sensed from his conversation that the love was mutual, and the respect. It was a sacrifice for him, I'm sure, to sit there and listen to me piss and moan about Karen and Elvis. "He pumps iron, of course, wears a big gold chain," I said, glumly.

"You'd probably kick his ass," Thomas said, sipping his pint of beer as if it were sherry.

"Why do you say that?"

"A lot of those guys have glamour muscles. They're not really that tough."

"Maybe I should kick his ass."

He squinted as if the beer had turned to whiskey. "I wouldn't recommend that."

"No. I guess I'm no Spencer Tracy. Remember *Bad Day at Black-rock*? He only had one arm and he beat the living shit out of Ernest Borgnine."

Thomas had this sort of embarrassed laugh, a laugh he seemed almost to be trying to suppress, while enjoying the joke at the same time. "I mean, listen, you know I'd be right there in your corner, like Burgess Meredith with Rocky, but I think it's time to move on. For your own mental health. Just be thankful you don't have kids. That would have been messy. Karen didn't appreciate you, but you will find a woman who does."

"I just hate all that dating crap and trying to pick up women. You have to walk up to some total stranger and say, 'Hi! I'm a loser whose wife left him for a guy who listens to sports talk radio all day in his auto body shop.' And then, even if she talks to you, what are the chances she and you will make a compatible couple?"

"Oh, stop it."

"Where am I gonna meet a woman, anyway?"

"There's Eva at work. She likes you."

"You think I could live with someone who has pictures of her five cats all over her desk? I'm allergic, for Chrissake."

I realized that this line of conversation must be getting old for Thomas. He would never let on that he was bored with me; he was too kind, but he was doodling on the back of our bar tab. Not really doodling, drawing—Thomas was an artist—that's what he did at work in the cubicle opposite mine: web design, graphics and all that. He'd graduated from Rhode Island School of Design. In a few minutes, he had produced a tiny cartoon of me running away from a bunch of cats. I laughed for the first time all day and decided to give him a break. "Oh well, as Bogart said, 'Everyone in Casablanca has problems.'"

I left off with the Karen and Elvis stuff and listened to him recount a trip he and his wife had taken to the White Mountains; he pulled out his phone and showed me some photos. One, in particular, struck me. At the bottom, the tops of pine trees were visible, and above and beyond them, the dark rolling bulge of a stony mountain. On the horizon, the sun had burst through the lower edge of a mass of purple clouds, showering brilliant rays on distant hills in a way that reminded me of how artists rendered God's grace in the religious books of my Catholic school days. I don't recall if he said it was a sunrise or a sunset.

We finished our beers and settled the tab, the bartender highly amused by the drawing on its back. Outside, it was overcast October. Thomas shook my hand and slapped my arm and said, "Dan, like I said, you're gonna meet a woman who appreciates you—I guarantee it. And you know what? It will be *when you least expect it*."

"Sure, if you say so. See you Monday."

Lane, our supervisor, called me on Sunday morning to tell me that Thomas had suffered a heart attack. I immediately pictured my friend sitting up in a hospital bed, surrounded by wife and kids, mildly accepting the admonitions of his doctor and the well wishes of friends. "When can we go and visit him?" I asked.

"He's gone, Dan. He passed this morning."

"*What?* That's impossible!" I said.

What a stupid thing to say.

The wake was—I don't know what it was. Everyone in the line kept asking *what happened*, as if there was some problem we could solve if only we knew what went wrong. How could a guy who ran every day, who belonged to the White Mountain Four Thousand Foot Club, having climbed all forty-eight peaks over four thousand feet, how could such a person have a fatal heart attack? He was still young! The story that circulated through the funeral parlor was that he was raking leaves and said he didn't feel good—he went in and lay down on the couch and died. *Wow*, they said. *God help us. Holy shit. It makes you think.* They said these things while the line moved closer to the body of Thomas Ashe, and then I saw his wife, stoically greeting co-workers and friends, their two children by her side. His son, who was probably sixteen, looked just like him, only taller.

A moment later, I stood in front of his wife, this figure, suddenly real, who had previously occupied the background of desultory work conversations with Thomas. I knew that with him she had enjoyed watching reruns of *Columbo*, and hikes in the mountains, that she managed the family finances. I knew that they had been a couple, a real couple, and that she seemed alone now, even in this crowd.

"Dolores Ashe," she said.

We shook hands. "Dan McLellan. I work . . . . I worked with Thomas."

She enfolded my hand in both of hers and said, "Oh, he mentioned you a lot. He liked you very much."

I nodded, unable to speak. Her face blurred. I averted my eyes and saw the body of my friend. She said something else—I don't remember now what it was. I only remember that I had come to comfort her, and that she was trying to comfort me. She was a strong person, and as I mumbled a prayer at the casket, I thought, "Thomas, you would have been proud of her."

We've all been to funerals for those who were relatively young and active at the time of their deaths. So different from the funerals for the aged who have passed quietly from feeble senility into the shade. I had not been inside a church in a long time. The stained glass and the Stations of the Cross, the flower-bedecked altar, the vaulted ceilings and low rolling organ brought me back to my boyhood, a timid being under the vigilant gaze of the nuns.

The organ ceased, and from the portico by the open doors, where a piper sheltered from the rain, came the mournful wail of the pipes. I recalled a couple of lines from the poem I'd seen tacked on the wall of my friend's cubicle, a poem which had been written by Sean O'Casey and dedicated to the martyred rebel ancestor for whom Thomas had been named. The lines read themselves in my mind above the skirl of the pipes:

> *The mountains of Erin are plaintively calling,*
> *Thomas Ashe, Thomas Ashe, we are mourning for thee.*

I stood, sat, and kneeled with the crowd, amid the smell of wet raincoats and floral perfume. The funeral was well attended; I was not the only person who had known the worth of the man. Women, and men too, cried openly when Thomas' son and daughter rose to bid him farewell. When they had finished, his casket passed down the aisle, followed by his wife and the whole clan. The title of a Maupassant novel I'd read in French class in college came to me: *Forte comme la mort.* As strong as death. And watching his wife move by in silence—austere, determined, a rock in a tormented sea to which her children could cling until time smoothed the waters—I thought: *Stronger* than death.

It was still raining outside. The funeral director instructed those who would follow the procession to the graveyard to put on their flashers. Lines of cars formed while I sat in my little Honda Civic trying to figure out how to turn on my flashers. I had never used them in the six years I'd owned the car. The wipers set a steady tempo which seemed to underscore the dull thud of my own heartbeat as I tore open the glove compartment and dug for the owner's manual. Through the rain-splattered windshield I could see the line of cars pulling out of the church parking lot. I threw down the manual and joined the line with headlights on, but no flashers.

The sad convoy issued out of the church parking lot while the rain rose to another category. It was no longer a hard rain; it was torrential. I twisted a stick on the steering column and the wipers ramped up to a frenetic back and forth, like the clock in hell that those nuns of my youth had described, the pendulum ever moving back and forth—forever-never-forever-never-forever-never. I gripped the wheel and followed the blurred red splotches of taillights that marked the dim procession ahead of me, wondering how it could be that I was on the way to bury a man with whom I had been drinking just a few days ago, in whom I'd confided all my stories, who, to entertain me, had drawn five cats with arched backs snarling at me. Just a few days ago. Forever. Never. Forever. Never.

I leaned forward in my seat to try to see through the bespattered windshield, and a phrase the priest had quoted from the Bible came back to me, *For now we see as through a glass darkly.* I focused all of my attention on the flashing lights in front of me, determined to follow the line, to take this last ride for my pal and say a prayer for him, even if I had no faith in prayer, because he'd had faith in it.

I was afraid to lose sight of those lights because I couldn't remember the name of the cemetery. But as I peered into that churning gloom, I saw that the line seemed to have pulled over, and after a moment that the cars in front of me were turning around! The procession seemed to be lost. I pulled into a side street and did a three-point turn. When I reached the main road again, I spotted a car with flashers on and gunned the gas so that I could pull up behind it before the traffic separated us. Then, through the curtain of rain I noticed other cars with their flashers on in different lanes, heading in different directions. The rain continued to hammer the roof of my car; the glass became opaque the instant the inadequate wipers had made a sweep, and a foggy dimness crept up the glass though I blasted the defroster. "Ah, poor Thomas!" I thought. His presence was still so fresh in my mind that I could clearly imagine his good-humored laugh, and self-effacing voice, saying, "I can't believe they screwed up my funeral cortege!" Doggedly, I pursued the car in front of me, hoping that the hearse was somewhere ahead of it.

Finally, the rain began to let up, though it did not stop; the sky remained dark. I reduced the wiper speed and was disappointed to discover that there was no procession, only two cars in front of me. However, a cemetery came into view on my right, and I followed the other two cars through the wrought iron gates. The three of us opened our doors and met under our spread umbrellas, where decorum, or our common plight, seemed to demand a brief introduction. The first car was driven by an older gentleman whose wife had volunteered with Thomas on charity drives in the parish. The second driver was a young woman, a cousin of Thomas's, named Bridget Ashe. We established quickly that we were lost, and that the cemetery we had entered was not the burial site. The older man said that he and his wife would return home since he felt we would arrive too late for the graveside service; he moved off toward his car.

"I don't know," Bridget said, uneasily. "What shall we do, Dan?"

"I got an email with information about the funeral." I laid my umbrella down as I pulled out my phone and began to scroll through my email list. Bridget stepped closer and held her umbrella over the two of us.

"Here we are ... 'Following the Mass, we will proceed to St. Mary's Cemetery in Derry, where Thomas Ashe will be laid to rest.'" I tapped out of the email and put the address into the GPS.

"I'll follow you," she said.

"All right. By the way, do you know how to turn on flashers?"

"There's usually a triangle on the button," she said.

She returned to her car and our small procession headed off to St. Mary's. She was right about the triangle, and my flashers were belatedly flashing, against the chance that the downpour would recommence. The toneless feminine voice of the disembodied guide led us onto the highway for about four miles and then directed us through a series of rights and lefts. A stone wall came into view, and then rows of headstones beyond it. "You have reached your destination," the voice said.

I pulled over, and Bridget pulled up behind me. The rain had finally stopped; there was just that swirling mist in the air, then, what the

Irish call "a soft day." A row of cars was parked along the road into the cemetery, but as Bridget came up to join me, we heard car engines turning over and saw that the people, no doubt damp and cold, were already leaving. "Too late. Well, we're here. Shall we go say a prayer?" I asked.

"Yes, I want to do that."

As we walked toward the grave, I explained how I had known Thomas, and she told me how much she had always admired her cousin, who had taught her to ski. "He was so patient," she said.

In the foggy distance, we saw the priest, Bible in hand and head bowed, walking away with Dolores and her children, and the last of a straggling line of mourners exiting from under a canvas awning set on poles over Thomas' freshly dug grave. Bridget joined her hands together as we approached the open grave, and I felt some guilt, in that place, to remark that she wore a Claddagh ring with the heart facing outward. She was single. We stood shoulder to shoulder, and I prayed with her, as earnestly as a skeptic is able, for one of the best men I had known. And if at the end of that prayer, her dark hair, and life itself, distracted me, it was Thomas' own voice, so clear, still, in my mind, that comforted me, telling me that I would meet a good woman, and adding, prophetically, "It will happen when you least expect it." God knows I had never expected this.

We made the sign of the cross together and my eyes welled once more to leave my friend in that bleak and friendless yard, forever. *Thomas Ashe, Thomas Ashe . . .*

Bridget shivered. "Can we go get a hot coffee, Dan?" she asked, handing me a Kleenex as she swiped at her eyes with another.

"Or something stronger. How about a hot Irish coffee at the Peddler's Daughter?"

"I'll follow you," she said.

I never lost her.

Kwaidan

Whenever I saw Finneral, I thought of the old folksong, "A Man of Constant Sorrow." He could often be seen walking the company corridors at TCI, tie askew, eyes rolling, every breath a muted curse or a forlorn sigh. Life had disappointed him, for he was only too aware of humanity's shortcomings. Their escapades, foibles, and at times, criminal behaviors were an open book to him. He was Director of Personnel. It was his job to investigate allegations of sexual misconduct, harassment, the myriad abuses committed on computers, complaints against bosses, complaints by bosses against employees, complaints of customers against sales staff, noncompliance with state regulations, every form of gender-identity and racial discrimination, inappropriate tweets, unbecoming social media posts, and union grievances. Is it any surprise then, that his unkempt head was so often shaken in disgust?

I knew Finneral better than most, better than anyone, perhaps, because we had discovered at a company outing that we were both amateur philatelists. *I* was an amateur; Finneral was nearly a professional. He dabbled as well in coins, antique clocks, toy soldiers, Sherlock Holmes memorabilia and Crimean War Light Brigade artifacts and prints. He was a member of several obscure scholarly organizations, such as the Brattle Street Antiquarian Society, the Speckled Band, the Grollier Club, the Wellesley Stamp Club, and the Cornish Horrors. It was at the eccentric gatherings of these societies that he felt most at home. The members of such groups were, in general, highly intelligent but oddball characters who shared his fascination with stamps, old books, or Sherlock Holmes. Finneral's devotion to Holmes may have explained why he could so readily get to the bottom of complex issues. Like his fictional detective mentor, Finneral might well have said, "It's my job to know what other people don't know."

When I met him during the day, exiting the café or at the copy machine, he would often entertain me with some uniquely Finneralian observation. "My mother was right. I would have been much happier in the basement of the British Museum of Natural History sorting piles of dinosaur bones."

He had a dozen old prints matted and framed in his office. There was a black and white portrait of Cornet Henry John Wilkin of the 11th Hussars in the full uniform of 1856, including, as Finneral pointed out to me, the snug cross-braided dolman jacket, the loose-fitting pelisse or over jacket, and the tall fur cap, or busby. Wilkin, he said, was a survivor of the Charge of the Light Brigade. Other prints and drawings reflected his idiosyncratic and eclectic tastes. His desk, too, was covered with a miscellany of books and curios, including a foot-tall samurai warrior in detachable plate armor.

My friend used these artifacts as a subtle test of the mental acuity of individuals with whom he spoke. He explained that if someone came into his office and began to study the varied antiquities, and to question him about them, or to show some sign of appreciation for their historical or aesthetic value, he was assured that he was dealing with a person of some intelligence and sensitivity. If, as more frequently happened, the person showed not a shred of interest in or curiosity about his collection, he was assured that he was dealing with a blockhead.

The full extent of his eccentricity dawned on me one day when I stopped before the workday had begun to sip a coffee in his office/museum. He looked even more haggard than usual and confessed that he'd had a spat with his wife. "Got a big ugly," he said.

I asked him what the issue was, since I didn't think he would have begun to tell me if he felt the matter was personal. "Well," he said, gazing over his shoulder to make certain the door leading out to the secretary's area was closed, "she indicated last night that she was in a, shall we say, 'frisky' mood, and she wanted to know if I was similarly minded."

I nodded, sipping my coffee, and waited for him to continue. A pained expression indicated that he recognized the mistake he was about to relate. "I told her that I would be in the mood, normally, but that I really didn't feel like moving all the books and toy soldiers off my side of the bed just then."

"Oh, boy."

"If I had known she'd already opened a bottle of Beaujolais . . . ."

"Of course."

"Anyway . . . ."

"She'll get over it."

"I suppose." He put his cup down suddenly and, still sitting in his chair, bent to rummage in his overstuffed leather bag. "I almost forgot. Take a look at this." He opened a book and took out a Japanese stamp in a transparent packet. It was a commemorative stamp dedicated to Lafcadio Hearn. Finneral explained that it was rare for a Japanese stamp to commemorate a non-Japanese person, but that Hearn, whose dates were on the stamp, 1850-1904, had done much as a translator to bring Japanese culture to an English-speaking audience.

It was a beautiful stamp, tinted in blue with the author gazing downward; three lotus flowers bloomed over his shoulder. "What does *Kwaidan* mean?" I asked. The word was written across the top of the stamp. I knew that Finneral would already have looked it up.

"Hearn published a translation of some strange tales, legends and ghost stories. They say it's difficult to translate the *kanjis* that make up the Japanese word *kwaidan* into English, but that it's best translated as 'strange tales,' or 'weird tales,' or 'odd stories,' or some combination of all those."

"Hmmm."

Finneral leaned back in his swivel armchair and said, "There's a lot of fucking *Kwaidan* around this place."

"Yup."

"I'm forty-four," he mused. "I just don't know if I can take it for another twenty years. People are *so* fucked up. Unfortunately, they pay me well, and I have to prepare to be robbed blind by colleges when the kids are a bit older." His head shook in disgust at the prospect. "Trapped," he muttered, then leaned forward and said in a lower voice, "Do you know—and of course this is in the vault—"

"Understood."

"A senior person in the company thought it would be a good idea to make up cards with his name and the company logo on them, also featuring a Confederate flag and the motto 'Make TCI great again!'"

"What the hell?"

"And he was giving them out! Including one to an African-American employee!"

"He didn't see a problem with that?"

"He says he's just proud of being from Georgia and he didn't realize people were so *oversensitive*." Finneral registered my look of disbelief and said, "Oh yeah. Then I have this guy in shipping that . . . do you know what an 'Onionhead' is?"

"Not familiar with that one."

"Neither was I. Apparently, they want to burn candles on their desks, and they are supposed to tell everyone they work with 'I love you,' every day. Now I have several women who feel they're being harassed because this dingbat keeps telling them he loves them. One of the women is his supervisor. He says it's his religion. I tried to talk to him. He thinks the women who complained are at best unenlightened, and at worst under a demonic influence. He sat here and gave me a load of horseshit Onionhead principles, like, 'Peel it, feel it, heal it.' He also said, 'You are never alone, because 'alone' spells out 'all one.' I almost screamed at him, 'No it doesn't you fucking dope!' I do worry that I'm going to lose it one of these days. I worry."

The phone on his desk rang. He looked at the caller ID and rolled his eyes as he picked it up. "Finneral," he said. It was time for me to log on to my computer, but as I headed for the door, I heard him say, "An emotional support hamster?" His day had begun.

I retired not long after that. We didn't lose touch entirely, but our communications became sporadic. Finneral's story, like everyone's story, could have ended in any number of ways. One day I was at Home Depot looking at snowblowers when I met Davenport, a former colleague at TCI. He still worked there. Of course, I asked him how my old friend Finneral was doing. "You haven't heard?" he says.

I felt a chill of apprehension when I heard those words. I prepared myself for the worst. "No, I haven't talked to him lately . . . ."

"He was fired."

"No! For what reason?"

"Not many people know, but Browning gave me the details. Seems there's this guy Cummings, in Accounts; apparently, he has a foot fetish. So, Lorraine, one of the accountants down there, good-looking woman, wears her boots to work in the winter and leaves her heels at her desk. She comes in and finds Cummings fondling and kissing her shoes."

"Jesus Christ."

"So, they had a meeting. Finneral, Lorraine, Cummings and their supervisor, Browning, and they all tell the guy to cut the shit, right?

But a week later, as she's working, she feels something under her desk."

"My God."

"Yeah, Cummings is under her desk, trying to caress her foot and pleading with her to let him do whatever they do with feet—I don't know. So, they have another meeting, and now even the CEO is involved, and Cummings is there sniffling and saying he's sorry and talking about Lorraine's feet, and all of a sudden, Finneral starts cracking up, and the CEO is shooting him dirty looks, but the guy just loses control and starts laughing hysterically, and like, he can't stop, and everyone is looking at him, and he's practically on the floor. Cummings is bawling now, and says he's feeling like he's in a hostile work environment or some shit, and Finneral pulls himself together and says to the weeping Cummings, 'What do you want, a safe space to grovel under women's desks, you fucking pervert? You like feet so much, how about if I put my foot up your ass!' And he lunges for him!"

"Jesus!"

"Browning and the CEO grab him, they all fall on the floor wrestling while Cummings runs out screaming like a child."

"Yikes."

"Meeting is cancelled. Another meeting, now about Finneral. Security is called. Browning likes him—tries to defend him, but the CEO is having none of it—he was holding his neck, and he was pissed. Told Finneral to pack up and hand over his ID. The guards helped him carry most of his stuff out to his car. What wouldn't fit, they left in the custodian's closet until he can come back."

Poor Finneral. I had imagined the harried man plugging away at the company until he'd gone gray and bald, 'trapped,' as he had said in the office whose contents were appreciated by so few. But the shit had finally gotten to him. A man of integrity and erudition can only tolerate so much contemptible and ludicrous behavior.

When I got home, I told my wife the sad tale. Being a woman

of great faith, she assured me that these things often work out for the best, but I couldn't see it. I thought about his three kids and their stagnant college fund and Finneral looking at Help Wanted ads without a recommendation from the company for which he'd suffered years of absurdity.

Sometimes, though, great faith is warranted. One Saturday afternoon I cracked a beer, took a seat on the porch, and called Finneral. I was surprised by the cheerful tone with which he responded. "How the hell are you?" he asked. "I've been meaning to call you, but we're so busy here, packing for Yevpatoria. Taking the whole family over February vacation and one extra week."

"Yevpatoria? Where in God's name is that?"

"The Crimea. Lake Moynaki. Vacation and a bit of Light Brigade research."

"Well—half a league onward!" I said, trying to match his cheerfulness, but I was dumbfounded. How could he be taking such an extravagant vacation when he'd lost his job? He gave me the story. It appears that an antiquated member of the Brattle Street Antiquary Society with no living descendants had had his eye on a certain tireless scholar and collector as a worthy heir. Upon his death, he had left his considerable fortune to the erstwhile forlorn Finneral. The sole proviso of his will was that the heir should undertake to organize and catalogue his extensive rare stamp collection, medieval illuminated manuscripts, early maps, oil paintings, Korean pottery, and the wide-ranging library in his mansion on Elmwood Avenue, which would be open to research scholars in several fields.

It was the job that my friend was born for. It took me some time to accustom myself to the newfound gusto in his voice, the buoyant enthusiasm for what was his new life, and now I imagined him growing old amid his books and stamps, speaking only to other scholars in the hushed sanctuary of the Elmwood Library. "Character is destiny," the Roman writer said, but it doesn't always work out that way. How wonderful it is to see a man who carried his erudition like a torch among the ungracious herd rewarded at last with a destiny befitting his character. "What a kwaidan!" I thought, as I raised my beer. *God bless you, Finneral.*

•

El Greco

Uncle Billy warned me when I agreed to rent the Broadway apartment from him, not to become too friendly with Andreas, the
Greek who lived downstairs. "He looks like a homeless guy, but he's
some kinda mathematical genius. You'll see the rich Greeks coming
to pick him up. He tutors their kids in Calculus and whatever. He's
all right, but he'll talk your ear off, start asking you for rides—drive
you crazy. He's obsessed with how the Americans never treated him
right, you know . . . he got fired from different teaching jobs because
he's crazy, but he thinks it's because he's Greek."

"How old is he?"

"Sixty or so. Hard to tell. He's looked the same for twenty years.
Looks a little worse lately."

"Doesn't he have family?" I pitied the man before I had even met
him. I was busy, though, teaching classes at the university during
the day and writing my dissertation on Herman Melville at night. I

didn't have a lot of free time, but the idea of brushing off this Andreas went against my nature.

"He's got an ex-wife, and a couple of kids who hardly ever talk to him," my uncle said, his cigar reeking a thick column of smoke out of his chubby fingers.

"Why is that?"

"Why?" Uncle Billy shrugged and blew a white plume into the air above us. "Hell, I don't know, Robbie. Maybe because he's a crazy Greek." He found this amusing and chortled, or wheezed, to himself for a moment. "I mean he's harmless. I'm sure he'll come up and introduce himself," he added. "Just don't . . . ." He squinted as he ran a hand over the white stubble at the back of his nearly bald head so that the smoke seemed to rise out of his cranium. "Just don't . . . *engage* him, know what I mean?"

The apartment took up the top floor of a depression-era tenement, one of a row of flat-roofed human warehouses standing like broken teeth set crookedly in the hag's jaw of Broadway, which was the main thoroughfare through this old section of the city known as the Acre. Irish and Greek mill workers had long scrabbled in the Acre for a foothold to begin the long climb upward. They worked and saved and waited and died while bank accounts grew so that they or their children could move out of the choking confines of the Acre to a neighborhood with oaks in the yard and a long front walk.

Though newer immigrants, Hispanic and Asian, had taken their places, some of the older families grew attached to the Acre or were so frightened by memories of the Depression that they were determined to live below their means and would never strike out for suburban grandeur. My parents met at a dance in the Acre when my father returned from the war, and after a decade on a cobbled street that ran parallel to the railroad tracks, moved out to the leafy Highlands. I felt in some ways that I was regressing, flipping the American dream by moving back to Broadway, a stone's throw from where my father had grown up on Wiggins Street, but my uncle rented it to me cheap, and it was a good place to save while I studied. Still, I felt a tinge of renter's remorse when Uncle Billy said, "I put the motion detector lights in the back 'cause we had a junkie break-in, but what the hell, you're a young guy! I'm sure you could handle a junkie!"

Louis helped me move in. He was an amiable sad sack who lived with my sister. It was one of those "Smart Women Dumb-Ass Choices" situations as far as I could see. He'd been trying to pay alimony to his ex while hiding his income by working all kinds of odd jobs under the table. He wasn't a bad carpenter. All this subterfuge eventually became too complicated for him, though, and the economy went in the tank anyway. He took to just lying on the couch. But the sister made enough money for the two of them, and for some unfathomable reason he made her happy, so who am I to judge? He did have a pickup truck, so I told him I'd get him a case of beer if he gave me a hand with the moving. I didn't have a lot of stuff.

The Greek never emerged as we carried boxes and furniture by his door. Finally, we sat upstairs amid the clutter, drinking a couple of Sam Adams. Louis is the only person I've ever seen eat a donut with a beer. He was regaling me with tales of his triumphs as a *chef de cuisine*. "Some time I gotta have you over to try some of my grilled tequila chicken. I got a recipe for that shit will knock your socks off. I serve it with an eggplant casserole. Nice bottle of Merlot. That's good eatin'. Amy loves my grillin'."

"How did you become such a great cook?"

"Since I been unemployed for a while, I watch a lot of the cooking channel."

"Time well spent, apparently."

We heard the door from the street open downstairs, the rattle of keys, and within a few minutes, bouzouki music. I told Louis that I had heard there was an eccentric Greek living downstairs. "I got no problem with the Greeks," he said.

"That's big of you, Louis."

Sarcasm was wasted on him. "You know it was the Greeks who

invented Democracy, Robbie," he said. "I saw a documentary about it on the History Channel."

"Is that right?"

"Now they specialize in pizza parlors," he said. I laughed, but Louis was quite serious, as if pizza and democracy were rough equivalents. From the apartment below, I heard a voice, pained and pleading, winding among the notes of the bouzoukis, and the rolling percussive rhythms of the hand drum, and though I understood no Greek, I sensed the man must be singing of loss. Louis wasn't as dense as I supposed, because, after a thoughtful pause, he added, "Nothin' wrong with makin' pizza, Robbie. That's honest work."

I nodded, listening to the foreign words, buffeted like a ship in a tempest amid the roiling cross-waves of notes, rising, falling, and rising again. Louis went on his way, and I spent the early part of the evening organizing the apartment. When I had my desk and table set up, I sat down with my yellow highlighter and began to pore over some of the notes I'd taken on *Moby Dick*. March was coming on like a lion outside, and I noticed that the steam didn't rise with any force to the radiators on this top floor. I thanked God the winter was winding down as I pulled an Irish sweater over my head, but as I did so my breath caught, and my heart seemed to constrict. She had often worn this sweater, and her fragrance still lived in its thick rows of cable stitches, interwoven diamonds, and honeycomb panels. I recalled her huddled in its ample *báinín* wool, sitting sideways on the worn corduroy couch, her hands wrapped around her coffee mug, her dark eyes on me. I tore the sweater off and pressed it to my face, closing my eyes and whispering her name into its softness. *Monica DeLucci.*

I folded it reverently and put it on the shelf in the closet. I told myself I should take it to the cleaners, but I knew I wouldn't. I imagined her in her nurse's uniform, making some invalid's day with the bright coin of her smile. I almost wished I could be taken gravely ill and lie in one of those beds with some critical complaint, so that I might see her leaning over me, adjusting my pillows and encouraging me in low tones.

What nonsense! I chided myself, recalling a line from a Graham Greene novel, "For God's sake man, pull yourself together!"

I refused to allow myself to wallow. There is no person more tiresome than the man who pities himself for disappointment in love. Self-pity should be reserved for parents whose children are fighting cancer, or soldiers who leave a limb on some foreign field.

Still, in truth, I couldn't help but feel it. I closed my eyes and pushed my fists into my forehead, banishing her image with an effort of will. I played tricks on myself to forget, to fix my attention elsewhere. My thesis would be a work of redirected energy.

I put on a pot of coffee because I intended to work late. The CD player and speakers still sat on the floor of the living room. I crouched and slipped in a CD of Isolde Ahlgrimm playing Bach's harpsichord piece, "Contrapunctus I, XIX." It helped me to focus as I read over my notes on the doomed captain of the *Pequod*. "Oh, Ahab! What shall be grand in thee, it must needs be plucked at from the skies, and dived for in the deep, and featured in the unbodied air!" Footsteps sounded on the stairs in the barren corridor, and four knocks on the door startled me out of my contemplative mood.

I opened the door and saw a small wild-haired man standing with an empty cup held out like a beggar. His great brush of a mustache was the kind that one usually only saw in old tintypes. He wore dark pants, a tee-shirt, and suspenders. "You are making coffee?" he asked. Ah, the Greek whose coming was foretold. The water still seethed over the grounds. I heard the thin stream of coffee trickling into the pot.

"It'll be ready in a minute," I said.

He considered this an invitation, stepped into the kitchen, and took a seat at the littered table, stroking his mustache. Only then did he ask, "I do not disturb you, eh?"

"No, happy to meet a neighbor."

"My name is Andreas." He leaned forward and extended a hand.

"Robbie Ahern, how are you?"

"How I am?" he said, gazing thoughtfully at the dusty glass of a hanging light fixture. "How anybody is in this rotten country? Why the gods they put me here, eh?"

I imagined Uncle Billy shaking his bald head in disgust. *Don't engage him.* "How do you want your coffee, Andreas?"

"Little bit sugar." He handed me his empty mug. I had no sugar, but I rummaged through an empty Dunkin Donuts bag Louis had left on the counter and found a packet. "The gods?"

"They worship one God, you see. I worship twelve."

"You mean Zeus and . . . ."

"Yes, of course, my friend. The Olympians. Why not? They were the gods during the golden age of Greece. They are good enough for Homer, then they're good enough for me. What the Greeks have done since they accept Christianity? Nothing, you see?" I recalled Louis's remark. *Now they specialize in pizza parlors.*

"Why don't you go back to Greece?" I asked. "I mean, I'm not saying I want you to leave. I'm just saying if you hate it here . . . ."

He accepted the coffee with a satisfied sigh and muttered something in Greek. "Yes, I like to go back to the village. Only I have two daughters here," he said. His face crumpled in thought as he stroked the gray stubble of his cheek. "Besides," he added, "I'm *Americanologist*, you see? Yes, I study them."

"How old are your daughters?" I ventured.

He peered over his mug at me as he sipped his coffee. Then he said, "I don't talk more about my daughters unless I know you little better." He began to examine the books piled on the table. "Shakespeare, eh? Why you read this plagiarist? He steal from the Greeks, from everybody. Why you are laughing?"

"Shakespeare is generally accepted as the greatest writer in English," I began.

"What does this mean, 'greatest writer in English'? English is good language for plagiarizer because you steal all your words. You steal words from the French, from Africans, from Indians, from Latin, from everyone, especially Greeks. You go in English from the 'embryo,' from the Greek *embryon*, *'a young one'* to the 'cemetery,' from *koimeterion*, *'a sleeping place'* all your life with the Greek words you steal, see?"

"You don't like the English language because it's not pure?"

He put his coffee on the table, leaning toward me with open hands as if he were explaining a simple truth to a child. "Is not a language at all, my friend. Is bastard mixed up system with a lot different words that cannot be pronounced and rules impossible to follow and spelling that is not sensible."

I was too tired to argue and was pretty sure it would be pointless. "Okay, then. English is not a language."

"Of course not, you see, my friend." He sat back and stroked his wild hair, satisfied that he had won the first round with his neighbor. Then he looked at me and said with decision, "I like you, Robbie, eh."

"Probably because I'm a pushover in an argument."

"You see, you're not typical American."

"Why do you say that?"

"I tell you why, my friend. You don't know me, and you invite me in, yes." I was going to remind him that he had invited himself in when he rose and pulled open the back door. "Look at this." I followed him out onto a small deck from which a stairway descended to the lower apartments and the backyard. The lights of the nearby downtown dimmed the stars, but I saw Venus unblinking in the southwestern sky. "You see?" he asked. He was pointing down at the other tenements and houses in the neighborhood.

"What am I looking at?"

"You see the light from the televisions?"

"Yes." In many of the windows, I saw the blue-gray light or caught the flash of color on a screen. "That's the Americans what they do. I live over there for twenty years on the Salem Street." He stretched a

141

hand over the lit pavement of Broadway to the street beyond. "Twenty years, the house beside me, the Wolfe family, I am never invite into that house. On the other side, the Silvas. I was inside that house one time. The neighbors across the street, they are Greek, Coconis, you see, but they become Americanized."

His voice grew hard remembering an old insult. "The mother, Stella, she was dead for three months before even I know. Her daughters don't come to tell me, they never dress in black. I never pay respect to the dead woman or bring the food to the family." He shrugged and concluded, "This is America, my friend. You see even these Greeks they are not Greek. They put them into the big melting pot, and they melt them." He shook his head sadly and then fixed me with slightly narrowed eyes. "Where your people are from?"

"My grandparents came here from Ireland in the twenties."

"Ah." He nodded gravely and seemed satisfied with this fact. "Your people they fight the Anglo-Saxons for centuries, eh? Now my friend, don't lose your Irish soul. When you lose your soul, you lose *everything*. Don't let the capitalists melt you."

I poured him another coffee and we talked a while longer. He talked a while longer. His favorite topic was the degeneracy of the United States. He spoke of the injustices committed against Blacks and refused to accept my point that there had at least been some progress since the days of segregation and burning crosses. "Progress? Is no progress, my friend. They fool the public, that's all."

He summed up his views with the simple declaration, "The symbol of your civilization, my friend, is the mushroom cloud of Hiroshima." He leaned forward, nodding, his eyes open wide to emphasize the unassailable truth of the symbolism, and added, wagging a finger in the air, "Stop to be an American, my friend. When you become an American you reach the bottom. You can't go lower than that."

I probably should have been offended, but I was amused at the way he continued to moderate his insults with the words: *my friend*. I considered telling him how my father had been with an infantry unit in the Philippines in 1945 preparing for the invasion of Japan. He had told me he remembered the men sharpening bayonets and oiling rifles; it was said that the land invasion of Japan would make Normandy look like a walk in the park. The *Enola Gay* put an end to that, and the old man wound up in Japan with the Army of Occupation rather than in smithereens on the beach at Miyazaki. I didn't bring it up, and in fairness, even my father used to say that Truman could have made a desert of some uninhabited mountain. Andreas wouldn't have heard any defense. His opinions were unalterable and argument a waste of breath.

When the Bach CD ended and the harpsichord no longer filled the spaces in our conversation, I was reminded of the time. "Not to act like an American, Andreas," I said, "but I have a couple of hours of studying to do tonight."

"No, my friend, you don't act like an American. They don't study you see. They know only how to play with the computer, or they are looking at their television or their little phones. They are watching basketball, football." He appeared to wince in pain as he rose but said nothing. He took his cup, opened the door, and paused there for his parting salvo. "If you take all the footballs, basketballs, and baseballs in this country, and put them in a big bag, your culture will collapse."

I heard him laughing as he descended the stairs and he called up, "Zeus be with you, my friend! Stop to be an American!" He's crazy all right, I thought, yet it crossed my mind as I returned to my writing table that more Americans were watching tonight's Celtics game than would ever read *Moby Dick*.

Teaching freshman writing helped me to support myself while I finished the dissertation, and for this reason, Andreas occasionally referred to me with the moniker he had devised for all professors: "Blackboard Terrorist." Teaching, meeting with my advisor, scanning the library shelves: the ensuing days unwound their threads in the usual routine, and I arrived home after supper. Later, I would hear the Greek ascending the stairs, empty coffee cup in hand, his wild hair sometimes covered with a black Greek fisherman's cap, and we would sit for a while and drink coffee and talk. I had even bought a bag of sugar for him. Finally, I asked about his family, why he and his wife had broken up. In a matter-of-fact voice, he said, "She lost her Cypriote soul, my friend. She was melted."

I imagined the Wicked Witch of the West sinking into the floor, screaming imprecations. "How was she *melted*?"

"Ah, the capitalists they put her in the melting pot and they melt her. She start to go to the gymnasium. Kickin' over here. Kickin' over there." He shook his silvered head. "Fools! The Greek *gymnasion* was a place to develop the mind and not only the body."

"Well, exercise is a good thing . . . ."

"My friend, if you want exercise you work in the garden, you see? Produce something. She start to read stupidities in the magazines. Oprah gains weight. Oprah loses weight. She watch the television about the celebrities what they do, they walk on a red carpet and other kind of bullshit." He leaned back, laughing whimsically, "They fool the public, my friend! Yes, and they turn my daughters against me because I tell them what is true. Don't do what the Americans they do! Open a book! Learn Greek! Don't lose your soul, you see? If you study just little bit in this country, you will be ahead of the Americans! They are lazy! They care only about footballs and basketballs and to play with the little phone. Fools! Fools! Fools!"

One Thursday morning I had free, and I slept until nearly 8:00, which was late for me. When the coffee had brewed, there was a knock on my door, and there he stood, neatly dressed and even combed, but pale as a ghost, with the empty coffee cup in his hand. I took it and waved him in. He sat at the finally uncluttered table and asked, "You have a mechanical donkey?"

"A what?"

"This what I call the car, you see. It's a mechanical donkey and the Americans, they take care of this machine more than they take care of their parents."

"You need a ride somewhere, Andreas?"

"Yes, you see, Robbie, I like to visit the grave of my father. It's Edson on the Gorham Street."

"Yeah, sure. I'll stop at my father's grave too. He's right next door in St. Patrick's."

I took a quick shower and got dressed while Andreas sat at the table and studied vocabulary cards he had made up; he was teaching himself Portuguese. I almost reached for the Irish sweater but left it on the shelf and tore a windbreaker off a hanger. We drove to Edson Cemetery and found Andreas' father in the back lot: Bedros Spheeris.

I wandered among the markers in the Hellenic section of the necropolis, with their Orthodox crosses and inscriptions in Greek. I stopped before one stone, incised into which was a quote from Aristotle in English. "Sex is the first principle. Birth connects us to the universal mind. Death separates us from the universal mind." Only a member of a race of philosophers would sleep under such an epitaph. *To sleep, perchance to dream?* No, Aristotle probably had it right; no dream in death would reconnect us to the universal mind.

I gave the Greek time to reflect or pray to God or Zeus by his father's stone, and when I returned, he seemed to have done. Before we left, he stretched his hand out and placed it on the curved top of the granite stone: "I will take your bones back to the village!" he declared to his father's ghost.

I was going to stop at my father's grave, but Andreas had begun to look as if he was in pain, so I headed back toward the Acre. He was quiet, ashen, and seemed almost to be holding his breath at times. Finally, he let out a quiet gasp and said, "You can to leave me at the Lowell General."

"Are you in pain, Andreas?"

"Little bit you see."

Monica was a nurse at Lowell General, but whether I saw her or not, I had to take my friend there. A hospital receptionist took his information and we sat for a while outside the Emergency Room until they walked him into a curtained cubicle, put him on a gurney, and started the monitors and tests and questions. I felt in the way and went to get a coffee and a newspaper and sat outside reading it. When I went back in, I saw a doctor with a folder in his hand walking out of the room. "Excuse me, doctor. I'm a friend of Andreas Spheeris. I brought him here. Is he all right?"

His medical eyes, heavily lidded, fell on me with all their weight, with their god-like knowledge, with their awesome familiarity with the first principle and the ultimate disconnection. In a thick Greek accent, he said simply, "Andreas has a bad disease."

He said no more, and I asked no more. It didn't matter because his eyes had filled in the missing word: *terminal*. I suppose I should have asked "How long," but instead I went to the bathroom and locked the door. I stood at the sink and found that tears had filled my eyes. I splashed cold water over my face and tried to put on a smile. On my way back to the main desk of the emergency area, I saw her.

She stopped short, and after a few seconds of indecisiveness, came toward me, smiling, what was it, politely? "Christine said she saw you. What are you doing here, Robbie?"

"I brought a neighbor of mine, a friend. He just saw a Greek doctor."

"Fotopolous."

"I guess. I just brought him over 'cause he wasn't feeling well. It seems . . . he's really sick."

"What's the patient's name?" She sounded professional, distant., but not so distant that I could not inhale that scent, a hint of which had kept me from washing the Irish sweater. What was it? Her shampoo, some store-bought fragrance, or oils? Perhaps, but more particularly *her*—her essence—like a rare spice that I could recognize amid an Arab marketplace full of spices.

"Andreas Spheeris."

"If he stays, I'll try to get him in 1207, where I can take care of him. There's a vacant bed there."

"Thank you," I said. I didn't want to say more, because I had become attached to this crazy Greek and I was afraid I might start getting teary-eyed again, over the doctor's sentence, and over seeing this woman that my gut told me I still loved. We Irish are inclined to maudlin. *For God's sake man, pull yourself together.*

"How are you, Robbie?" she asked, putting aside the mask of professional courtesy for a moment.

How am I? My stomach is tied in a knot that only the touch of your lips could ever loosen. I hear the echoes of your voice even in my sleep, and sometimes I think I'll go mad if I can't hear it again, but now that you're speaking to me here it doesn't matter because your voice is only friendly and no longer warmly tender. How am I? I'm like a junkie that's lost his fix, and the drug I crave is your love.

"I'm good," I said, attempting an earnest tone. *Why did you leave me,* I wanted to ask, but this was neither the time nor the place. There was no time nor place for that question. It was a craven question, one I would never ask. She didn't have to explain her reasons to me. Who could explain the heart anyway? The reason didn't matter, no more than it mattered what 'bad disease' was eating the Greek's life. It just *is*. Pull yourself together.

She touched my arm and said something, that she was glad or something. I felt her touch, but I didn't hear her words. Maybe I didn't hear her words because I felt her touch. And she was gone, leaving a pair of double doors swinging into stillness. I took a deep breath and felt my nerve returning.

I sat in the waiting room with a sullen mother cradling a pouting child, a tattooed teenager slouched beside his crutches, his cap visor pulled over his eyes, ashamed of his sudden vulnerability, and an old woman with a rosary wrapped about her knuckles, silently mouthing her pleas to the Virgin. I heard whispered conversations in half a dozen languages, the reassuring tones, the attempt at banter, the commonness of our humanity while the television above us droned a cooking demonstration, and I wondered if Louis was watching. I tried to read the newspaper, but the words appeared as they were, black marks on paper.

Finally, I went in to see how things were going. Andreas appeared to be sleeping. His head on the pillow reminded me of a photographic series I'd once seen by Hans Olde, "The Ill Nietzsche," with his arrow nose, sunken eyes, and wild Hussar's mustache. A rotund nurse came in on quiet sneakers and blue nurse pajamas, a blood pressure gauge hanging about her neck. "He may be sleeping for a while," she said, implying, I suppose, that they had given him a sedative. She picked up a chart hanging at the end of the gurney and said, "If you want to come back tomorrow, he'll be in room 1207."

The first thing I heard when I went into 1207 the next day was Andreas speaking to the man in the next bed, a sad-looking Hispanic with long white hair and an oxygen tube in his nose. I'd had to learn to read two languages as a PhD prerequisite. Spanish was one, but I was by no means fluent. I heard a lot of *Americanos* and *capitalistas* and *futbols*.

"Where did you learn Spanish, Andreas?" I handed him a coffee from a shop downtown.

"Ah, thank you, my friend. This is Ricardo from Honduras." The old Honduran raised a thin arm.

"When I was in the Army was stationed at Fort Bliss in El Paso. And when we have a pass, you see, my colleagues, they go to the whorehouse, and I go to the library and study. I speak to the people, yes. My friend, I tell you while the Americans they are watching football and baseball, I am studying, mathematics, languages, philosophy, yes, you see? Never they will get me into the melting pot."

"I didn't know you were in the Army."

"Naturally, my friend, I want to serve the country when I come, but still they never treat me as equal."

"How are you feeling?"

Without a trace of apprehension, he replied, "Ah, this doctor he says probably I will die soon. This is bullshit, my friend. The Greek priest come by this morning to give me some kind of blessing. I tell him stop to say the Mass in English! And that he has only one God and I have twelve! He's upset you see, and he leave. That's all right." He sipped his coffee and added casually, "Monica, she is not working today. The one was your girlfriend."

"How did you know . . . ."

"Anyone can see. She ask me how I know you. I tell her he's my neighbor and he's good man has not been melted. He has a heart and a soul, you see? Now I will tell you how to win back this woman. You have a pen?"

"Why?"

"Must be an American. To write with, my friend."

I decided to humor him and got some paper at the nurse's station. When I returned, I heard him telling Ricardo, "*Esos gringos no saben nada de amor,*" which I did understand.

"OK, I'm ready," I said, like a dull Christian with his Greek Cyrano.

He cleared his throat and said, "Let me see. All right. I'm going to tell you how to write. It's . . . the beginning. *Monica, beloved woman, princess of the race of Aeneas . . . .*"

"The race of Aeneas?"

"Yes, you see the Italians are descend from the Trojans escaped from Troy. Just write what the words I tell you." He tilted his coffee into his mustache, took a sip, and continued: *Princess of the Esperia, the great tribe so famous over the world. Since I see you, I am in love with you. I think of you during the day and in the night I dream of you, so you see I have no peace. I can't eat. All the time I am thinking of your loveliness like the goddess Aphrodite; your eyes can see my soul and in your eyes I see your gentle soul also. You are good woman. I only want to kiss you and to be nice to you. So please love me and make me the great honor to be my wife.*

You sign it, see, and I give it to her tomorrow."

"I'm going to hold off on that, Andreas."

"You don't love the woman?"

"It's unrequited. I can't..."

"Ah, she's afraid, you see. Probably she thinks your head is full of basketballs and footballs."

"Maybe. All she said she was not ready, she needed time, you know, that sort of thing."

"Naturally. You Americans want instant coffee. You must let the coffee percolate, my friend. If you force the key in the lock, you will break it. So, we don't give her the letter in this case. This is special case it requires what they call in the army the *tactics*, eh?"

They kept him for a few more days, and I learned that he had been treated for pancreatic cancer for over a year. I visited him in the evening, after Monica's shift. He would give me little hints of their conversations, or make some comment designed to keep her in my thoughts, as if she were not. "Ah, my friend, Monica came in today we talk. DeLucci—this means 'of the light,' you know. Yes. She makes a bright light. Even in her panoply of the nurse, she look so beautiful probably if you saw her you would throw yourself from the Pawtucket Bridge."

There was something odd about attempting to ascertain the details of a lost love through the filter of an eccentric old Greek, and I felt in any case that my concern should not be with my feelings or my problems when my friend was dying. Still, I couldn't stop my heart from rousing whenever he mentioned her name. I'd brought him on a Thursday; on Monday I came in and found him with pages spread all over his bed, long equations incomprehensible to me. I stood at the door and listened to him muttering to himself in English as he worked: "I bring down this capitalist, and multiply the variable of this little imperialist you see . . . . "

He was always happy to be interrupted with good strong coffee. "Yes, my friend, this Monica. She is confused, you see, but when you live in America, of course, you are confused. This is natural." He paused and looked over as if he were going to say something to Ricardo, the Honduran, but the bed was empty. He handed me his coffee while he stuffed his notebook with loose leaf papers and slid it all into the math book which he placed on the table beside his bed. He took his coffee and sat back. "Yesterday, Monica, she say to me, 'He must hate me.'"

"I must *hate* her? What did you say?" I heard a doctor being paged on the intercom, and the nurses laughing outside at the station as Andreas sipped his coffee. I became aware, as the seconds passed, that I was holding my breath.

"I say, 'Darling, he's a Christian. He doesn't hate anyone.'"

He gave me the look he used when he wanted to emphasize a point, eyes round and wide over his flourishing mustache, and said, "The coffee is percolating, my friend." His laugh died on his lips when two teenage girls stepped warily into the room as if the floor were thin ice. His daughters, Cora and Elara. I left them with him, hoping he could speak to them of something other than the horrors of capitalism and the melting pot and all the perceived injustices that had become the focal point of his immigrant rage.

Andreas came home to die. Uncle Billy was good to him, too. He used to bring him supper, sometimes pizza from Yianni's, with the sea and the blue domes of Santorini drawn on the lid of the box, or lentil soup and spinach pie from the Athenian Corner. The Greek refused to acknowledge his impending demise. He spoke of Death as a being and said that like Odysseus, he would escape from the clutches of Hades to return to his own Ithaka, which was, coincidentally, Corfu, just north of the home of the old master mariner. "I will blow out the candle that they light for my death vigil, my friend, yes." We listened to the plaintive cry of a Greek singer and the bright, clear notes of bouzoukis and sipped a Metaxa.

But it was Death who blew out his candle, and I helped to carry his coffin, so light, to the hearse. He was buried beside his father, far from the village. He must have faced the truth at the end. He left a coin of the Ionian Islands to be placed under his tongue: Charon's obol, a final act of defiance to the priest.

Monica and I stood before the stone on which the engraver had still not come to cut his name. In the light of late August, the shifting branches of the maples stirred the shade. "I was confused, Robbie. I needed time to think, but I kept thinking of you. And Andreas said to me, 'Robbie has a heart and a soul,' and I knew that was true." The shadows of the swaying branches shifted, but her dark eyes shone in sun and shade. "I'm not confused anymore."

Not confused anymore. In my mind, I heard my friend's voice in its simple wisdom, "You have to let the coffee percolate, my friend. If you force the key in the lock, you will break it." A sort of delirious affection that I knew was love flowed through me, and I moved closer to Monica and wrapped her in my arms.

The world was right again, except that my friend was gone, and I had him to thank for setting it right. Obsessed? Yes, he was. A dissident Don Quixote, lowering his lance against an America that had somehow betrayed the dream he'd held of her. His continuous expression of this *idée fixe* drove many away, yet he had reunited us. To me, above all, there was something authentic in his wild refusal to compromise with the state or the priest—with the world—to hold fast to his values and his pantheon. I had to admire one, like Ahab, "who, against the proud gods and commodores of this earth, ever stands forth his own inexorable self."

Work, Music, and Love

"Ah, music," he said, wiping his eyes. "A magic beyond all we do here!"
—J.K. Rowling, *Harry Potter and the Sorcerer's Stone*

Often, when I wake in what the old song calls "the wee small hours of the morning," and sometimes even in dreams, I revisit all the jobs I've had and the men who worked beside me. I bless them, and I bless every truck I loaded and unloaded, every cracked or broken slate I ripped from a roof to replace with a whole one, every sheet of drywall I finished, with a trowel in my right hand and a hawk in my left, alongside old Steve Quinlan, a Chesterfield hanging from his lips, both of us smiling as in another room my father sang "I'll Take You Home Again Kathleen" while he mixed joint cement into a bucket of sand finish. I remember with gratitude the work that made me—the snow I plowed, the garbage I hauled, the shingles I nailed, the boxes and the furniture I packed onto the freight elevator at Bon Marche, the clattering machines whose tireless jaws I fed with stock, the forklift I wove between columns of raw lumber with a palette of plywood balanced in the air before me.

There is no compliment a man like me loves more than for someone to tell him he's a solid worker. "Arthur McNeil Junior, eh? You work like your father," a builder told me once on a job site when I was a young man hanging the drywall. "How's that?" I joked. "Slow?" He shook his head. "No. *Steady*." Nearly forty years later, I find satisfaction in those words.

I was a working man. I tried college, and I wasn't a bad student. I've always enjoyed reading, but I wanted to work, not shuffling papers in some cubicle in an office, but doing a job that you could see was done at the end of the day. I took pride in whatever I did, and I would never be the one to ask is it time for lunch or to say let's call it quits or it's too hot to strip a roof today. I would work until my back ached or my hands bled, and when the boss called to wrap it up and I sat down for a beer on a Friday with the roofers and the framers, sometimes I could hardly get up, and it felt good.

It was the summer of '78. Things were slow in the building trades. I had started working on my electrician's license at night. By day I was "setting the heads" on the machines at a cardboard box factory. This involved pushing a button so that the body of the machine separated along a track and the "head-setter" could enter the newly formed crevice with a set of measurements and an L-wrench to loosen the screws that fixed the great circular blades on a ruled axel, slide them to their new position, and tighten them there so that they would slice the cardboard at the requisite lines to produce whatever sized boxes had been ordered. There was a safety switch of course, but I always kept one eye out for a psychotic who might come along and try to close the machine while I was inside setting the heads, and more than once in dreams I saw those blades closing in on me.

So, when Frank Duggan, an old high school friend, said he could get me a job with the city DPW tossing garbage into the big orange trucks, I jumped at it. The idea of working outside appealed to me. I gave my notice at the box factory and looked forward to my new career as "garbage man," at least until I completed my 144 hours of technical training and found an apprenticeship with an electrician.

Things went smoothly at first. In the morning, I'd get to the City Barns and hang around waiting for my job to be called. Eventually, a short guy with a thick mane of white hair and a stubby cigar would appear and read off the assignments, coming eventually, on most days, to "Pelton, Totten, Lowry, Ortiz, McNeil—Ashes and Waste," and off we'd trudge to the garbage trucks. I enjoyed making the circuit of Pawtucketville or Centralville, hanging onto the back of the "honey wagon," hefting the barrels and dumping them into its steel maw. With a gloved hand, I'd pull the lever to bring down the sweeping hydraulic compressor jaw that slowly crunched and snapped and mashed the garbage into the insatiable stomach of the truck-beast. The maggots took a few days to get used to, but you'll get used to just about anything if you're willing to work—even the little shits who called after us, "How's business? Pickin' up?"

Around the third week, I was surprised when one day I didn't hear "McNeil" called out on the Ashes and Waste detail. I stood around listening to other assignments as guys filed out, until I heard, "Croswell, McNeil—Collections." This referred to a dump truck that was sent out to pick up discarded kitchen appliances, furniture, anything too big to throw in the garbage truck. We joined the driver, a knucklehead named Tony. I call him a knucklehead because the previous week I had been eating lunch on the tailgate of my pickup. My buddies Mike Pelton and Johnny Ortiz weren't around, so I was reading a book my father had given to me, *The Guns of August* by Barbara Tuchman.

This Tony walked by and gave me the stink eye, as if I was sitting there cooking a spoonful of heroin. He seemed to think that reading a book was a subversive activity, and maybe he was right about that. Anyway, I was none too happy to have to spend the day with this moron who was a loudmouth around the Barns, a popper of mints after his liquid lunch, and a guy who knew a lot about sports and nothing about anything else. I had worked with another driver named Harry Charity one day; the name suited him. He was kind and smart and told riveting stories about working for the Lowell Locks and Canals during the Depression. I'd work with Harry twelve hours a day, but this blunt-faced dimwit—I knew it would be a long day, though I had no idea how long.

Croswell was the quiet type, and when Tony realized I didn't know shit about the Red Sox, his suspicions about me were confirmed. We picked up a stereo console with its speakers removed, a decrepit picnic table, an old Magnavox cabinet TV, and some tires that had been abandoned in a parking lot. Under the Lord Overpass, we loaded a lop-sided recliner and a frayed two-legged couch. Tony took out a jack knife and slit the backs; he said you could usually find some change that had fallen out of people's pockets in the crevices, and he did come up with 55 cents, enough, as he reminded us, for a bottle of Bud with his lunch at the Highland Tap. Lunch at the Tap was great so long as it was a pickled egg and a Slim Jim.

We had one more pickup before we could head out to the dump and then to the bar—that was Tony's plan anyway. I never drank at lunch, but you have to go where the driver goes or walk. He checked his clipboard. "Walden Street? Where the hell is that?"

"It runs between Oakland and Parker," I said, and he put the truck in gear. Getting little response from Croswell and me on some remarks that Dick Stockton and Ken Harrelson had made during the Sox game the night before, he turned on the radio and started to sing along with the Commodores' "Three Times a Lady." I wondered once again what the hell 'three times a lady' was supposed to mean. "I'll Take You Home Again Kathleen"—I know what that means, and anyway my father had a great voice. But "Three Times a Lady" was just an awful song. I don't mind sentiment, but I hate syrup, and Tony did not improve upon it with his warbling. It was worse for

Croswell, because it was his turn to 'ride bitch,' in the middle of the truck's bench seat, so in addition to having his knees jostled with the stick shift, he had to listen to that tuneless crooning in his ear.

Eventually, we pulled up at the house on Walden. There was an Emerald Flooring truck out front; that was Mario Santiago's company, and I could hear the floor sander buzzing inside. Tony began to back the truck into the driveway. I leaned out the open window and looked over my shoulder, and there it was—an upright piano sitting in front of the garage.

A minute later we were standing around it, a trio of rubes in front of a fine instrument—a work of art. I lifted the keyboard cover and read:

Concord Piano

Upright Grand

Chicago, 1918

Croswell tapped a few keys—some of them worked, others were muffled and out of tune. Tony pushed his Red Sox cap back and scratched his head. "How the hell you guys gonna get this monster on the truck?"

"I can't believe someone is throwing this out," I said. "Are you sure this is what's going, Tony?"

"Whattaya think I'm stupid?" I didn't answer that. "It says piano right on the order."

The whine of the floor sander inside died, and Mario came out with his respirator hanging from his neck and lit a cigarette. "Hey, Arturo!" he called out, seeing me. "How you doin'?"

"Hey, Mario. What's up with the piano? They wanna throw it out?"

"Yeah. This guy he want the floors done pronto. He don't care about that piano. He wanna throw it away. He just get the place from his father, died in some nursing home. He's a lawyer an' he got plenty of bucks, so he jus' wanna throw that piano away. It don't work."

"Who got it out here?"

"Some guys that clear out the house. They get it off the floor for me, but they say they don't take no piano. Man, that sucker, guy say it weigh like 700 pound."

"Shit," Croswell said.

"You think the four of us can get it on the truck?"

Tony stepped backed, offended. "I'm a driver. I don't load shit. It's against union rules for me to do anything but drive."

Mario shook his head. "Man, I need my back for my job. Besides, the three of us try to lift that thing, we all end up with balls like grapefruit."

Tony checked his watch and said, "Well, we can't stand here with our thumbs up our ass." He went to the truck and pulled a ten-pound sledgehammer out from behind the seat. "We'll take her in pieces." He handed the sledge to me.

"Wait a minute, Tony. This is a beautiful old piano. Somebody would love to take it, fix it up. Look at the carving on the front."

"Yeah, it belongs in Carnegie Hall, I'm sure. But our job is to get it the fuck out of here, and the only way to do that is in pieces, so let's go. It's almost lunch."

Now I would willingly have followed his directions if he had handed me the sledge to break up a doghouse or a couch or smash through a wall—but this was just a shame. It was like being asked to smash a stained-glass window in St. Patrick's Church. This piano had stood, upright and grand, from the end of the Great War, through Prohibition, the Depression, and my father's war. And who knows what songs had been played on it, what voices had risen in chorus around it, what dreams it had inspired? Concord Piano. Upright Grand. Chicago, 1918. *Chicago, 1918*! "We can't destroy this piano, Tony."

He made a big incredulous puss. "What?"

"Come on, look at the workmanship."

Tony was losing patience. "I don't give a fuck!"

I was in too deep. I've already told you I'd stood in the heart of a machine setting blades. They asked me to shovel shit, I'd shovel shit. I'd pull my weight on any crew, maggots and all, but behind me stood the creation of some other workman—a *craftsman*—long dead, and I was not going to hammer the fruit of his labor, and maybe all that remained of him, into rubble. That was a job I couldn't bring myself to do.

Tony tried to grab the sledgehammer from my hand, but I jerked it away. "Hang on, Tony. You're a driver. It's against union rules, remember?"

"Give me the fuckin' sledge!" He grabbed at it, and we each held on.

My blood was rising. With two hands, I yanked the long handle out of his grip. He snorted angrily, stomped back to the truck muttering threats and obscenities, and pulled a crowbar from behind the seat. I stepped in front of him. "Get outa my way!" he roared.

There was nothing for it. I said the only words I was sure he'd understand. "You whack that piano, I'm gonna whack your head."

Croswell stepped in with palms raised. Mario dropped his cigarette and said, "Whoa, Arty, *cálmate hombre*."

He raised the crowbar and held the claw a foot from my face. "Are you threatenin' me, you son of a bitch?"

"Get that crowbar out of my face before I shove it up your ass."

"OK, Tony," Croswell said, "let me talk to him. Listen, Arty . . . ."

"Your ass is off this job, McNeil!" Tony bawled. "And you know what? After we dump this load, I'm going directly back to the Barns! I'm gonna tell Rainier personally that we couldn't do the job because *you* wouldn't let us do it and that *you threatened* a co-worker."

"I'll take the piano," I said. "I'll come back and get it."

"We're supposed to get it out of here *now!*"

Fuming, he climbed back into the truck, and I heard the crowbar clatter on the floorboards. Croswell got in. Mario went back inside, shaking his head, and I threw the sledge in the back of the truck and pulled myself up there. I sat on one of the tires we'd collected because I didn't want to listen to Tony's simpering—or his goddamn singing—all the way out to the dump and back to the Barns.

Well, there's no need to dwell on the scene in Rainier's office. "You've only been working here five minutes, and you think you're running the job? You screw up a simple pick-up and threaten the driver? You're fired, and I'm docking you an hour of this morning's pay for wasting the city's time."

On my way out, I saw Tony lurking by the gate wallowing in his smugness. "See you around, McNeil!"

"Not if I see you first." I flipped him the bird and left. He was correct though. I did see him around. If the reader will allow me a brief digression: a couple of years later, I was at the American Legion bar minding my own business, listening to Nip Ahearn tell stories. Tony approached with some bottled courage under his belt and called me an asshole. That was the most original insult he could muster. I stood up and asked him if he wanted to repeat it. He did. I couldn't believe it. I was like a kid at Christmas, thinking, *I'm finally going to get to knock this guy's lights out.* I won't waste words on the ensuing affray, except to say that Tony proved once again the truth of the old Irish adage: "It's often that a man's mouth breaks his nose."

Back to my story: since I've already told you that I thought of myself as a team player and a solid guy on a crew, getting fired was a blow to my pride and an embarrassment. I couldn't hold down a job on the DPW? I felt bad that Frank Duggan had vouched for me, and I'd let him down, not to mention old Arthur McNeil senior and my mother Eileen, who knew people in the city. The thought that they might be embarrassed bothered me more than losing the paycheck. I could always find work.

The only good thing about getting fired was that I had time to consider the piano dilemma. What I needed was a truck with a

Tommy Gate, a hydraulic lift, and a few guys. That afternoon, I was able to borrow the lift truck from George Dabilis at Olympic Construction. I stopped at the Tap and enlisted three guys from the bar to help me move the piano. There was a load-moving dolly and some straps in the back of the truck, and within an hour I had the piano in the living room of my apartment.

After I'd paid the guys and returned the truck, I went home and cracked a beer and studied the piano leisurely for the first time. I noticed a Latin inscription carved into one of the three square panels on the face of the instrument, amid clusters of grapes and intertwining vines: *Musica donum Dei.* I didn't know what that meant then. I lifted the cover from the keys, and tapping some of them, felt as if the hammer inside was not striking anything cleanly. I knew little about pianos, but I lifted the lid to have a look inside and used common sense to figure out the principles.

I saw as I struck the keys that there were tuning pins set in a steel plate and a neat row of hammers that would strike the piano wire as a damper lifted to let the note resound and fall to mute it when the pianist's hands moved on. The hammers attached to the higher notes' keys struck three of the thinner strings while the lower note hammers struck only one of the thicker ones. All the strings were attached to two great crisscrossing harps, though I could see only the tops. The felt pads on some of the hammers seemed to have dried out and fallen off, and even I could hear that the instrument had not been tuned in many years. It was certainly a piece of precision work, and I hoped, not beyond repair, because I felt proud of it, and I wanted to hear it played. I even thought I'd like to take some lessons.

I was about to close the lid, when I noticed, tucked between the metal frame and the housing, an edge of pale blue paper. I reached down and pulled it out—an envelope addressed to a Gordon Rosser in Ithaca, N.Y. The return address—S. Fayette, in Aurora, N.Y. I opened it and unfolded a handwritten piece of music and a letter.

Dearest Gordie,

I dreamed of you last night, and today I wished so very much that I could see you. When will you come down to the lake again? Mr. K says that you will marry Janine DiPetro or her sister Eva because their father is wealthy and has connections. Is it true, Gordie? Then tell me, but if you marry another, I will never marry at all. You are my last love, and you have spoiled me for any other. Did you not feel it from the beginning or was I mistaken? That afternoon that you played through the rainstorm at Glencoe Cottage, though we were both drenched to the bone and the fire was weak and smoky—I have loved you since then, or maybe before, maybe before I ever met you. Your playing drew me close, so close to you. I hear in your music a deep connection to the great soul of music, which shows us the truth of all that it is to be fully human, and that is why I tell you that your name will someday be known, but whether that is true or not, it is a name that I will always love as I love the gentle man who bears it.

At Christmas, you said that I might not be happy with you. I will never be happy without you. Visit me as soon as you can and let us kiss again the way we did on the bridge at Taughannock Falls, enveloped in white mists as in a dream, and then tell me once and for all that you can see a future without your Sarah. I attach the piece I wrote for you. I am a simple girl, and it is a simple piece, but you will understand it if anyone can. Love fades sometimes, they say. But my love for you will live so long as I breathe. Do not think me a silly girl; I am young, but I know my mind when I declare that I will love you always. Come soon to me because my heart is breaking without you. And if I am deluded and you decide to stay away or to form other attachments, then I will live forever with the memory of the hours we spent together, and the comfort of the certain knowledge that at times, at least, you did love Your Own Sarah

I examined the faded postmark on the envelope—1938. I read the letter over and over. I carried it with me for days until I felt that I was in love with Sarah myself, and I wished I could go back and shake this fool of a Gordie by the shoulders and ask him, "What's wrong with you? Damn the money! How many men ever have a love like this?" I doubted whether such a love was even possible anymore.

When I tried to study my Electrical Code Book, the image of a woman came before me, blotting out the diagrams of circuits and the words on the page. Sarah Fayette stood at the crossroads of love on an arched bridge gazing toward the thundering falls, shrouded, like her own future, in mist. And I heard her solemn question: "Is it true?"

In the meantime, I located Jacob Mudge, a semi-retired fellow from Carlisle who could repair and tune the piano. I left the key under the mat for him because George Dabilis had called me to ask if I could sheetrock a house with a couple of his guys.

When I got back, Jacob, a grizzled tradesman in a plaid shirt and wire-rimmed glasses, was reassembling the piano. He had brought in a chair from the kitchen because there was no bench. "A fine instrument," he said. "You had some sticky keys," he continued, "mainly because the key slip was too close to the front of the keys—sometimes it gets a little bent over the years. I just put a shim in, so it doesn't touch the keys now. Let me see, some of the front rail pins needed to be smoothed and polished, the bushings tightened—that can make the keys stick, too. And I glued some of the jacks back on to the whippens and replaced the hammer pads, and now I just have to tune her."

"Looks like you know what you're about, Jacob."

"Oh, I've been at it a long time. By the way, I found those things inside the piano." He pointed to a pile by his toolbox. "Six pencils, a toy soldier, two puzzle pieces, three marbles, the skeleton of a mouse, and ... when I had the music desk and the fallboard out, and tried a little arpeggio, I heard a kind off fluttering sound in the base. Look at this—a Christmas card—from 1939!"

He handed me the yellowed envelope, saying, "Three cent stamp. Celebrating the centennial of baseball."

It was addressed to Mr. & Mrs. Gordon Rosser, which told me nothing, but there was a card inside. A pair of cardinals sat on a holly bush singing silently above the words "Seasons Greetings!" I was almost afraid to open it. I felt that if I saw the name of Janine or Eva, I would lose my faith in humanity. A weight seemed to lift off my chest as I read: *Tweet Tweet! Merry Christmas Gordie and Sarah! Hope you two lovebirds keep making beautiful music together in 1940! Shirley and Stan*

I produced Sarah's letter and her musical composition and handed them to Jacob. He nodded appreciatively when he'd read her words and said, "Mrs. Mudge never wrote me a letter like that." He smiled and added, "However, she does put up with me." It took him two hours to tune the piano, and I didn't have to request that he play the piece that Sarah had written. The old man set the music before him and began to play. He named the chords: "C minor 7, F minor 9, D minor 7, G7, ..." None of that meant anything to me, but I was filled with wonder as the voice of the old piano, rich and renewed, filled the room. Mudge spoke to me over his shoulder as he played, "Yes, it's really a lovely composition."

I realized that up until that moment I had seen the piano merely as a beautiful piece of workmanship. Now I saw it as something much greater, a being, nearly, with a voice that evoked thoughts and moods and ideas that words would be inadequate to express. It made me feel that the human soul was capable of nobility, of connecting to 'the great soul of music,' which must live within the men and women who compose it and all those who appreciate it, and which, as Sarah had written, "shows us the truth of all that it is to be fully human." In a strange way, the music made me feel that young lover's presence; her composition was not nearly as sad as it might have been had she been left, in my mind, standing forever alone on the bridge by the falls.

My wife sometimes plays the piece on the old Concord piano. It may not surprise you that I married a pianist, my teacher, who was a music student at the university. And so, much of the course of my life, it seems, was charted in one moment's refusal to swing a sledge.

Since there's no title on the composition, my wife calls it "Sarah's Song." When she plays it, I'm reminded of the passionate woman who composed it, and of the truth of the old inscription: *Musica donum Dei.* Music, a gift of God.

Happy to Meet, Sorry to Part

*B*aile Átha Cliath. *The "town of the hurdled ford."* Better known as Dublin, also from the Irish, *Dubh Linn,* the "Black Pool," which is a reference to an ancient "treacle lake." It survives today as a bathing pool for the penguins in the Dublin Zoo. I confess I'm not sure what a treacle lake is, but I'm looking into it.

Dublin was founded by the Vikings in 988 AD before their move to Minnesota. It was a stronghold from which they could sally forth to pillage, plunder, murder, rape nuns, rape monks, and lord it over the Irish until Brian Boru fixed their gallop. More of that anon.

Now that you have a solid historical background, let me bring you forward one millennium to 1980, a Victorian house on 64 Mountain View Road in Ranelagh, south of Dublin City and the Grand Canal. The house, with its stolid bricks and wrought iron fence, had at some point, (probably before penguins began to disport themselves in the treacle lake), been divided into "bedsitters," and "flats." A "bedsitter" is a single room equipped with a bed, a sink, and a "cooker." A flat, as you probably know, is any kind of apartment.

Downstairs, in one of the flats, dwelt a drunken turf accountant named Grogan, who always seemed to catch me when I came home late and half-lit, and insisted I drink whiskey with him and listen to his grandiloquent Jameson-soaked recitations of Yeats. He was living with a petite but tough strawberry blonde when I first moved in, but one night I came home to find all of her clothes on the front sidewalk. This was Grogan's subtle way of letting the woman know that their relationship had faltered. She, in response, had thrown a brick through the windshield of his Morris Minor and bid him good riddance.

Upstairs, Vincent Martin, a Trinity College graduate who worked for the Electric Supply Board occupied another flat with a separate bedroom where he spent much of his time reading Camus and contemplating suicide.

Then there were the two upstairs bedsitters. One provided a refuge for an indeterminate number of young men 'up from the country' to make their fortunes on construction sites in Dublin. The other inhabitants of number 64 referred to them collectively as "the lads." When the pubs closed, they lurched and zigzagged homeward, singing "He wuz me bruther, Sylvest" or some other boozy ballad in a variety of musical keys.

Upon their return, doors slammed, music blared, and the house shuddered and rocked for about an hour with wrestling matches and all kinds of misdirected sexual energy. A few nights previously, one of the lads had been thrown against my door, which flew open as he was sent sprawling on the floor beside my bed. "Sorry Jackie!" he said and flew out of the room again. The other lads had locked him out and were trying to hold the door closed against his repeated charges. The result of this particular pissing contest was that the bottom half of the door was shattered. The lads closed the top half and they all stretched on the floor for a hard sleep.

The final bedsitter was occupied by me, Jack O'Brian, a "Yank" from Lowell, Massachusetts. I had come to Ireland upon news of the inheritance of a cottage in Clontarf, north of the city, from an aged great-aunt named Doll. I had met Doll once, as a child, on a visit to the old country with my father. I recalled a smiling spinster with a marmalade cat in her lap sitting by the fire, shawl-covered and benign, a picture of what the Irish poet Raftery called "undistracted calm."

And now this gentle old woman out of distant memory had gone and left me a house, perhaps because my mother had written so often to tell her what a wonderful boy I was, and that I was "the image" of Doll's nephew, my father, who had died years earlier, and whom she had loved. While the solicitors shuffled papers and arranged the thing, I helped my cousin out at his shoe store and did some elementary repairs and cosmetic work at the Clontarf cottage. Until I had the place fixed up and was ready to either rent or sell or inhabit, I thought it wise to take the bedsitter in Ranelagh on this street that the real estate agent had described as "an idyllic retreat in a mature residential enclave." Apparently, no one had explained this exclusivity to the lads, or to Grogan the drunken howler.

To return to number 64. The toilet, or "loo," was in the hallway, as was the telephone. There was also a shower that stood just outside my door, like a moldy upright coffin. Hot water was generated by feeding 5p coins into a ticking meter beside the shower. It must have gone cold on one of the lads that Saturday morning, because I heard him shouting, "Payther! Put two bob in the mayther!"

I rose stiffly out of my lumpy bed. The landlord had nodded sadly in its direction when he showed me the room and admitted, "The bed is banjaxed." He shrugged as if to say, "What can you expect for eight quid a week?" Certainly, not an idyllic retreat. I splashed cold water on my face and was just finishing brewing a pot of Campbell's Perfect Tea when the shower outside my door was turned off and I noticed that the phone was ringing in the hall.

I threw the door open and nearly collided with one of the lads as he stepped out of the shower. We wished each other a good morning, and the lad said, "Ah, Jackie . . . ." and something else in his broad Naaavan accent, interlaced with a lot of "fooks" that I couldn't make head nor tail of, though I laughed anyway and said, "If you say so!" The lad laughed too, and added something about "a right quare fella," but I didn't know if it was myself or someone else who was supposed to be a right quare fella or why. I didn't pay much attention to the lads.

Proinsias O'Kelly was on the phone. Now he was a right quare fella. He made no morning salutation. It was as though by picking up the telephone, I had interrupted a soliloquy. "Yeah," he was saying. "Yeeeaaah. I'm in a phone booth near the G.P.O. The tricolor waving against a blue sky. *Right proudly high over Dublin town they hung out a flag of war.* The Irish women, walking arm in arm. God, they are full of life, laughing and joking and capering . . . capering, that's a good word."

Proinsias was an American student from Philly, though his parents were Irish born. "Full of the owl' palaver they are, sure," he continued, affecting a Dubbalin accent, which he could do well.

I had met him at Birchall's, a pub down on the Sandford Road that we both frequented. Proinsias was high strung and liable to launch at any moment into a tirade or a fit of nervous laughter. Sometimes, when he returned to his bedsitter from the pub around midnight, he would open his window and stick his head out and yell a lot of rubbish. I seemed to have a calming effect on him, though, in general.

"Hang on," I said, and I dashed into the loo and took a quick slash. Then, I trotted up the four or five stairs to the room, poured a cup of tea, and tossed in a spot of milk. I ran back to the phone. "Go on," I said into the receiver.

"Capering and laughing and tossing their hair about and giggling. Always laughing about something. And teasing. *Slaggin'* as they say. I heard this beautiful blonde in the Chinese take-away on Abbey

Street. Her friend says, 'Sure, this food isn't kosher.' The blonde fires back, 'Are ye slaggin' me religion?'"

"Proinsias? Any reason you called?

"Yeaah. Ah . . . instructions from The O'Brian."

"Right. Had your tea?"

"Tea . . . tea. Yeah. Yeeaah. Had my tea at Bewley's. So, what do I do now?"

"All right then. Walk up to Mary Street, buy some fresh fruit and a piece of cheese at the farmer's market for lunch later. You have your briefcase I presume?"

"Yeah, but I have no notebook or pen or anything."

"Hmmm. Then what's in your briefcase?"

"Ah, it feels like it's empty."

I paused and sipped the reviving liquid. "Well, stop at the stationers near the Kilkenny Design Center, buy a cheap pen, and a pad of paper, and head over to the National Library. Work on your thesis until 12:30, then eat your fruit and cheese, take a stroll up to the National Museum, check out the dead Viking they have in the glass case, and return to the library to work on your thesis. I'll be working in the shoe store this afternoon. Come by and see me at 5:00, and we'll go for a pint."

"Yeah. *Si señor. Me voy.*" Proinsias had been in the seminary for a few years, which, I thought, might account for his partial insanity. Having been saddled with the name 'Proinsias,' the Irish form of Francis, hadn't helped either. The fathers of the church had sent him to Mexico to learn Spanish before packing him off to work with the poor in East Philly until one day he got fed up and broke a lamp over the head of one of the poor.

"See you later, then," I said.

There was a brief silence at the end of the line. "I saw Malone in Bewley's," Proinsias continued.

Malone was a poet, the self-declared voice of the Irish Diaspora, returned to Ireland to reconnect with the lost Celtic heritage and celebrate its mystical depth and terrible beauty in lyrical verses that he enjoyed intoning for the females at drunken international gatherings in the back of Birchall's Pub. I found him amusing. Proinsias loathed him.

"Don't get upset. Just ignore Malone."

"He was wearing a tie."

"That's all right. He can wear a tie."

"Yeah, but when he saw me, he kind of put his hand on the knot and you know, raised his eyebrows and adjusted it in this condescending way. So, I went down to Harrods and bought a tie. I went back and found him sitting on the terrace writing one of his wretched poems on a napkin. I went out there and fucking glared at him and adjusted the hell out of my tie, right in his face."

"Well, I guess you showed him . . . something. Go work on your thesis."

I hung up the phone. I can't tell you how it had happened exactly, but Proinsias had latched onto me and had gone quickly from seeking occasional advice to total dependence. He was good at theorizing but bad at doing anything. He was indecisive to the point, at times, of total paralysis. He called every morning now for his 'instructions.' I assumed that it was affected to some degree, though I admit I rather liked playing Caesar to Proinsias's Rufio. In any case, it was easier to tell him what to do than to listen to him wallow in indecision.

There is one other aspect of our relationship that I should mention. Proinsias referred to me as "The O'Brian," the article as prefix to the surname indicating a chieftain of the clan. He saw cosmic significance in the fact that I'd inherited a home in Clontarf, where in 1014, Brian Boru, the eponymous ancestor of my clan, had driven the Vikings into the sea. Boru was killed in the battle, but was horribly avenged by his brother, Wolf the Quarrelsome. You can Google it. You'll also find, that Tadhg Mór Ua Cellaigh, or Big Tadhg O'Kelly, commanding the army of Connaught, responded to Brian's call to arms and covered his left flank in the battle. He died that day, too.

Coincidence? Yes, of course, but one not lost on the O'Kelly who had just requested his own marching orders.

Vincent came out of the loo, and I followed him into his apartment, inquiring in a phony brogue that irritated the hell out of the Irishman, "How are ye dere, buoy?"

"Please don't address me in that repulsive voice. And if you want to know, I'm awful." He spoke with a fine educated West of Ireland pronunciation, as if every word had been chiseled with diamond-edged tools in an elocutionary machine shop.

"God, Vincent, you need to water your plants." I fingered the brown withering leaves in the pots near the window.

"I've decided that the happiness of plants depresses me."

"I don't know about happiness, but they're going to die."

"Oh, fuck them."

"Hmm. So, what's up for today? What's on your sheh-jool? Nice pajamas by the way."

"They happen to be comfortable." He poured water into the kettle and put it on the burner.

"And attractive. I have some tea all brewed, if you like, Vincent."

"I hope I won't offend your sensibilities irreparably if I tell you honestly, and in the spirit of friendship, that you make the vilest and most loathsome cup of tea I have ever tasted."

"Well, that hurts," I said with as much sincerity as I could muster on the subject of tea. "Cuts me to the quick. And for your information, big shot, it's *perfect tea*. Campbell's Perfect Tea."

"The label on the tea is irrelevant. You must learn to brew it properly, and before you return to America, I will have to teach you."

"Ah, when I get back to America, I'll use tea bags."

"*Tea bags*, he says. You might as well put your tea in a Durex condom and let that steep in the hot water."

He turned on the radio. A man was speaking in Irish. Vincent was from a place in Galway called Muckanaghederdauhaulia. In Irish, *Muiceanach idir Dhá Sháile,* meaning "a piggery between two briny places." My host began to chuckle. "What's so funny?" I inquired.

"It's the weather for the west. The man said, '*an ceo ar an aill ard*,' 'there will be fog on high cliffs.'"

"Say, that is funny," I said, in an attempt at irony, or sarcasm. I'm not sure I know the difference. Maybe it was irony seasoned with sarcasm.

Anyway, the tone was not lost on the keen mind of my host. "Well, it's funnier than my perfectly decent pajamas."

"Your water is boiling."

"See now, you're off to a bad start. The water is not boiling. Come here 'til I show you."

"Tea lessons in Dublin," I muttered, "Chapter 62 of my autobiography."

Vincent had drawn the lid from the steaming kettle. "Look at the bubbles there," I said. "It's boiling."

"Is that what you call 'boiling' in America?"

"What do you call it?"

"I call it simmering. That water is simmering."

"Well, I have things to do, and a watched pot never boils . . . ."

"All right, here we go now, it's starting to bloody boil. Now Jack, take your teapot and rinse it with the boiling water, like this." He swirled the steaming water in the pot and poured it in the sink. Now take your teaspoon . . . ."

"That looks a little smaller than an American teaspoon."

"Of course, everything is bigger in America. Now it's one teaspoon for the pot, and one for each cup."

"Now the water is really boiling."

"So it is, Sherlock. It must be well boiling to burst the tea buds; otherwise, you don't get the flavor. Now I put in four teaspoons, that's three cups you see, no more. Pour the water over the tea, turn the flame down to low, place the teapot beside it, and just let it steep for a bit."

I watched the thin column of steam rise from the tiny vent hole in the top of the pot. I dumped what was left of my tea in the sink, and said, "I'll try yours, since you're such a tea freak."

Vincent disappeared into the bedroom and came out wearing some dark brown dress pants and buttoning a white shirt. "Can I pour a cup yet, plant killer?"

"You Americans want everything instantly. Let the damned tea steep a minute, will you?"

"Where are you off to all dressed up?"

"A fella that I work with is taking me up in his little airplane, a Piper Cub or some damned thing. We're going to fly over Howth Head. It's his first time flying on his own, so I thought I'd keep him company. Do you want to come and fly over your property in Clontarf?"

"First time flying on his own. Are you crazy? He may crash into Howth Head."

Vincent shrugged. "I hope he does." He inspected my cup and rinsed it disdainfully to make sure that every drop of my "vile and loathsome" brew was washed away.

"There you go again with the death wish. You have sixty years of life in front of you."

He snorted. "Don't remind me."

A minute later, he poured me a cup of tea, and placed it on the table with a milk container. He took another cup from the cupboard. The steam rose around his pale face and rust-colored hair as he poured.

"Just do me a favor and don't hang yourself anywhere where I'll find you because it would ruin my dinner—probably for days."

"I would regret ruining your dinner far more than quitting this insipid life. Put a napkin under your cup there, would you?"

"The guy wants to kill himself, but he can't have any cup rings on his table. Water your plants and cheer up for Chrissake!" I sipped the rich brew. "All right, your tea is better than mine."

"That's like telling me I'm better looking than the elephant man."

"Very amusing. The elephant man had charisma. You exude—I don't know—*death*. I need to get you fixed up with one of these Dublin girruls."

"I must warn you that my sexual spark when I am in the company of Irish women, is weak, intermittent, and unreliable."

"Why the antipathy to your national females?"

"I am not sure I have an antipathy *per se*, but I am aware that my views on life and the world are different and unlikely to be shared or indeed understood by most Irish women. I am an atheist in a Catholic country. Many women my age, even the college ones, have been molded by their convent education and formative Catholic upbringing. I am twenty-three years old. I've had one rather trying relationship that ended inexplicably. Moreover, my outlook on life has been influenced by the nihilism in Europe, the ongoing situation in Northern Ireland, the European reaction to the Cold War, the Bader-Meinhoffs in Germany, and Brigatas Rosas in Italy, and the Fundamentalist Revolution in Iran. There is a climate of doom, which combined with the grayness and rain that plague this island, is not conducive to positive vibrations."

"Maybe you'd better kill yourself."

"You're right, Jack."

"I was only kidding, Vincent. I would be depressed as hell if you did yourself in, 'topped yourself' as they say over here. As would your poor mother and father. Think of them." Guilt was supposed to be the greatest argument among the Catholic Irish, but perhaps Vincent's atheism made him immune to such an appeal.

He was quiet for a moment, and I sensed a real melancholy below the banter. "You'd get over it," he said quietly. "So would they."

"No, I really wouldn't, and neither would they. Ever. I've got to get to work," I said. "I'll save your life later. Try to enjoy yourself, will you? It's not raining today. If you're back, will you join me and Proinsias for a drink at Peter's Pub after 5:00?"

"I will under no circumstances drink in the company of Proinsias O'Kelly. The man is completely unhinged. He belongs in a psychiatric ward under the care of a competent physician."

"Ah, he's all right. Cheer up! Bader-Meinhoff . . . Jesus!"

Vincent's bad opinion of Proinsias had arisen out of an episode a few weeks earlier in my bedsitter. The two of them had gotten into a discussion of . . . well, I disremember the nature of the discussion. I'd a drop taken. But I do recall that at some point Vincent said, "For God's sake man, be reasonable!" In response to this plea, Proinsias poured a full bottle of Guinness down his pants. Did it flow? Yes. His underwear held it in check for a moment, but soon it ran out of his pant leg over his shoes and onto my already well-used carpet.

"What are you about?" Vincent cried. To which Proinsias responded in a professorial tone, "Oh, well, you see my good man, I'm being reasonable," before bursting into a fit of laughter which did sound, I'll admit, a bit unhinged.

I left Vincent, hunched beside the radio, listening to a stream of rapid syllables that was now comprehensible to so few of the world-scattered tribes of the Irish. I put on a clean shirt, and on the way out, I saw Tony, the landlord, politely knocking on the intact upper half of the lads' door. "The door is banjaxed," I pointed out, helpfully.

A few minutes later, I was heading down Mountain View Road toward Ranelagh Center to catch the 11D bus into Dublin, where, as I said, I worked at my cousin's shoe store. The housewives were already out in their aprons, polishing their knockers . . . their door knockers. The Irish have the shiniest brass door knockers in Christendom. The seagulls wheeling around the chimney pots reminded me that I was near Dublin Bay and called to mind the local politician with the unforgettable moniker of 'Sean D. Dublin Bay Rockall Loftus.'

The shoe store was slow that Saturday, partly because the storm clouds had finally, and predictably, charged in from the mountains around *Baile Átha Cliath*. The rain was rolling down the windows of the shoe store, and I imagined Vincent, intensely depressed, hurtling through a fog around Howth Head with a nervous pilot.

The gloom of the day was banished in mid-afternoon, when I spotted a fine-looking young woman with hair as raven black as her umbrella, gazing into the shop window. She came in, collapsed the umbrella, and picked up one of the open-toed high heels in the window display. She studied it for a moment and asked to try on a pair, in red. "Would you ever bring sizes eight and eight-and-a-half, please?"

A pretty girl is like a melody; indeed, her perfume enveloped me in a fragrant and musical air in which I sensed an alto of lavender and jasmine over a bass of musk. I inhaled deeply and trotted into the back room to fetch the shoes. I slid the boxes out from under a tall column of boxes, but before I returned with them, I stopped and slipped a Tom Waits record onto the turntable. I took a seat on a stool in front of the woman, gripped her nyloned ankle gently, and removed her flat-heeled shoe. "I'll try the eight first," she said. I gently pushed her slender well-arched foot into the red high heel, as, from the speakers near the cash register, Tom Waits began to rasp, "I'm goin' out tonight in my red shoes! Red shoes!"

She didn't seem to notice, consumed as she was in her shoe dreams. "Sure, you can't wear stockings with open-toed shoes, can you?" she asked.

As an employee of a shoe store, I had of course become an expert on women's footwear. "That would be a fashion *faux pas*, in my opinion."

Her head tilted, and her hair fell, long and full as she extended her leg to study the red shoe from different angles. I wondered why it was that the vanity of men was so appalling and the vanity of women so appealing. "Try the other one," I said, and when I had helped her into it, she rose, a goddess, taller and instantly sexier, stepping toward the full-length mirror, riding the three and a half-inch heels, her legs suddenly longer, the thick raven hair playing over her shoulders and back as she moved.

"I suppose the open toes are not very practical in the rain, but they are darling. I love the little crisscross strap." How beguiling, her feminine observations. Still playing the expert, I examined the product information on the box. "It's called a 'vamp strap.'"

All at once she stopped and looked up, a quizzical expression on her face, showing off a fine neck. She had become aware of Tom Waits, that voice like raking gravel, chanting over and over, "Red shoes! Red shoes! Red shoes! Ahhgh! Red shoes!"

"Did you do that on purpose?" she asked. "Slaggin' me shoe fetish, are ye?"

"I suppose it was my idea of a joke," I admitted. "I guess it was kind of sophomoric." Thankfully, the song ended.

"You're a Yank," she said definitively.

"Jack O'Brian, from Massachusetts," I said, and we shook hands.

"Funny name."

"I thought it was a fairly typical Irish name. My friends back home call me 'Obie' or 'Obi-Wan.'"

"No, I mean, your county, or state rather. I remember it appears in *Finnegans Wake* as Masses-of-shoe-sets." Her attention focused once again on the shoes, a thin line of concentration creasing her brow. She retrieved her bag from the seat and pulled out a checkbook. "I'll take the shoes. I think the eights are grand."

"I do hear the women say that the Nine West shoes run a half-size larger anyway."

"Do they, so?"

"They look great on you. I mean you would look great in flip-flops."

She laughed; her large brown eyes full of that warmth that blue eyes can never attain. "Why thank you, Jack." Tom Waits was croaking out "Blue Valentine," now, and I was, if not falling in love, at least smitten hard. I saw the name on her check, and on the license she held out to me: Lydia Balcombe Stoker.

"Stoker? You're not by any chance . . . ."

"Yes, Bram Stoker was my great-great grandfather."

"I pass his house every day on Kildare Street."

"That's right. He wrote *Dracula* there."

"How interesting." I deposited the check in the drawer. "I read *Dracula* just last year."

"A bit chilling, isn't it?" she whispered.

"Yes, it is." We talked for a little while. She was studying at UCD, the School of Business and Law. I told her how I'd just graduated, and about the cottage in Clontarf, thanking God all the time that the customers who paused to gaze in the window kept walking. As my grandfather used to say, *Faint heart never won fair maid.* I cast the die. "Say, any chance we could get together for a drink, maybe tomorrow? I don't usually ask customers out, but . . . ."

"Well, yes, I suppose. It's not just because I'm related to the famous Bram Stoker, is it?"

The Stoker connection had piqued my interest to some degree, but let's face it, a woman like this didn't need a pedigree to pique a man's interest. "Of course not, Lydia. Good book, but to tell you the truth I don't understand the fascination with vampires."

"Do you not? I believe I can appreciate, at least from a woman's point of view, the fantasy of the vampire." She tore a piece from the bottom of her shoe receipt and wrote her name and number.

"Can you?"

"Rather!" she said with playful slyness. I experienced what the less graphic brand of fiction writers call 'a stirring in my loins.' I had no desire to sink my teeth into her neck, but the suggestion that she was capable of entertaining fantasies that were on the fringes of sexual conduct, or misconduct, was intriguing.

I took the paper she offered (*Lydia Stoker*: such a fine hand) with as much nonchalance as I could muster, and said, "Perhaps you can explain it to me over a drink."

"I suppose I can try to explain it," she said.

"Wear your red shoes," I said, and immediately wondered if the remark was appropriate.

"Would that make you happy, Jack?" Her eyebrows arched over almond eyes, upswept at the outer corners, as if the blood of Andalusia flowed in her veins, along with Stoker's. God Almighty what a creature. "As I said, they look smashing on you."

She pushed me gently. "You're quite the salesman, aren't you, Obi-Wan?"

"I'm just being honest. And remember, don't wear stockings with the open toes!"

"Why, what will you do? Spank me?"

Now as I'm sure you know, the Irish drive on the other side of the road. Here in the States, we look to the left before we step out onto the road. In Ireland, you must look to the right. A few days previously, I had made the nearly fatal mental error of looking to my left and stepping onto the street. A double-decker bus swept past me, about six inches from my nose. The subsequent heart-shock and rush of adrenalin I felt as I leaped backward onto the sidewalk was not unlike the feeling I had when she posed that question. I opened my mouth to speak, but nothing at all came out, not even breath.

I slid her shoebox into a bag as she pushed her feet back into her flats, stood, and put her coat on. "I'll call you tomorrow," I managed.

"Right, so. I'll talk to you then, Jack," she said merrily, as though we were old friends. I held open the heavy door for her, inhaling her fragrance once more as she passed.

I saw her for an instant tugging her coat closed and squinting in the rain in front of the store. She smiled and waved at me through the window and then the umbrella mushroomed over her, and she receded along the pavement gray as the rain-washed Dublin City and Tom Waits chanted, "Blue valentines, blue valentines, blue valentines . . . ."

Proinsias came in at five, wearing his new tie, hollow-eyed and haunted, pursued by a thousand imagined insults, plagued with a thousand unanswerable questions. "The O'Brian!" he said, in a sort of hail-to-the-chief voice, as if my presence reassured him in some way. I was feeling like the true leader of the clan with Lydia's number in my pocket.

Before locking up the store, I called number 64. Meanwhile, Proinsias ambled around, touching the women's shoes reverently. I had to let the phone ring about thirty times, but finally, I heard Vincent's clipped hello.

"Jack here. How was the flight?"

"Uneventful."

"I guess that's good. Listen, Vincent. You're the brightest person I know. Here's a question. What would you say is the appeal that vampires have for women?"

"I should think it quite obvious."

"Not to me. What is so sexually exciting about being bitten?"

"It's not being bitten. It is the universal feminine desire each woman has to surrender herself, as Joyce says, 'body and soul and blood and ouns,' to a dominant male who passionately desires her in a raw and animal way, thus immortalizing her in the eternal experience of the union of opposites."

"But then she's one of 'the undead.'"

"Metaphorically, she has only freed the societally constrained and perhaps unladylike beast within her, dangerous and sexually aggressive."

"Holy shit."

I locked up the store. The rain had let up, and now a wind that blew in from the Irish Sea swept away the storm clouds that hung over the capital. The dampness was in my bones, though. I had begun to long for a day at Rye Beach in the sun, for an evening sipping beer on the screened-in porch in my shorts and tee-shirt, listening to the crickets. That was before Lydia. Now I began to convert the cottage in Clontarf to a castle in the air which I inhabited with the dark-haired beauty, raising the descendants of an Irish literary genius on the site of Ireland's greatest military triumph with one of Ireland's most lovely (and sexually aggressive) women. In memory, I saw her eyes kindle and heard the suggestive word: *Rather!* I imagined her surrendering to my passionate desires as the Clontarf hearth fire suffused the room with a flushed and rosy glow.

From O'Connell Bridge, Proinsias and I watched the setting sun spilling its own rosy glow over the Dublin Quays, while gulls coasted the sea breezes that coiled up the Liffey and about the city.

"The Viking in the glass case looks the worse for wear," Proinsias said.

"Yeah, well nine hundred years in a bog will do that to you." My gaze ran along the quays down to the silver arch of the Ha' Penny Bridge and beyond it, the darkening silhouettes of construction cranes against the pastels of the sky. "Speaking of the Vikings, I hear they had to stop the construction at Wood Quay because they've uncovered a Viking settlement."

Just then, a burly, bearded Dubliner was passing. Looking back on it, I'm sure that he was already in a stew about something, but he stopped short when he heard my American accent. He stepped up to us and pointed westward along the Liffey. "What do yiz tink a dat?" he wanted to know. He appeared agitated.

"It's beautiful," I said, in soothing tones.

"Well let me tell yiz sumtin. I'm fookin Dubbalin born and bred in the Liberties. I'm down at the Gas Works like me fadther bafore me. An' I'll tell ye sumtin'. The Kennedy's are not gonta buy this fookin place!"

"Yeah, well I don't think that's an issue," I said, my patience running thin.

"A pair a' feckin Yanks tossin' yer dollars at de Irish, are ye? Ye feckin whores' gits!"

"No, señor, I am no a Jankee," Proinsias retorted, the Dublin man looking puzzled. "I am from Habana, Cooba. And een my countree we call the people like you *los pendejos*. Thees mean in English, fuckeen assholes." And then, of course, he was taken with a bout of hilarity. The laughter ceased when in one rapid motion the Dubliner hoisted him up and, his torso twisting as if he were throwing a discus, tossed Proinsias, briefcase and all, off O'Connell Bridge. I heard his cry of "Whoooa!" and then a splash. Peering over the balustrade, I was relieved to see him surface and begin to swim toward a stairway in the Bachelor's Walk, pulling his bobbing empty briefcase along beside him. A crowd was gathering, and people were calling out to Proinsias and cheering him on.

The burly Dub, satisfied with himself, was starting to slip away, trying to lose himself in the crowd. How could I tell my friend that the O'Brian had just let his attacker walk? That wasn't how our ancestors had thrown back the proud invader! I ran after him and tackled him the way Coach Piwolski had taught me, and he went down hard on the footpath. We wrestled for a minute, and then we were both on our feet. He was a strong bastard, all right. I was holding him by the collar and trying to push him against the bridge railing, just hoping to hang onto him until the gardai arrived because even in Dublin there must be a law against throwing people off bridges.

He grit his teeth and glared into my eyes. I didn't know what a "Dublin kiss" was then. What we would call a "head butt." I must have taken a double kiss, or maybe a kiss and an uppercut. I woke up in the hospital with a broken nose manifested by two black eyes, and my jaw wired shut. A vague recollection of fond ruminations concerning cottage romance returned as dream-like fragments, floating pleasantly above the Liffey until a bolt of pain shot behind my eyes. I heard Vincent's voice. "He's waking up, but I believe he's still in great pain." A stout nurse delivered an injection. I said to Vincent, between clamped jaws: "My panch."

"You can't leave yet Jack."

"De number. Caller pleash."

"I'm sorry. I can't understand you."

"Calla number. Teller I'm shorry. Ah calla whena can."

"Right."

"Ponsias alife?"

"Proinsias tried to board the ambulance with you but was eject-ed. Having been assured that you would recover, he climbed back up onto the balustrade of O'Connell Bridge and startled the crowd by giving a short rambling speech about the Battle of Clontarf and jumping back into the Liffey, laughing madly. He's been taken to St. Patrick's University Hospital for observation."

"Aw, heesh awright." When you're from Lowell, Massachusetts you develop a high tolerance for eccentric behavior.

The next time I awoke, I inhaled a familiar fragrance of lavender and jasmine. Through half-opened eyes, I saw Lydia Stoker sitting with Vincent, her head inclined toward him in earnest conversation.

"I don't care about looks, really," she was saying. "What appeals to me is a masculine intellect."

"That is your way of telling me I'm as ugly as sin."

"Sin can be quite appealing, can't it?"

"I have no concept whatsoever of sin, to tell the truth. And like Camus, I reject all things that erase the consciousness of the absurd, such as sin, religion, God, the whole lot."

"Isn't murder a sin?"

"There can be no sin without God. There is only behavior that causes others pain, and that, for empathetic reasons, one should wish to avoid."

I closed my eyes again, but not before I saw that Lydia was riveted by Vincent's masculine intellect, and it killed me to think that she was probably wearing her red shoes. I had to lay there seething for another hour listening to him astound her with tons of Existential rubbish. If I'd not had my mouth wired shut, I would have cried out "Camus? Sartre? Jesus, the man is from a fucking piggery between two briny places!" In retrospect, I'm glad my mouth was wired shut.

The insubstantial pageant of wild nights of passionate romance before the cottage fire was vanishing, like the wind-swept clouds of the previous evening, replaced once more with the long-held image of Doll and the marmalade cat sitting in Zen-like placidity by the fire.

Vincent was a good friend. When I got out of the hospital, he often brought me soup that I sucked through straws and assayed various hints about his feelings for Lydia, their feelings for each other. I could see that, despite his belief in the absurdity of life, he had a strong notion of loyalty, and he was eager to know if accepting Lydia's interest in him was a betrayal.

"Not at all, Vincent. What am I to her? Just a guy that sold her a pair of shoes. Not my cup of tea anyway." I was relieved when he smiled and said, "I hope you are never involved with a woman who could be compared to *your* cup of tea."

"Well, that's a good point."

"But you really don't mind . . . ."

I continued with the blandishments. "I was hoping to introduce her to you. Remember I said I'd have to fix you up with a Dublin girl? She'll ignite that faltering spark."

"Oh, I should think so," he said, and my heart sank even as I laughed with him. She was a Stoker all right, and she'd have no trouble stoking any spark to flame, no matter how meager. A month later they were engaged, and Vincent inquired about purchasing the cottage in Clontarf. That, as they say in Dublin, "put the tin hat on it." It was done, and the following week, I helped Vincent move in with Lydia. I had to admit they were good together. I saw her watch Vincent with warm sympathy and keen admiration. Her kisses had banished his death wish, so I suppose he was "un-dead."

Meanwhile, the lads were out looking for the "fooker" that broke my jaw. "We'll foind de fooker, Jackie. We'll do for 'im boy. We'll fix his fookin wagon." It was unlikely they'd find him since I said I couldn't remember a thing. I certainly was not going to tell them that he was employed at the Gas Works, for fear they might blow up the city.

Proinsias was let out of St. Patrick's Hospital. They told him to stop drinking. The two of us got drunk that night at Birchall's. I got drunk fast because I'd lost about twenty pounds with my mouth clamped. My ticket home was in my pocket, and it made me feel as if I was only half there. If you've spent time in foreign parts, particularly in your youth, you know the feeling.

You're a part of everything, of all these people and places and events. And you feel the weight of history in the Dublin stones, in Bram Stoker's house, in the National Library where Joyce held forth to the Quaker librarian. You sense it on the bench where Patrick Kavanagh sat by the Grand Canal, on the stone bridge near Harold's Cross where Robert Emmet was taken. You hear the echo of rifle fire where Cathal Brugha charged out of the Four Courts like Butch Cassidy. The place seeps into your being. And then you step on an Aer Lingus jet and in six or seven hours it's all just memory, insubstantial stuff, and you know you'll never have a shot with a woman like Lydia again. Christ, you'll never even meet a woman like her again.

Proinsias and I drank the parting glass and I told him I should not have taken on the role of his chief. I was not 'The O'Brian,' just an O'Brian, and it was time for him to set his own course. "Yeaah," he said. "Yeah." I hugged him and slapped his arm and walked up Mountain View, never to see him again, but I could still hear him on the corner of the Sandford Road, bellowing into the night:

Oh, all the money that e'er I spent, I spent it in good company
And all the harm that e'er I've done, alas it was to none but me
And all I've done for want of wit, to memory now I can't recall
So fill to me the parting glass, good night and joy be with you all.

Back at number 64, Grogan's door was open, and there he was at his kitchen table—a wrinkled shirt and wild hair, waving me in. A glass was waiting for me. He poured the Jameson, pushed it across the table, and launched grandly into Yeats, "*Come away oh human child, to the waters of the wild, for the world's more full of weeping than you can understand."*

He threw back his whiskey and fixed me with his bloodshot eyes. "That's so true, Jackie," he said. "That's *so fuckin' true.*"

A Fireside Chat

The woman leaned out the front door and looked up and down the street. "I think that was about the last of them," she said.

"Turn off the front light, then, Honey," her husband said, inspecting the nearly empty bowls of candy that sat on the hall table beside a porcelain jack o' lantern, its grin illuminated from within by an orange bulb. "The fire still has some life. Let's have a glass of wine in the living room before we go to bed."

"Sounds lovely," she said. She drooped onto the couch with a sigh that bespoke the long day she'd had, while he went into the kitchen and came back with two balloon glasses of Cabernet. They settled comfortably and watched the flames. They always lit a fire on Halloween night. It was seasonal and cast a warm light over the room. Tom, the tiger cat, sauntered in, blinked at them placidly, and sat down on the rug before the fire.

She sipped her wine and said, "Reminds me of when I was a little girl. Joanie Gillick and Sharon Herbert and I used to love to sit around on Halloween and tell horror stories, try to scare the crap out of each other."

"Kids love scary stories, all right," he said.

"Do you remember any, Dan? Tales of horror?"

"None that would scare you." He paused, then, and the easy smile faded. "Well, maybe one," he said.

She edged closer to him, shivering happily in anticipation. "Tell me!" she whispered.

"I'd rather not," he said.

"Oh, come on. Why?"

"Because once I tell it I can't take it back, and you might wish you didn't hear it. I think you'll wish you didn't hear it."

She laughed and shoved his shoulder lightly. "You really know how to set this up!"

He stared into the fire, saying nothing.

"Dan, you're scaring me!"

"It is scary. It scares me now more than it did at the time because I'm older and . . . ."

"And you've never told me?"

He shook his head and gulped some wine. "I preferred to put it out of my mind."

"So, it involves you, personally?"

"Yes. And I didn't want to lose your good opinion."

"My good opinion? Dan, we've been married for twenty-six years. We have two grown children. I think I know who you are."

His eyes were troubled when they met hers. "Maybe you don't know who I am. Maybe I don't know who I am, or who anyone is, but I did what I did."

There was no sound but the hiss of the burning logs, and the sharp intake of the woman's breath. Nothing moved in the room but the shadows of the restless flames. The cat was a statue outlined in fire.

She gripped his arm, not in excited anticipation of a Halloween story, but as an affirmation of love. "Tell me," she said softly.

After a moment, he began. "Well, you know through college, I worked summers for Billy Drollet on slate roofs. That summer there was a guy who used to drive his truck down from Peterborough. His name was Bobby. I don't even remember his last name. I don't want to remember. We worked on expensive houses in Winchester, Newton, Wellesley. So, we would meet Bobby somewhere down there every morning early and go to the job. I didn't know the guy before that, but I liked him at first. I admired his skill. I was a summer roofer, but he was a real craftsman. If you see those roofs on expensive houses that have designs in the slate—maybe a gray roof with designs in red slate, diamond shapes, or scalloped designs on the front of a mansard roof. He could do all that. He could bend metal, too, on this thing they call the break—anyway, he was skilled. I also liked the way he talked, again, at first. He had a lot of funny expressions, old expressions, like World War II slang that he used. "Stick that up your gigi!" and "Blow it out your barracks bag!" He had been in Vietnam, too, and sometimes after work, he'd get in his truck and light up a big joint he called a 'Bong Son Bomber.' He called me 'Number-One-GI.' He could be funny."

The fire was burning lower. The cat's tail coiled like a separate being with a life of its own. He continued. "But as I got to know him, or as he got to know me and feel more comfortable with me, he started to say strange things. He would say them as if they were perfectly normal, in an offhand way, as though he might be kidding."

"Like what?"

"Some of it I think I've pushed out of my mind. But he told me not to ever try to get a cow to lick my dick because their tongues are like sandpaper. I think it was a cow—some fucking animal."

"What?"

"Bizarre shit. I would just dismiss it and say, 'What the fuck are you going on about?' And he'd laugh and start to tell me how great it was to have sex with sheep or something. I remember I asked Billy, Billy Drollet—'Is this guy for real? What the hell is he talking about?' Billy says, 'Oh yeah, he's fuckin' scrambled eggs, but I need him—he's a good roofer—just don't pay any attention to his bullshit.' And that's what I tried to do.

"But the shit he said got weirder and weirder. He said he was watching some little girl, a neighbor, with binoculars. She was fourteen, and he would try to see into her bedroom window."

"Oh, my God."

"How do you ignore that? And if I told the police up in Peterborough, he would just deny it. But the guy was starting to make my skin crawl. Then, one day we're up on a roof in Brookline, ripping some slate to put in new copper valleys, sweating gumdrops. And he starts up. 'I think I'm going to kill somebody.' Out of the blue. He says the one thing that bothered him was that in Vietnam he never got to kill anyone, and he just wanted to see what it felt like. 'So, Number-One GI, I made up my mind. What I'm gonna do, I got a nice bolt action Winchester hunting rifle. I'm going to take that somewhere, maybe down to New York City, rent a room. Find a nice spot—hidden somewhere, and I'm just gonna pick someone off. Throw my rifle in the truck and leave. No motive. No way of ever finding me."

"What did *you* say?" his wife asked.

"I don't remember exactly, but I'm sure it was why would you want to hurt an innocent person? You need help—all that. But he just said he wanted to see what it was like. And what really scared me, and what I remember vividly, was that he said, 'I don't give a shit about people.' He tapped his temple with a finger and said, 'I'm missing something up here. The conscience part.'

"I was getting freaked out. I told him I didn't want to hear any more of his bullshit about his little neighbor or barnyard animals or killing people. 'Cut the shit, Bobby,' I said, 'it's not funny.' And he says in this phony Asian accent, 'You not worry. You beaucoup

Number One. I not kill *you.*' And he had a big laugh at that.

"A few days later, a Friday, we're finishing up in Brookline. He set the ladder up in the back of the house, and I'm out front getting something out of the truck. I noticed that Bobby had taken his car that day, a beat-up Corolla. Hot day. The windows were down, and I looked in his car. I remember he had a cooler in the back and some empty beer cans, a *Hustler* magazine on the floor. I popped his trunk and went around. There was a long bag in there. I pulled the side zipper down. It was a rifle with a scope.

"When I went back up on the roof, I asked him why he hadn't brought his truck. 'Less conspicuous,' he said. I asked him why he wanted to be less conspicuous, and he just laughed. Said something I didn't catch, but I knew."

He paused, looking into the fire for a moment. "We had finished up the valleys. The only thing left was to replace some broken slate, here and there, across the roof. The normal thing to do would be to lay down a hook ladder beside the broken slate, but he wanted to do it fast. He ties a rope around his waist and throws the other end to me up on the ridge and immediately starts to clamber down the side. Now, this was a big old tall brick house, a Tudor-style mansion with a very steep pitch to the roof. Bobby goes over the side suddenly, before I even had a chance to get my gloves on and pick up the other end of the rope, and he was a big guy. I grab the end and shout, 'Jesus, Bobby, let me know before you go!'"

He calls up, 'Either I trust you or I don't.' He seemed to care as little for his own life as he did for everyone else's. I brace the rope against the chimney and watch him sliding the ripper under the broken slates and hooking the nails, pulling nail and broken slate down. Then I'd slide him down a new slate from the pile behind the chimney. All the time I'm thinking about the gun in his car and trying to tell myself that he was probably full of shit. So I call down, 'What are you doing this weekend, Bobby?'

"He says, 'Tonight, like the song says, I'm gonna get down and find out what it's really all about!'"

My stomach turned a bit. "What the hell does that mean?"

"He chuckled and said, 'Oh, no, Number One G.I. You not wanna know.' He looks up at me. I can still see him smiling there at the end of that rope. There's a strange light in his eyes, like some kid who's excited for a day trip to the beach.

'Why don't I wanna know?'

'Cause you got a conscience is why.'

"He taps the nail in with his punch, then he pulls a copper bib out of his nail pouch, a little patch of copper to slide up under the slate and cover the nail hole between the slates. I see the copper flash in the sun. And when he had driven it up, he stands and begins to scramble across the roof to the next cracked slate. Then, in the roof beneath him, a rusty nail gives way. A slate slides out under his foot. I brace my shoulder against the chimney, and for an instant, I feel his full weight on the rope. I make no conscious decision. I just open my hands. And close my eyes. The rope flies away from me, and I hear him crash hard onto the roof—a fleeting silence, and finally the shattering of the windshield of a Mercedes in the driveway as he landed. Broken neck—broken everything. Dead."

The fire was dwindling. "God help us," his wife said.

He felt relief that she was still holding his arm, still close to him. As the shadows swallowed the corners of the room, she said in a low voice, "You have it, don't you, Dan?"

"Have what?"

"The rifle. You took it and put it in your car before the police showed up."

He stiffened. "How did you know that?"

"They were ready to chalk it up to an accident. You didn't want anything that might hint at another motive."

"I suppose it was something like that."

"And you still have it."

"Well, yes. Up in the rafters of the workshop. I always meant to get rid of it, but . . . ."

She squeezed his arm. "Go get it."

"What? Why?"

She leaned closer, her head bowed, toying with a button on his shirt. "Because I asked you to. Because I...I want to touch it."

He raised her chin and looked into her eyes. In the flicker of the dying embers, they had a strange light, one that he had seen before. In Bobby's eyes.

A Literary Evening

On Friday night, as usual, Mike Duchamps appeared at the back door with a few typed pages rolled up in one hand and a six-pack dangling from the other. "I told you I have plenty of beer," I said.

"Come on, Stan. I never arrive empty-handed," he shot back, which was true. Mike is a fiction writer from Pawtucketville, which is a section of Lowell named after the Pawtucket Indians, who lived here for millennia and are no more. I live in the Highlands, which is another section of the city, and not a part of Scotland. I'm Mike's only close friend who reads a lot, and so the only one whose opinion of his craft he values. He's been reading me his stuff over beers on Friday nights for years. In return, he never comes empty-handed.

We cracked a couple of brews and I poured them into mugs I had stolen from the Highland Tap when I was a kid. I used to drink with Mike and play bumper pool down at the Tap, or the Trap, as we used to call it. That was back when the drinking age was eighteen and the beers were 55 cents.

We went to sit in my living room. The furniture may not be showroom quality, but it is comfortable. Everyone says that. Everyone who comes, which is not many people. I live alone. I took the end of the couch, and he took the stuffed armchair so we could both put our beers on the end table. Very comfortable indeed. We're both big guys—not fat, yet, but unless we start hitting the gym, probably in another ten years we will be fatties. And neither of us has made a resolution. I wear glasses for reading—he wears them all the time. He's a bit unkempt, I must say. Not a mess, but unkempt. Nondescript. You wouldn't see him in a crowd. Brown hair, untrimmed. Jeans. Plaid shirt. Soiled and well-worn olive field coat that now lay on the couch beside him. Light beard you can hardly see. He's bordering on middle-age, bordering on everything, a bit downtrodden, I guess. But smart—he always had that going for him. And his wife, Gladys, she's a sweetheart. He's got a couple of kids in college, and he slaves away teaching History at Lowell High. He had written some pretty good stuff, and even gotten a few things published in respectable journals.

"OK," I said. "Whatcha got?"

"I don't have a title yet," he said as if this was a disclaimer or what lawyers call a fact in mitigation.

"OK."

"All right, let's see. OK. So."

I knew he was going to clear his throat, and he did. People never have to clear their throat to talk, hardly ever, but if they're going to read, especially if they wrote what they going to read, they have to clear their throat.

"Ahem. OK," he said again. "Here goes." And he began to read:

I don't remember exactly when it was that I lost my fear of death and even my respect for it. It was not a loss that left me fearless; on the contrary, I became a greater coward; the fear of death was replaced by a far more profound fear of old age. A fear tinged with horror. And having crossed the milestone tombstone of fifty, the truth of Jacque Brel's words stands like a granite pillar in the foreground of my mind at all times. To die is nothing, it's a beautiful thing, but to grow old, ah, to grow old.

Dependency, second childhood, and the loss of faculties. Condescension in the vapid eyes of nurses, some nephew who wants you dead shouting in your nearly useless ears: "Why don't you sit here! Do you want to sit here?" And thinking ‹Ya deaf old bastard, the shrunken guardian of the few thousand yer keeping from me by inhabiting six feet on the wrong side of the ground.›

I'm not there yet, I hope not by a long shot, but the harbingers come on stealthily. The blurred page, sore knees, a slight paunch, and the longing, that sad longing. The old songs that formed the background music of my youth twist my gut, or mock me like carnival music, reminding me of what I was, and all suggesting the same refrain: Those days are gone—forever.

And soon, you're so out of it that you're not even aware that you look ridiculous in your striped polo shirt, your shorts pulled up to your hoary chest, your knobby feet in socks and sandals. An old man, shuffling along in all the spiffy clothes they gave you on the last grim superannuated anniversary of your antediluvian nativity, growing tits and hair in the ears and wild eyebrows. And some perky guest on Good Morning America *says that people in their eighties, people like you, can still have a healthy sex life, and everyone looks at you and the wizened wifie, and feels like they want to vomit.*

He paused and picked up his beer mug, eyeballing me over the rim as he drank. I sat there, nodding, pensive, trying to give his work the attention it deserved and to say something that might be useful. "What do you think so far?" he asked as he set down his beer.

"You don't like the idea of getting old. Where's the story?"

"Never mind the story for now. It's voice-driven."

"Voice-driven." I tried to dull the edge of skepticism in my voice. "People do like a story. But go on."

He wet his pipes with another swig and continued: *Yes, to die is nothing, but to grow old . . . what horror. If one is not religious, where does one find solace? Shakespeare was right about everything else, and he offers a philosophical consolation on the point in question. You remember,*

When forty winters shall besiege thy brow,
And dig deep trenches in thy beauty's field . . . .

Forty was old in Elizabethan England. And with forty-one winters now having begun to blueprint the trenches in my own face, like the bard, I look at my children. My son, lean and taller than ever I was. My daughter, bearing the stamp of her mother's beauty, and the easy grace of a confident young woman.

How much more praise deserv'd thy beauty's use,
If thou could'st answer 'This fair child of mine
Shall sum my count, and make my old excuse,'
Proving his beauty by succession thine!
This were to be new made when thou art old,
And see thy blood warm when thou feel'st it cold.

Let me sink then, and let them grow, and when I'm a dribbling old fool with a bulbous nose and a boney chest peeking out of a tattered housecoat, I may still catch a glimpse in my half-blind eyes, of some facial expression or gesture in which I'll see living again my own old man, when, with hammer in calloused hand and nail pouch at waist, he could shingle a roof in a day.

"I like that last line," I interjected. The positive reinforcement warmed him up and his voice took on confidence and urgency.

These thoughts were comforting once. The old Micmac Indian, Ed Guilmette showed me a decorative belt, a series of green triangles, the apex of each piercing the base of the next, the ever-renewing tree, death and rebirth, the eternal earth. You could slip away easily with that ever-renewing tree in your mind. But those consolations are harder to cling to because now the world decays with us. Ineffectual senators discuss the vanishing polar ice caps; hurricanes brood and gather in mighty columns above the warming oceans, and the men in black war turbans broadcast jihadist threats of global destruction against all of us infidels.

Words. Infidel. Semper fidelis. Fidelity. Fiel. I have been faithful to you Cynara, after my fashion. Mountains of words, rivers of memories, springs of ideas, but all constrained by the immutable borders of birth and death, and now, the shadow of the death of all. Lyrics, lines, songs remembered. And the brilliant young woman who died, the philosopher, the scholar, and at her funeral my cousin said, "Isn't it strange that her experience, and knowledge, and understanding will never be combined in another human being in the same way." And how can we imagine the day when all knowledge dies, when all our pages are gibberish, all our violins mute, all our technology a world-wide-web of unpowered circuits. Never, raven, nevermore.

His head tilted thoughtfully for a moment, and he said, "Maybe I'll call it 'Nevermore.'" He stared at nothing for a few seconds, in what old writers called a "brown study," then roused himself and said, "Not sure where to go from there." A siren grew louder outside, and we waited until it had faded along Pine Street. Then he asked again, "What do you think?"

I've known Mike too long to beat around the bush. "It's fucking depressing."

"Depressing or sad?"

"Not sure I know the difference."

"You know the song, 'Danny Boy'? It's sad, but it's not depressing. Elie Wiesel's book, *Night*? Depressing."

"Then what you read is depressing."

Resignation tinged his voice. "I think you're right. But then a lot of depressing works have made it big. *The Road. Angela's Ashes. 1984.*"

"But those all had a story. Are you setting up a story here?" I asked. "I know it's voice-driven, but whose voice is it? Who is this guy who's talking, and what else do we know about him? I know he has a couple of kids and he's over forty, and he's depressed about it. Why is he telling me this? What happens? Otherwise, you're getting into 'experimental fiction,' and you know what I think about that."

"But do you find the voice compelling at all? I ask because these thoughts struck me with a certain force when I wrote them down."

"Compelling? Yeah, yeah, maybe compelling in a way, but you know, it's a hell of a lot of old age and death and hopelessness and world destruction in a page and a half. If you can frame the ideas . . . ."

"In a story."

"Sorry to be a philistine, but people do like a story. Think of your most popular pieces. The ones people liked the best. There's a reason. Something happens, Mike. Beginning, middle, and end. Can't be just a guy thinking thoughts, whether they're depressing or sad, and even if they're true. I mean we all know old age sucks."

"Yes, but when I wrote it, the idea of how much it sucked, the totality of the pointlessness, the mystery and the . . . ."

"Depression."

"All hit me. But you're right. It's random. That's why I say I'm not sure what to do with it."

"How about this—you, I mean the narrator, you're a writer, and you have a friend like me, and you go over his house and read him a voice-driven, sad, depressing, random, *thing*, and then you find out the next day that he fucking killed himself."

I thought he might laugh, but his glasses turned upward, and he stroked his thin beard. "Hmmm," he said, looking at the plaster ceiling, where the cracks spread out like a river with its tributaries. Finally, he nodded. "That's not a bad idea."

"Yeah, then, you, ah, you throw your manuscript into the fireplace— you'll need a fireplace in the story and a good roaring blaze, and the paper flares and crinkles black like the earth when the exploding sun consumes us, or nuclear war, and then you hug your wife hard and look at the picture of your kids on the piano."

"And so, the theme is—just cling to what you have, like a drowning man clinging to a plank."

"Right. You don't question the quality of the plank, or its purpose, or what it's drifting toward or anything. You just cling to that sucker 'cause it's all you got. And finally, maybe, you whisper a prayer for your dead literary critic friend. And there's your title: 'World Without End, Amen.'"

"Jimmy Breslin already used that one. But I like your idea." He nodded judiciously as if I were the sommelier and he had just tasted my best chianti.

We talked about titles for a while, and books and movies and drank another beer and Gladys texted him to ask him to pick up some Pepto Bismol on the way home. She had an upset stomach. Anyway, it was near 9:00 pm and we were both yawning, and he got up and put on his coat and rolled up the typed pages and stuck them into his coat pocket. At the door, he smiled and said, "God, remember when we used to head out for the night at this time?"

"Those days are gone."

"Now don't kill yourself after I leave."

"I don't like the idea *that* much," I said.

"Right. Good night, Stan. And thanks for the input."

"Night, pal."

When Mike had gone, I opened another beer. What the hell. It was Friday night. I looked around at my bookcases and at the old family photos that sat above them, at the pile of *New Yorker* magazines on the mug-stained coffee table, the few framed prints I'd collected in my travels. Not a very elegant plank. Maybe, I thought, I should start working out, shape up, ask Marian, that pleasant, divorced secretary who worked in I.T. and was not unattractive, to go out for dinner. Sex. That would be nice. Of course, I'd have to cheat on my girlfriends at hotbabes dot com, sadly my only female companions these last few years.

I remembered that Marian had a ten-year-old kid. "I could be a good father," I told myself, and pleasant images of fishing with the boy and reading Harry Potter to him flashed through my mind. Wasn't that what my old friend and I had affirmed that evening? In the end, nothing matters but our bonds with other people. I wouldn't see my parents in him, as Mike would in his kids, but that's all right, I might still feel the bonds of wife and child. It would be nice to go together to see the boy in a school play, maybe hold hands with Marian in the darkened auditorium, or even to have a woman text you and ask you to pick up a bottle of Pepto Bismol. To depend on you for that. To need you.

And yet, as I was, I didn't feel lonely or depressed or sad. Yes, Mike's story, or whatever it was, was true. We were barreling down the road toward pathetic old age and death, and if I turned on the television news, I'd see suicide bombers and a divided country and ballistic missile tests and shootings in schools and malls. Felt like "The Eve of Destruction" all right. And I was alone in the middle of it all. Alone. Soon to vanish, like the Pawtucket Indians. Yet I didn't mind. How strong must be the will to live, just any kind of life. Still, it could be better. I made a sudden resolution. I would ask Marian out. If she said no, maybe I'd get a dog. I always wanted a Boston Terrier.

The View from the Summit

"The beauty of things must be that they end."
—Jack Kerouac

Elbows on the bar, Spider McNulty was giving careful directions to the bartender. "No, no mixes. No juices. Just Patron agave tequila, right? Splash of fresh lime juice. A splash of Cointreau. Shaken with ice, but no ice in the drink."

"That's all booze," she said.

Spider was nonplussed. Like he needed a college coed bartender to remind him what he was drinking. "Yes. Like a martini. It's a Mexican martini."

"Okay."

"Thank you. Oh, and I'm going to sit at that table by the window."

"I'll bring it over."

"That's grand . . . ." She was walking away when he added, "as they say in Dublin."

He picked up his Barnes and Noble bag and lumbered over to the window, where he lowered his bulk onto the seat. He spilled the contents of the bag over the table. A copy of *The Last Temptation of Christ*, a CD of Emmylou Harris, and two postcards of Key West, which is where he was and had been for over twenty years. One postcard featured the sign for Route 1, and the words, "Key West, The End of the Road." The other, a hot babe in a stringy bathing suit holding a conch shell up to her ear and smiling invitingly. Spider had been unable to decide between the two. As a Jack Kerouac guy, Buddy would appreciate the subtle reference to the road. Spider had been thinking a lot about Buddy, his old pal back in Lowell, Mass, since Norm Brunelle had told him that Buddy was not in the best of health. Cancer. He thought a postcard might cheer him up, but upon consideration, he decided that you could not send a pal who was sick a card that mentioned the end of the road. He turned over the card with the hot babe and began to print his old friend's address.

The bartender arrived with Spider's single drink on a tray. "Would you like to see a lunch menu?"

"Maybe in a while."

She set a napkin on the table and placed the brimming drink on it.

"Thank you."

She smiled, nodded, and left, swinging the tray beside her like the carefree little girl she had probably been not so very long ago. Probably, but who knows what anyone's life has been.

Spider lifted the drink carefully and sipped. "First of the day," as Buddy used to say. He looked out the window across the deck, where a small crowd sat eating lunch or perusing menus. A rough-hewn sign pointed south: "Habana 150 Miles." Two young women seated at a bistro table leaned toward each other as they ate. The one facing him, a blonde, was listening intently to her friend, who was recounting a story, no doubt, from the animated movements of her head and hands. The blonde's eyes widened, her fork suspended over her plate.

Then, covering her mouth, she sat back and laughed, her shoulders shaking. Spider's chest filled with a hollow ache as he watched her. It was not a longing for her, nor the certainty that such a woman would never desire him again. His libido had receded with his hairline. It was her youth itself he envied. Her eyes shone, and her thick hair shone, too. Grace and power and confidence and strength; she held them all within the aura of Beauty.

There was a time, he knew, when he had been, in his way, the complement to what she was now. Lean and strong and damned near fearless. A man in his prime. He remembered the day he was carrying a bundle of shingles, shirtless, toward a ladder at a job site. A carload of women had driven by honking the horn, hooting at him. They were laughing in the sun as they passed, and he laughed, too. God, it was good. Youth! He and Buddy Brooks on the road to Montreal with the windows down, blasting Derek and the Dominoes *Live at the Fillmore*. "Why Does Love Got to Be So Sad?" But nothing was sad back then, really. The 70's. He had no bad memories of the 70's. A lot of years and a lot of pounds ago. Life was a book then, with many pages yet to be turned, many chapters to be written, many women to meet.

Buddy had his arm in a sling during their first trip to Montreal; he'd broken it just the day before they left, having slipped on a patch of ice outside the Press Club. He was in some pain, and Spider stopped at a packy and bought him a bottle of Jameson. By the time they got to St. Johnsbury, Vermont, Buddy had killed most of the bottle and Spider realized that the music had stopped because his drunken friend was putting out his cigarettes in the tape player, thinking it was the ashtray. Fuckin' Buddy—beautiful.

Spider took another sip of his Mexican Martini and settled down, staring at the blank postcard, sucking the tip of his pen and considering what to write. "Weather is here. Wish you were beautiful!" No. Something more serious. Norm didn't know how sick Buddy was, or what kind of cancer he had, but he said he had heard that he "wasn't good." Spider McNulty shivered in the sun recalling those words. "Not good," was generally a euphemism for "dying."

Amigo! He wrote across the top. Spider closed his eyes and thought. Back to Boy Scouts, where he had first met Buddy, who was still Arthur Brooks back then. They grew up together, looking for Indian arrowheads on Fort Hill, building lean-to shelters in the woods, and later carousing and drinking and chasing women in the days, and nights, when the drinking age was eighteen. Once they took the train into Boston to see Stephen Stills at the Garden and ended up in the Combat Zone after the show. Two guys came up; one held two fingers in front of his lips and said to Buddy, "Hey, man, gimme a smoke."

"I got no cigarettes," Buddy said. Spider could still picture him standing there on the sidewalk with his unkempt blond hair and his Fu Man Chu mustache.

The guy said, "What you mean you got no cigarettes? You're smokin' a fuckin' cigarette. You got a pack in your pocket."

"I mean I got no cigarettes for you! Screw!"

Spider didn't really feel like getting in a brawl in the Combat Zone, and he said in a low voice, "Just give him a cigarette, Buddy. What's the big deal?"

"No. He didn't ask me politely! I'm not gonna give him shit!"

"Gimme a fuckin' cigarette, now!" the loudmouth said, bouncing on the souls of his feet, fists clenched like he was showing his friend how to get respect in the Zone.

Buddy got that wild glint in his eye. It was a look Spider had seen before that said, *I'm tougher than you. I'm crazier than you. And if you are not willing to go all the way—all the way, until one of us can't get off this sidewalk, then walk on. It ain't worth a smoke.* He threw down his cigarette, and it sprayed motes of orange cinders at his feet. "You lookin' for trouble? You came to *the right place.*"

Spider was not happy that Buddy had chosen this moment for his display of pride or principle and was glad that the guy's friend stayed out of it, which allowed him to stay out of it. The fight lasted about thirty seconds, maybe less. It was a toe-to-toe exchange, with Buddy gradually pushing forward, fists slamming his opponent. The loudmouth was soon reeling, and he backed off suddenly and put his hands up to signal he'd had enough, but Buddy kept swinging, pounding the guy until he went down, staggered to his feet, and ran, followed by his less enthusiastic friend. Buddy pulled a paper bag out of a bin and wiped some blood off his knuckles. "Let's see some strippers," he said, and off they went to the Naked i Cabaret.

Amigo! When they got a little older, they got into mountain climbing, returning to their childhood scout training, and Buddy was reading *The Dharma Bums,* in which Kerouac and his poet pals climb Matterhorn Peak in California. Spider recalled the best of their trips. They had camped by Greeley Pond, at the foot of Mount Osceola, where they met two French Canadian women, Nicole and Bernice. They hit it off right away. It was August in the White Mountains, and that night the Earth was passing through the Perseids. The four of them climbed onto the roof of the shelter to watch the meteor showers, lying on their backs under the bright wheeling stars. The sky was so thick with meteors shedding trails of sparks across the black sky that Nicole said that they should get down or they might be hit, and the others had a good laugh about that.

Later, sitting around the fire was a mystical experience, as if they were alone on some alternate plane of existence, four hearts beating within a small circle of light. Beyond the glow of the fire, the world was curtained in impenetrable darkness, a darkness so dense that it seemed to press against the light. Was it an ancestral foreboding that made them sense the glint of eyes peering at them from the heart of that profound night? No, the owl was certainly hunting, and after they had huddled on the raised deck of the shelter, they heard the cry of a fisher cat like the howl of some forlorn child.

Spider had said a quick prayer, and the women had, too, in French, but Buddy only laughed and invited Bernice into his sleeping bag, where he could "protect her better." The girls were not easy, though, and insisted they would have to get to know them, which was why he and Buddy had taken so many later trips to Montreal. When Bernice finally did get to know Buddy, she asked him to marry her, and he said he thought she'd never ask.

Amigo! What next to say? He hadn't seen him now in eight years. That was the last time Spider had been in Lowell, for his mother's funeral, and Buddy was there with Bernice, and after the funeral, they went to the Rainbow Café and Dan Webster played, "When Irish Eyes Are Smiling" and "Danny Boy," slowly and jazzily on the piano, and Buddy told him he was damned sorry to see his mother go. "She always loved you, Buddy," Spider said. His old friend draped his arm around his shoulder. "Christ, how many times did she feed me at her table over the years?" He shook his head and dabbed at his eyes with his fingers. Then he said, "But—the wheel turns." Words that were simple and true. And now the wheel was turning again, throwing Buddy to the ground. He leaned over the postcard and began to write.

A hospital bed was set up for Buddy Brooks in the living room. After some months on what he jokingly called, "the hospital-rehab merry-go-round," he had been sent home for the final time. There would be no more chemo, no more ambulance rides, no more surgeries; only heating pads, and oxycodone, and now, morphine. He slept a lot, most of the day, it seemed, but then Bernice would look and see those eyes of startling blue, suddenly open in his pale, drawn face, and Buddy watching her, and she would stroke his forehead and talk to him, and he would smile, and sometimes he would say a few words and sometimes she would understand him. And she was so happy when he stayed awake for a long time, a half-hour or more, because she could feel his presence, a presence that she knew might cease to be at any moment. She would try to get some broth into him, or some Ensure, though the doctor said he would lose the will to eat, soon, and that trying to feed him would only prolong the inevitable or maybe cause him to choke.

On Thursday night, his children, John and Kate, spent hours by his bed, but Bernice told them to go home and sleep, there was nothing they could do. The doctor came on Friday morning, saying once more that the end was near, but that she could not predict the day or the hour. The children called out of work and returned. Buddy opened his eyes in the morning and Bernice said, "John and Kate are here." They all heard him say, "God bless 'em," before he drifted off again.

The mail arrived just after lunch, and Bernice came in and took the chair beside his bed. "Buddy, you have a postcard from Spider McNulty," she said. "From Florida." The eyelids lifted and once more the eyes appeared, not fuddled and glossy but bright and even observant. "A postcard from Spider," she repeated. She held the photo of the sexy beach woman in his line of vision, but his eyes fixed on the window and the pale March sky beyond the bare oak branches. She turned the card over. "He writes: *Amigo! Norman says you're sick. Very sorry to hear that Buddy. Get well if you can, or . . . .*" She paused and stroked the chemo-thinned hair the color of the pillow on which it rested. "*Get well if you can, or like Hendrix said, I will see you on the other side. I'm toasting you right now with the first of the day. Ever your good friend, The Spider.*

The stricken man said nothing; a single tear crept from the corner of his left eye. Buddy's wife and children leaned toward him, gripping the metal rail of the hospital bed as they whispered words of comfort to him because the doctor said he could hear them. In the afternoon, the intervals between his breaths became longer until it seemed he was suspended between life and death, and Bernice clutched her rosary and whispered *Je vous salue, Marie, pleine de grâce; le Seigneur est avec vous.*

The doctor was right. He did hear her voice. His mind rushed backward across the plain of life. He walked with his children along the Merrimack River, pointing at the boats moored under the pink and purple stippled sunset sky. The murmur of that dear voice drew him toward a night beneath the stars. *Vous êtes bénie entre toutes les femmes et Jésus, le fruit de vos entrailles, est béni.* He did not know if that night was behind him or before him or if he was there now. He stretched out a hand to pull Bernice up the granite back of the Chimney on the Eastern Approach to the heights above. From the stony summit of Osceola, they saw great mountains of shivering pine rolling toward the horizon like waves on the sea. Sweat glistened on their sun-drenched brows as they paused to drink some water and look across the vast expanse of Waterville Valley. The four of them were young and smiling, forever. Osceola!

"Sola," they heard him whisper. He raised a hand toward her, and Bernice took it in hers and held it tight. "Sola," he said once more, but they did not know what that meant. They waited, their own breath nearly as suspended as the dying man's. After what seemed an impossible hiatus, Buddy Brooks pulled a last ragged breath, and his wife and children waited for some time for another. They were all quiet as Bernice continued to whisper her prayers for the soul she sensed departing: *Sainte Marie, Mère de Dieu, priez pour nous pauvres pécheurs, maintenant et à l'heure de notre mort.* When at length she leaned over to kiss his forehead, he was already growing cold.

This Ever New Self

Camila! He had thought of her so often, though he hadn't seen her in many years, several decades really. And there she was! As he cast a sidelong glance along the glass case full of arrowheads, curving bowls and archaic stone chisels, her Aztec profile, unchanged, though the wild dark hair of former days was now clipped and silvered.

She leaned over the glass, studying an ancient face graven in a stone the size of a walnut. She seemed to sense his gaze, but rather than look toward him, she turned away, checking the gallery guide she held in her hands. He continued to watch her from across the room, a stylish figure in a blue oversized cashmere with the sleeves rolled away from her braceleted wrists. He stood wondering whether he should approach, or wait, or leave her wandering the paths of his memory in the glory of youth, though now the image he'd long held of her was fading, to be replaced with the one he watched ascending the winding museum stairs toward the upper level. At the top, she paused and looked back. His head sank immediately into his own guide: *As you make your way upstairs, notice the unique architecture of our 1930's building. Many of the stairways, ceiling moldings, floorboards, and doorways in the museum were preserved from 17th and 18th century homes.*

Ghostly relics, sad remains, he thought, whispering still with the swish of lace bustle skirts and the click of stovepipe boots. But it was more than the disunited artifacts of Concord's past that cast a gloom over him, for over these floorboards and through these doorways where the long dead had walked, now moved this ghost from his own past. Was it the jolt of mortality that shook him when he saw the reality of the woman he had, until then, held in some part of his mind untouched by time? She had been a beauty. He felt a hollowness in his core, a troubling emotion he could not name because he did not know the cause. Was it only the recognition that strikes all of us at certain moments, of the rapid passing of the years? Those lines of Marvell came to mind.

But at my back I always hear
Time's wingèd chariot hurrying near;
And yonder all before us lie
Deserts of vast eternity.

Yes, the years had flown, it seemed to him, like something that happens quite suddenly when one is looking the other way. But this swelling sadness was due to something more than just the passage of time, and finally he asked himself the question that had been gathering in his mind since he had first recognized Camila. *Were we in love?*

Still standing among the stone art and implements of vanished peoples, he gazed up the staircase into the well-lit space, and saw her in the Upper Gallery, moving into Room 18, which, his Guide informed him, held the exhibition of Thoreau's journals, manuscripts, letters, books and field notes. The exhibit was entitled "This Ever-New Self," and it was the reason he had come.

His indecision rooted him to the ground floor as he tried to answer the question he had put to himself. His mind ranged far, out of this staid museum and back through the years that seemed so turbulent to him now that he had become accustomed to the static home-life of a man approaching his sixties. He recalled the early days when he had first noticed her in the college library and was as reluctant to approach her as he was on this day. He tried to "create coincidences,"—today it might be called "stalking," but in those days, it was the normal behavior of the smitten male. She also confided, much later, that she used to drive by his apartment to see what cars were parked in his driveway.

In those early days, though, they exchanged only harmless greetings, polite words. Things changed when he mentioned he was having a hard time with Calculus. After all, he was an English major. She offered to help. She had always been good at math, she said, and was majoring in Electrical Engineering. He could recall the scene so clearly. They sat together at a table in the back of the library as she filled papers with strings of differentiation formulas in her neat hand, patiently describing trigonometric functions. One night she asked if he knew how to find the area between two curves. "I'd like to find out," he said, and immediately regretted the remark when she looked away.

They became friends, though, and then one evening near the end of the Spring term she put down her pencil and stared at him for a moment, her dark hair tussled from running her hand through it in her mathematical exertions. Almond eyes fixed him objectively, and she said, "I think you would look good with a mustache." The words thrilled him because that was the first thing of a personal nature she had ever said to him, and he felt—what? Desire? Infatuation? Love? Certainly, at the time he would have said it was love. He grew a mustache.

When did she begin to requite his deeper feelings? It took some time. For how long exactly were they together? Why did they break up? He found it surprising that it was difficult for him to say, now. It was so long ago, and so difficult to see through the clouded intentions of the ever-new self. He only remembered that at some point he began to distance himself—from her—from his own feelings. They saw less of each other. When he'd heard that she was engaged, he was somehow surprised, and sad, and yet he sensed that he had lost her through his own lack of determination, passion and commitment. Wasn't that it? Yes. He had let her slip away, and she was a proud woman, too proud to demand an answer or press her case. She moved on.

Camila. Why had he let her go? He recalled how, at that age, he'd felt that marriage was a trap: the business of raising kids and buying a house and bringing home a paycheck for the mortgage and tuition and home improvements and lawn care. And years later, when his options had narrowed, he had married Laura because it was time. And for seven years they pretended to be a couple, and for years after maintained a cordial relationship for the sake of their son Thomas, who now lived in California and returned once or twice a year. There was always something missing with Laura. And the sight of Camila today confirmed what it had been. Yes, he had loved her. They had been in love. But as the poet had said, "Hearts are to be earned." What had he earned? A solitary place in the world. Acquaintances, yes, and nothing more.

These thoughts kindled a desire to speak with Camila, but as he moved toward the stairs, he imagined their conversation. It would have come full circle, back to the innocuous and circumspect greetings of their first acquaintance. How are you? What have you been doing? Oh, that's nice. Do you have pictures of your children? And this time there would be no math lessons in a quiet sanctuary of books. Maybe better to let her remember the man that he had been, and not this shadow, not the balding, bespectacled, new self that stood with one hand on the banister. And what was there to say, really? *What happened to us?* Or, even more impossible, *I miss you?* No, no. Old ghosts pass in silence. Say nothing. Do nothing. It was over a long time ago. He did miss her, though; he had always missed her. Sex, of course, but it was getting late for that. Her friendship, her voice, her laugh, were what came back to him now and resonated within a soul as empty as a church at dawn.

He went up the stairs warily and entered Room 18. There was no one in it but an old woman, a docent who sat reading in the stillness. Under glass, various journals of Thoreau lay open. He caught sight of Camila through a passageway exiting Room 19 and heading toward the stairs. She appeared to be alone. The room felt close and warm. He turned away and began to try to focus on the opened journals in the display cases, but the words bore only a distant relation to things; *Shepherd's purse, cerastium, slender spikes of Lycopus*; the words took flight and circled her image and her name like wild geese before they turn southward in the fading days of an Indian summer. He moved mechanically from one case to the next, and finally, inclined over hand-written lines of his old mentor, he read with some difficulty: *March 10, 1859. There are some who never do or say anything, whose life merely excites expectation. They are like fine-edged tools gradually becoming rusty in a shop window .... I exclaim to myself: Surfaces! Surfaces!*

He straightened so abruptly that the old woman looked up from her book. A moment of thought, or maybe emotion, and he rushed toward the stair head. All his being was gathered into a single purpose. Just to tell her—not to win her back, not to save himself—just to cut below the surface for once with the fine edge of truth. He descended quickly and was searching for her among the first-floor rooms when he paused by a window and saw her in the parking lot getting into her car. By the time he made it to the exit and out to the lot, the car was receding along the road to Concord Center or Walden Pond or Cambridge. Or to anywhere.

He walked back to his own car and began the drive to Lowell, considering the multifarious roads that spread before a man in his youth and how each decision narrows the number of roads that offer themselves until you are on the one with no exits, and you wonder why you passed those that might have led to some tranquil harbor, a home where love could be felt. He drove through Concord center, recalling Brutus.

There is a tide in the affairs of men.
Which, taken at the flood, leads on to fortune;
Omitted, all the voyage of their life
Is bound in shallows and in miseries.

Bound in shallows. Surfaces. Never a definitive action! Never a risk! Never a—

Camila! It was her. She was just putting money in a meter outside the wine shop. He pulled into the first space he saw and hurried after her, finally catching up to her on the corner. "Camila!" he called.

She stopped short and turned her gaze on him. "What, me?" She spread a silver-ringed hand over the blue cashmere sweater just below her throat. "I'm not Camila," she said—not angrily, but indulgently.

He saw that he had been mistaken. Camila's eyes had been darker, her face narrower. "Yes, now that I'm closer, I can see. I'm sorry. You look very much like a dear old friend." He inhaled the lovely scent of what he knew was patchouli oil because he had always loved it.

"Oh, you don't have to be sorry. I hope at least she's good-looking."

He laughed. "Yes, very. That kind of Latin beauty you—well, you have, if you don't mind me saying."

"Not at all. Italian beauty—in bygone days." Her head moved slightly so that a silver pendent earring caught the sun. "Didn't I see you at the museum exhibit?" she asked.

"You did, and I thought then that you were this, Camila, but I wasn't sure if I should approach, because—I'm sorry—you don't want to hear all this. Sorry to bother you."

He had taken only a few steps back to his car when he felt a tap on his shoulder. Turning quickly, he met the inquiring gaze of the woman who was not Camila.

"Maybe I do want to hear it," she said.

He wasn't sure how to begin. "Well, you know, it was years ago." He seemed to stand before the gates of what he had considered formal social rules for a man of his age, and he knew that he would no longer be put off by such weak and wobbly barricades. "Listen, if you do want to hear the story, could we get a coffee?"

She hesitated for less than a second, just enough time for him to wonder whether she thought him too forward. "Let's get a coffee, then," she said.

"Are you sure you have time?"

"Yes, I'm sure. I'm just rambling around," she said, waving an arm that was meant to encompass all there was to do in the center of Concord.

They introduced themselves and walked toward the Main Street Café, conversing with no awkwardness; at first, about the Thoreau exhibit; they both admired Thoreau and the other Transcendentalist writers. As they drank their coffees, he told her about Camila and the lost lessons of the past. He realized how much he had missed feminine company and was reassured or felt somehow completed by a hundred small things, the lipstick on her cup, the careful observation of details a man doesn't see, and the heartfelt "Oh!" at the sight of a baby in a carriage. Later, they browsed through a used bookstore, where she bought a copy of Margaret Fuller's essays, and they strolled through the old colonial graveyard where the weathered stones bore names like Ezekiel and Obediah and Abigail. She shared the story of her losses, too, simply and sincerely—a husband gone, a son estranged. He supposed that at their age, everyone lived with regrets.

He sensed that perhaps another road was forming on the horizon. It was too soon to say, but he could see that at least he'd found a friend, that her mind was sharp, and her soul was kind; that they understood one another. And already he knew that if ever he earned her heart, if ever the tide was at the full and the wind blew fair, he would set sail, and that voyage would be his last.

What It Takes to Write a Story

Late in the day, Larry McShee and his wife Laura sat in wicker chairs in the shade of a wrap-around porch at the Seagull Inn, enjoying a long weekend getaway on the Maine coast. Before them lay a short stretch of marsh grass, and just visible beyond that, the Atlantic, a slim glittering ribbon under a sky that seemed at this hour, Larry thought, to have the "purple glow" that the poet had once described over the Lake Isle of Innisfree. Laura put her feet up on the railing and closed her eyes.

"You can hear the waves," she said.

"It's high tide. The surf is just pounding the slope of the shore."

They were quiet for a moment. Larry watched the sandpipers or plovers or whatever they were dipping and skimming over the salt-marsh grass. He had been thinking, for some reason, of an old folk song he used to listen to in college and began to sing softly to himself.

A diamond ring I own I gave to you
A diamond ring to wear on your right hand.

His wife turned her head toward him and said, "You're a writer. Write about this."

"About what?"

"This." Her arm made an arc in the air before her. "About harmony and beauty and perfect happiness."

"No one would read it," he said. He pulled his wallet out of his back pocket and put it on a side table before sliding deeper into the chair.

"Why wouldn't they read it?"

"The best-selling books I've written are the books in the Agent Dan Mattigan series, right? They sell because they're full of murder, kidnappings, hostages, terrorists, brutality, gratuitous sex, all played out to the background music of explosions, car crashes, and gunfire. So, the only way I can think of working this perfectly beautiful scene into a book would be if we suddenly heard a scream."

"And of course, it would have to be a 'blood-curdling scream.'"

"Well, I hope I don't use *every* cliché, but it's a fact. Harmony only serves as a prelude to stress and disaster."

Her dark hair seemed to shimmer in the sun as she shook her head. "Why does it have to be that way?"

"That's what the public wants. The hit movie is *Titanic*, not *Queen Mary*." The phone in his left hand vibrated and he tilted it to peek.

"I wish you would write me a beautiful story about right now. About a whole summer of love and breezes from the sea and sails gliding across the blue and moonlight over the water and the sound of waves and you and I just being happy."

He felt a sudden tenderness for her, and a twinge of guilt. "I'll write something for you."

"About us being happy?"

"Wildly happy."

"You are happy, aren't you?"

"Of course I am, sweetheart."

She smiled and stretched out her arm. He took her hand and leaned over and kissed it. Then he got up and said, "Stay right here. I'm just going to run up to the corner and get a bottle of wine. We can take a cup down to the beach and watch the waves for a bit."

"Sounds good, my love."

When he had left the inn behind, he paused and read more carefully the message he'd received. Then he deleted it and tapped a number. It had hardly rung before a woman answered.

"Larry."

"Rose. Listen to me. Stop texting me. It's *over*. I love my wife. We have grown children."

"I know. I know," she said, and he could tell by her voice that she'd been crying. "I just miss you. I thought maybe . . . ."

He stopped and stood under the awning outside the Beach Mart. "Stop. Stop thinking anything about us. I never misled you. I told you what it was. Like the song says, 'Just one of those things.'"

"I think you just wanted the experience of screwing around so you could write about it. I was just a literary experiment."

"Maybe you're right. I'm sorry if you were hurt. But you can't say I didn't warn you. You can't say I didn't tell you exactly what to expect. It's called a *fling*, Rose. You know what happens to flings? They end. This fling has ended. So, don't pull a *Fatal Attraction* on me. It won't end well for either of us. We had a good time. It's over. I'm not leaving my wife. So . . . ."

He felt a tap on his shoulder and turned to see Laura standing there, holding his wallet. "You forgot it," she said. Her dark eyes were full of tears.

He turned off his phone and said, "Laura, I . . . ."

"You're sorry if *she* is hurt?"

He saw the pain in her face, and strangely, it struck him that she and he were not characters in a fiction, that this was his life—their lives. *A diamond ring I own I gave to you.*

"How could you do it, Larry?" She flung the wallet at him. It struck his chest. Credit cards, insurance cards, and money, the paper part of his identity, scattered at his feet. "Now you can write the story the way you wanted it," she said, "the perfect happiness that was the prelude to misery and shit. The vacation is over. The marriage is over, liar, and you can *never* rewrite this chapter."

She left him there, picking up the contents of his wallet, wishing somehow he could rewrite the chapter, wondering how he had got this plot so very, very wrong, and how useless were all the words at his command.

Thy Sister's Keeper

And still there sits a moonshine ghost
Where sat the sunshine maid.
                    —D. G. Rossetti

It was back in '92. While I attended UMass, Lowell, working toward a degree in English, I had a job working for the Massachusetts Guardian Security Services. Armed with my radio and Maglight Tactical Flashlight, I would prowl the darkened alleys and hollow hearts of vacant mill buildings, where sluggish canals still ran like clogged arteries beneath the worn floorboards of the basement, oily with drippings from long-vanished machines. The Boott Mills, named for Kirk Boott, one of the city's founders, was my primary responsibility. "One hundred foot of John Street" was the curious address for the extensive quadrangular complex. Anyone who says that he can roam, without some trepidation, the winding stairs and vast empty silent floors where once sat row upon row of shuttling power looms with their churning belts; that he is not troubled by the darkness outside the beam of the flashlight, or by the dim moonlight that sometimes pales the endless rows of windows, is either a liar or a better man than I am.

Old Sullivan from County Donegal had done the job for years, but as he neared retirement, he was transferred to a post that did not require him to mount so many flights of stairs. He took me on a tour and explained my duties. "Look for vagrants, signs of squatters. Check the thermometers that are taped to the support columns in the different rooms on every floor. Make a note of the readings. If the temperature is slipping below 32 degrees, radio the property management. Can't let the water protection units freeze, you see. Sure, this whole place could go the way of many old mills before it."

I kept asking him about the strange sounds that distracted me from his explanations, "What was that?"

"Rats, Frankie. They run the place."

I shivered in the cold darkness, following as, haltingly, he ascended the stairs to the fifth floor. "Worn by the feet of the mill girls as they answered the bell, as far back as 1835," he said, "when as they say, cotton was king." Surprised by a sudden rushing clamor, I shot my flashlight beam wildly into the black void above us. "Pigeons," he muttered. The floorboards beneath our feet were covered with their droppings.

It was a creepy place, even with the calm Sullivan, but soon I was on my own. I became accustomed to the scurrying of rats. Joe Gamari, who did the daily rounds, was fond of leaving dead ones on the stairs for me. There were other things I did not grow accustomed to, such as the feeling that I was not alone in that old mill, that amid the scratching of rats or the clamor of wings or the sound of a siren passing in the night outside, I heard something else: whispers, sighs, and sometimes distant laughter, as if there were a radio on in another room. Every sound echoed in those spaces, but my flashlight showed nothing anywhere but rows of columns standing amid the barren plain of the floor.

How I looked forward to the dawn, when I would hurry away, traversing the courtyard under the brooding windows of the mills and cross the canal bridge, heading to the Paradise Diner, where Arthur and his wife would be unloading their station wagon of fresh bread direct from the Middle East Bread Company. The mysterious sounds and eerie stillness of the previous night would take flight as I sat at the counter drinking a coffee, watching Arthur prepare my Boott Mill Sandwich, smiling at the word spelled out across the back of his belt: DELICIOUS. I'd arranged my classes for the afternoon so I could go home and sleep for five hours or so.

I was able to do my job and banish my fears, or at least quell them, for a while. One night in mid-October, I had a particularly apprehensive feeling as I approached the Boott Mills. The bell tower, with its cotton bobbin weathervane, was silhouetted against charging ragged moonlit clouds. I thought of the old Creedence song, "Bad Moon on the Rise," and tried to shake the feeling. Surely, if Old Sullivan could do this job for so many years, so could I.

I passed the grim wasteway and turned the key in the padlock of the first gate. The heavy chain fell clanking against the bars, and I entered and turned to relock the gate. The basement, empty. No signs of break-ins or squatters. My footsteps resounded on the stairs. A dead rat hung from the door latch on the first floor. "Very funny, Joe."

The night was chilly, but not near freezing. Still, they wanted me to check the temperatures for "data collection." It was their way of making certain that I checked every room on each floor because there were no key stations in the mills. My footsteps seemed to fracture some skein of silence as I made my lonely rounds. Descending the stairs toward the third floor, I heard movement behind me. It was neither rat nor pigeon, but a hurried footfall and something like the rustle of fabric, the swish of a long skirt. I spun, flashing a stream of light into vacancy. The sound had been loud enough and distinct enough to suspend any courageous thoughts I had of charging back the way I had come, as if I might locate some reassuring source. It had been directly behind me. As I stood, frozen in that spot, I heard a voice, the light voice of a young girl, which seemed to come from the darkness of the stairwell above me. Some old song reached me from the vaulting dark above me.

Pray what do you want with us, sir,
With us sir,
With a ransom-tansom-tay?

I felt someone, I should say *something*, at my side, and I heard, close to my left ear, a sound like a breath exhaled, and in that breath, the words, "What do you want?" I ran.

Outside by the gate, I invented temperature readings, and waited nervously for dawn, when finally, I crossed the courtyard toward the bridge, feeling as if a thousand eyes watched me from the dark windows of the mills that surrounded me. The next day was Saturday, and I went to see Old Sullivan, who I knew lived above Gormley's Diner. He answered the door in slippers, his company pants, and suspenders over a tee shirt. He took one look at my face and said, "So you've seen them?"

"I haven't seen 'them,' but I've *heard* them. Jesus, Sullivan! What's going on in there? Why didn't you tell me? I ran out of there last night!"

"Well, not everyone hears them or sees them. You need some kind of . . . empathy. Coffee?"

"Yes, please." He poured two coffees, took a bottle of Bushmill's from the cupboard and fortified each with a shot. I didn't object. I noticed that his apartment was full of books. "The long and the short of it is this," he said as he set the coffees down. "An awful lot of young women came to this city long ago and slaved their youths away in those mills amid the deafening roar of the looms. They worked, they dreamed, they looked longingly out those windows past the river toward their homes in the countryside. They choked on cotton dust. Many were injured and some died in there. One woman's hair was caught in the belts, and she was hauled right up to the ceiling. Took her a while to die. The place consumed their lives, five days a week, twelve hours a day and half that again on Saturday. It was grueling, but you see they formed strong bonds with each other there, a sisterhood if you will, the way people do in very trying circumstances. Something so strong, it survived, somehow."

I shook my head in confused disbelief, yet I knew that it was true. "What did you see, Sullivan?"

He shrugged. "Entities, I call them. Shadows of the past, I don't know. Ghosts if you like. Donegal is full of them, Burt Castle, the rectory in Newtowncunningham, Drumbeg Manor. The first one I saw in the Boott was a very young girl, in skirt and apron, looking out the window toward the river. Such a sad look she had when she turned her gaze on me."

"What did you do?"

The old man muttered something incomprehensible, in another language. "That's what I said, for I grew up speaking Irish, and it sprang to my lips, you see?"

"It means?"

"Simply, 'May your soul be on God's right hand.' And the girl, for she was more a girl than a woman, spoke. Her lips never moved, but I heard her voice plainly, and she was Irish too, and spoke in the old tongue. 'And your soul, too, when you die,' she said. Then I heard one of the other many sounds you hear there at night, rats probably. I turned for a second, and when I looked back, she was gone."

"But there were others?"

"Oh yes, Frank. They are always there for those can see them. The ladies of the loom, as Lucy Larcom called them. I never breathed a word of it. People don't understand."

Before I left, he went and rummaged among piles of books and handed me several reprinted copies of an old literary magazine that was published by the mill girls, called *The Lowell Offering*, and a book of poems by Lucy Larcom. "Read those, and you'll know them. They never harmed me, Frank. They're not evil entities. And anyway, as Shakespeare's prince said, they can't ever harm your soul, which is a thing immortal, like themselves."

I wasn't sure if I was comforted or frightened by the old man's words. "I don't know if I can go back," I said.

"It's not a place for the faint-hearted." The unspoken question that hung in the air was, "Are you faint-hearted, Frank?"

I girded my heart and returned, and having immersed myself, in what little free time I had, in the books Sullivan had given me, I did feel as if I knew or understood those presences that still inhabited the spinning rooms and carding rooms of the Boott Mills. I carried Lucy Larcom's poems with me. As Halloween approached, I was more than usually jumpy in that ghost of a building. One night a sudden voice beside me nearly turned my heart sideways, but it was my radio. "Frank McClaren," I said. "What's up, Ken?"

"Frank, a body was just pulled out of the canal behind the Paradise over your way. Keep your eyes open for anything suspicious."

"Foul play?"

"Waiting to hear. Maybe the cholesterol from the Boott Mill Sandwiches got to him." Ken laughed. I didn't. "Okay," I said, "let me know what you hear."

It was cold in the mills that night. Currents of even colder air seemed to flow about the dark chambers and along the quiet stairways. I wrote the temperature of the various rooms of the third floor in my notebook, 36 degrees, on average. As I thrust my notebook into a jacket pocket, my breath caught. A woman stood by a window in the dress of a factory girl of the 1840's. The wan moonlight, or maybe it was an exterior light, fell over her face, from which her hair had been pulled back in a chignon. A wave of cold fear ran from the floor up my spine and caught my lungs in a tightening web as she fixed me with dark eyes that shone in that ashen face, and I sensed the question she seemed once again to project: "What do you want with us, Sir?" I cleared my parched throat and tried to remember Sullivan's blessing, but my mind was blank.

Though not a religious man, I now quietly called on all the saints to help me stand my ground, repeating to myself over and over the words the old man had said: 'They are not evil,' and recalling that my soul was a thing immortal, like them. Other forms, less distinct, but no less real to me, now gathered around this proud entity. There was whispering among them, and one of them was sobbing while others tried to comfort her. I almost ran, but then I reached for the book in my jacket pocket. I shone the light on the page, afraid to look up, but feeling as I heard the young woman's sobbing subside that something like peace had descended on us all as I read from the book:

> *All day she stands before her loom;*
> *The flying shuttles come and go:*
> *By grassy fields, and trees in bloom,*
> *She sees the winding river flow:*
> *And fancy's shuttle flieth wide,*
> *And faster than the waters glide.*
>
> *"I weave, and weave, the livelong day:*
> *The woof is strong, the warp is good:*
> *I weave, to be my mother's stay;*
> *I weave, to win my daily food:*
> *But ever as I weave," saith she,*
> *"The world of women haunteth me*
>
> *So up and down before her loom*
> *She paces on, and to and fro,*
> *Till sunset fills the dusty room,*
> *And makes the water redly glow,*
> *As if the Merrimack's calm flood*
> *Were changed into a stream of blood.*

Too soon fulfilled, and all too true
The words she murmured as she wrought:
But, weary weaver, not to you
Alone was war's stern message brought:
"Woman!" it knelled from heart to heart,
"Thy sister's keeper know thou art!"

Several things happened at once. As I neared the end of the reading, I heard applause, but the sound of it was closer than the "entities" had been. I saw that the space by the window where they had gathered was empty; a man was emerging from the shadows, smiling and clapping. "A rent-a-cop reciting poems in my crib! Who invited you? When I come home, I clear the rent-a-cop scum from my house!" At the same time, my radio crackled, and I heard Ken's voice. "Frank, that guy in the canal was stabbed to death. Keep your eyes open."

I dropped the book and lifted the long flashlight in my right hand. I went for my radio with my left, but the man lunged, and the radio skittered across the floor. I saw him reach into his belt to draw what weapon I did not know. I swung the flashlight, but he ducked. I felt a sharp sting in the arm and knew it was a knife and that I'd been cut. I dropped the flashlight and staggered backward, aware that he was drawing back to swing the knife again. I've been in my share of brawls in this city, but this was the first time the cold and fearful realization struck me with utter certainty: "This son of a bitch wants me dead." And I ran for my life.

I ran toward a wrought iron gate that set off the old bursar's office and a back stairway. It swung open as I approached. My hard breathing and the footsteps of my pursuer close behind were all that I could hear, but when I passed through the gate, I heard it slam shut behind me without my having touched it. There was no lock, yet the lunatic had stopped short, and I saw that he was unable to move it. The gate that had opened on quiet hinges for me had closed and was immovable for him! My fallen flashlight sent a beam across the floor like a single footlight on a barren stage. The madman was cursing and muttering as he tried to shake the gate free. I should have kept running, but something kept me there. He held the knife in his teeth and pulled at the gate with both hands. It did not even rattle; it was motionless. I smiled.

A shadow emerged from the surrounding darkness into the arc of light, a moving blot that crossed the floor directly toward the mad stranger. It was a rat, and the man jumped as it climbed his leg. The knife fell from his mouth and clattered on the floor. He shook his leg and swiped wildly at it. "Get away you little bastard!" Another rat ran toward him, then two more, and four; they rose from the floor and out of crevices in the wall; soon it seemed every rat in the silent mill complex was crawling over him. He danced screaming over the old floorboards under a dark squealing blanket. "The rats run this place," I shouted to him. "You bloodthirsty prick." I was not surprised when the gate opened easily under my hand. I picked up my flashlight, book and radio and notified Ken. "Third floor Boott Mills Number Four. Call LPD and an ambulance."

"Roger that. What's that sound, like screaming?" Ken asked.

"That's a man screaming," I said. "Make your calls." I tied my jacket tightly around my wounded arm and sat in the window casement where the factory girls had been. The screaming stopped. I read Lucy Larcom while I waited.

Captive

Just before noon, the cloud bank that had hunched over the city like a great gray cat skulked off to the west, giving way to light. Lowell always looked beautiful to me in the sun: red brick and gray stone under blue. Along the cobbled streets of the old center there are a few sidewalk cafes where the lunch crowd was beginning to gather. The day was heating up fast, and the interior of the café in what had once been a fire station looked cool and inviting. I ambled in and took a seat at the bar. Sports Center news was on; there was some big celebration in Boston for Tom Brady's 40th birthday. The bartender came up, a curly-haired blonde with a tattoo of a keyhole between her breasts. I ordered a pint of lager, idly wishing I was much younger, and had the key.

"How much longer you think he can go?"

I turned and looked at the guy on the next stool, who was gazing up at the TV, and copped on to his question. "He takes damn good care of himself. I'll say, barring injuries, three more years."

He considered my opinion, nodding as if it might be plausible. "Did you ever play?" he asked. I took him for a laboring man. His build was bullish, and while his clothes were clean, there were stains of tar, paint and caulking here and there. He was about my age, maybe a little older, fifty or so, hair thinning and graying, but blue eyes that were clear and intelligent.

"I played in high school, you know, small Catholic school."

The bartender stole my attention as she set my beer down and flashed a warm smile that was certainly worth a hefty tip.

"We had a pretty good high school team," my new barstool neighbor continued, "in Pepperell in '89, '90."

"Oh yeah?"

"Except we had a crap quarterback. Dan Huffman. The kid had an arm, too. He could throw the ball sixty yards, but it took him five minutes to throw the damned thing! And he was always bitchin' at the line. 'Mac,' he'd say, 'you don't block for Chrissakes!'

"Well, how much time do you need? I can't hold 'em forever!" It all came to a head during the Thanksgiving game. I was tired of his whining, and I said to the defensive lineman across from me, 'It's a passing play, and he's all yours.' On the second *hut!* I sidestepped, and the fuckin' guy charged in and demolished Huffman before he could take two steps back. Huffman got up with grass stickin' out of his faceguard, and I said to him, '*That's* what it feels like when I don't block.'

"Then, at half time, just before we're headed back out to the field, the coach runs up and grabs my faceguard and says, 'Mac! Huffman said you let that sonofabitch nail him!' The coach had one stub instead of a finger, and he would hold your faceguard and let the stub poke through in front of your eyes.

I said, 'Coach, I would never do that!' Then I got in the huddle and said, 'You ran to the coach, you little pussy?'

'Fuck you, Mac!' he says.

Then, of course, the coach says to me later, 'Did you call Huffman a pussy?'

'He is a pussy.'"

I could see that my new acquaintance, Mac, was getting angry remembering all this. His eyes narrowed as he sipped his beer. After all these years, he was still brooding over forgotten contests, and I had the feeling that I was not the first guy at a bar who had heard about Huffman, the whining quarterback. Still, I figured I'd let him get it off his chest. "So, what happened? How did it turn out?"

"I'll tell you how it turned out. That was the last game of the year. We lost by a touchdown, and the coach remembered. The next year I went out, my senior year, he sat my ass on the bench. First two games, I played about ten minutes combined, and the kid who took my place sucked. The coach wanted me back in, but his pride wouldn't let him. Finally, he says, 'Mac, I tell you what, you go apologize to Huffman for that Thanksgiving game, and you're back starting at left tackle.'"

He seemed to be staring down some long hallway of time where that scene was forever playing out, and his mouth turned down as if he tasted something sour.

"What did you do?"

"Couldn't do it. I quit. And do you know, that was over thirty years ago, and I still think about it all the time. We—*they*—almost won the championship that year, and I wonder if I could have made a difference. A solid left tackle makes a difference."

"Sure does," I said.

"But I'll never know. And sometimes I think if I could go back there, I'd eat the humble pie and apologize to that dink. Maybe I should have. Other times, I think I was right. I don't know. Everyone was just doing what their pride dictated, but I feel like I lost something that fall that I can never get back."

"Like Sinatra said, we all have a few regrets. But hey, you did it your way. The way that seemed right to you at the time."

He took a deep breath, like he was trying to pull himself out of a reverie, shrugging it off. "The coach died about ten years later. Had a heart attack during practice one afternoon. As for Huffman, I saw him getting out of his car one day at Home Depot in Nashua. Something welled up in me. I'm not normally a violent man, but I suddenly wanted to kick his ass. I walked over, ready to slam his head against the hood of his car, but as I come up, I see he's reaching into the back seat, and he pulls out his little girl. And I have to say, I was ashamed of myself."

"Yeah, you gotta let it go, my friend."

"Hey Mac," he says to me, "all friendly. 'How are you doin'?' You know, like he cared. And he put his hand out, and I shook it. I shook his hand. After all that."

"You did the right thing. You were kids back then."

"I don't know. I suppose."

"Sure." I thought it best to leave the subject there. I'm no therapist anyway, and nothing I could say would change the movie, or send him back to a time, maybe the last time, he felt the camaraderie of a team, and a place of honor within it. Gone, and like he said, you can never get it back.

I looked up at the sports highlights on the big screen. "Hey, did you catch the Sox last night?" I asked. "They were absolutely crushing the baseball."

He made no answer, and turning, I saw that he was staring intently into his glass of beer.

Austen Mania

My wife is fond of costume dramas of the British variety. There's nothing she enjoys more, on a rainy Saturday, than to get cozy and watch for the thousandth time, Mr. Darcy's attempts to win the affections of Miss Bennett. She holds her breath as the lady sternly rejects Darcy's proposal. She reaches for the tissue box when Miss Bennet, having learned that she had misunderstood certain reports, finally tells the lovelorn aristocrat, "My feelings are so different from what they were."

I won't catalogue them, but my wife enjoys any drama in which British men wear coats and tails and British women wear evening gowns and enormous hats. One thing that became a source of irritation for me was that every time we watched one of these dramas, my wife at some point would say, "Oh, I love the way they talk. How come you can't talk that way?"

After careful meditation on the subject, I thought, why deny my wife the one thing that would apparently make her happy. What sort of husband would do such a thing? If celebrities can reinvent themselves, why can't the rest of us? Consequently, you may refer to me as the gentleman formerly known as Stephen O'Connor. I've decided to reinvent myself as Sir Lionel Grenville-Primrose, Duke of Ashwood. Why not? First, I had to put aside the inherited familial prejudice produced by 800 years of feuding with the British, but dash it, that's all in the *pahst*. Secondly, to be a true English gentleman, at some point I will need a great deal of money, without condescending to work, or to disgrace myself with any fumbling in the greasy till. "I shall meditate on that while I drain a glass of Pomeray," I told myself, and so I did.

However, I was eager for my reinvention. When I woke up Saturday last, I turned to my wife and said, "Good morning, Dearest." It was my wish to ring for my manservant to order tea and toast with marmalade and the morning paper, but the domestics all seemed to be on holiday. I suppose they'll want Christmas Day off as well. I took matters into my own hands, telling my betrothed, "I shall descend presently, and it would give me great pleasure to return with a tray. Pray, stay where you are. I should be happy to accommodate you."

"Oh, thank you," she said, "Mr. . . . what shall I call you?"

"Why my name, Madam, Sir Lionel Grenville-Primrose, Duke of Ashwood. 'Duke' is acceptable, or 'm'lord.'"

Things were going rather smoothly. In fact, when I returned with toast and marmalade and a pot of Earl Gray, Lady Primrose was wearing a devilish smile. Knowing the sensitivity of the reader, Sir Lionel will draw a curtain over the ensuing scene. Later, however, I decided it was time to read my correspondences. I didn't have any correspondences, as it turned out, so I thought I should tour my grounds. Sadly, that activity was precluded by the sudden appearance of a paved road fifteen feet from my front door. Imagine my alarm. What else could I legitimately do as a gentleman? I could contact my solicitor to inquire after the progress of certain business interests in town. Damnably inconvenient for a fellow, but I have no solicitor, nor any business interests in town.

I called for a carriage, but, however, when none appeared, I walked to The Windsor Shoppe to purchase the morning periodicals. I couldn't find *The Times* or *The Observer* or even *The Tattler*. I was forced to purchase a local periodical called *The Lowell Sun*, and I can tell you I was deucedly disappointed because there was no news whatsoever of the queen, nor goings on at court, nor any humorous depictions of the Irish. The clerk inquired after my health in the quaint manner of you Lowellians. Of course, I'm incapable of duplicating the precise articulation, but it was something like, "Haza goin?"

"Exceedingly well," I said. "I thank you for your kind solicitude, my good man."

"Hey, are you a Britisher?" he asked.

"Hold your tongue you fool." Imagine addressing a peer of the realm in such a cavalier manner! I gave him such a look that he understood that another damned impertinence would result in a sharp crack from my riding crop, with which I struck my leather-booted calf by way of a shot across his bow.

I'm not given to violence, but as a gentleman I do study the art of fencing under the Italian master Umberto Carravaglio. One must always be prepared to demand satisfaction on the field when one's honor is impugned. Indeed, when I leave the house—the house— now there is a sordid sort of nomenclature for one's abode. I will no longer refer to my dwelling as *the house*. It is Essex Stairs. When I leave Essex Stairs in the morning now, I invariably kiss Lady Primrose and remind her, as if she did not already know, that "I could not love thee so much my dear, loved I not honor more." She bids me hasten my return, for how like a winter is my absence and that sort of thing.

We are planning a hunting party for Michaelmas. We will be wearing our red jackets. Oh, do join us if you are able! Since my grounds are devoid of any worthwhile game, and since horses have been banished from Lowell, we will skip the actual fox hunt, which is of little consequence. But we shall adjourn to the drawing room at Essex Stairs for cucumber sandwiches and punch, and Lady Primrose will play the piano forte and sing, "O Let Me Not Die of Love."

All the best people will be in attendance, and the conversation will be instructive. You needn't fret about any unpleasant encounters with vulgar persons. Colonel Cavendish, a most amiable if somewhat bibulous officer of the King's Own Fusiliers, will regale us with tales from some outpost of the Empire, and Lady Ellen Cavanaugh, Esquire, of The Royal Academy, will present a travelogue and slide show entitled "A Tour of the Mysterious Kingdom of Cathay."

I hear you even now, bemoaning your exclusion because you don't enjoy an independent income, or possess a vermillion jacket, or a high-waist puffed-sleeve long dress, or you haven't had the leisure to spend hours with a dancing master perfecting the Cotillion, or your parents owned a shop. Mere trifles, as is your race or religion, or lack of it.

Let me assure you that the only prerequisite for an invitation to dine at Essex Stairs with Lady Primrose and myself is that you have watched enough Masterpiece Theater, or read enough Jane Austin, or spent sufficient time in the company of Lord Grantham and those characters who always speak in perfect sentences, that your brain has become addled. You now secretly long for Britishness, and you feel more comfortable in the secure, orderly and predictable world of Regency Literature than you do in the messy, uncultivated, and pathetically democratic world we inhabit.

Confound it, here I am rambling on, and it's gone past high tea! Please accept my best wishes and allow me to bid you a good day, and we'll see you round the Stairs, shall we?

Acknowledgments

"The Dog, the Wife and the Friend"—*Lodestone Journal*

"Eschatology"—*Sobotka Literary Journal*

"St. Lucy's Day"—*Open Road Review*

"Happy to Meet, Sorry to Part"—published as "Red Shoes," *River Muse Anthology*, edited by Lloyd Corricelli and David Daniel

"September"—*Aethlon Journal of Sports Literature*

"Cast a Cold Eye"—*The Mark Review*

"Blind in Darian"—*The Font: A Literary Journal for Language Teachers*

"Jailbird"—*Rock and a Hard Place Magazine*

"Here to Stay"—*Literary Nest*

"The View from the Summit"—*The Dimeshow Review*

"What He Lived For"—*Sandy River Review*

"July 19, 1969"—*RichardHowe.com*

"Down to the Crossroads" published as "Woke Up This Mornin'" *Southern Pacific Review*

"The Goldfish"—*The Mark Literary Review*

"A Literary Evening"—*Literally Stories*

"Thy Sister's Keeper"—*RichardHowe.com*

"Austen Mania"—*Lowell Sunrise* Radio Program

I must also acknowledge Paul Marion and Rosemary Noon of Loom Press. They have been valued editors and great supporters of mine and of other writers, poets, and historians in the Merrimack Valley. I'm indebted to all the people I watched being uniquely themselves over the years, and all those who told me stories or said interesting things that found their way into my writing. Many are gone, now, and if I were to try and name them, I'd leave too many out. Thanks to Brian R. O'Connor for the fine cover art. His work can be seen on Instagram @briman_draws. Finally, thank you to my lovely wife, Olga Maria Ortiz O'Connor, our son Brian and our daughter Molly, and my siblings Rory, Ellen and Annie. And farewell to my old friend, the late Thomas J. McArdle, who once told me, "O'Connor, if you don't become a writer, I'm gonna kill you."

Notes

As I wrote "Down to the Crossroads," I had questions about chords and tunings which I directed to Jim O'Connor, (no relation), of Boston Blackthorne. He read the story and asked if he could put the lyrics I had written for Van Dinter's song to music. Anyone who is interested in hearing the result can listen to "Manville Bells" at https://www.bostonblackthorne.com/listen.

My nephew, First Sergeant Patrick M. O'Connor, USA Retired, along with his wife, Major Natalie J. O'Connor, USA Retired, served three tours of duty in Iraq and Afghanistan. Patrick told me he was never more uneasy there than he had been as a lone night watchman making his rounds through the deserted Boott Mills; his recounting of those nights gave me the idea and many of the eerie details for "Thy Sister's Keeper." The poem quoted near the end is "Weaving" by Lucy Larcom. I quoted selected lines for my purpose in the story, but the entire poem is worth reading. It is a heartfelt cry against slavery in which she refers to the cotton used to make the textiles of Lowell as "poisoned cloth," since it originates in the slave-worked fields of the South. She wonders if working in a Lowell cotton mill makes her in some way complicit: *The blot they bear is on my name/ Who sins and am I not to blame?*

The story "Jailbird" was inspired by conversations with Gary Boyle of Lowell, who made some bad mistakes in his youth and paid a hard and a long price for them in prison. Today, he's a different man, and a good one.

A Note from the Author

Loom Press published my first book of stories, *Smokestack Lightning*, in 2010. After that, I spent much of my time writing novels; I published three novels between *Smokestack* and *Northwest of Boston*, (2023). In the intervening years, a few things happened. I watched our children grow. I got older, and as the previous generation began to disappear, I often thought of the words of James Joyce: "One by one they were all becoming shades." Inevitably, these changes found their way into my writing; however, I always feel that as a storyteller my job is not only to connect emotionally with the reader, but also, to make him or her laugh, even if it's at the precariousness of our position. The reader will find stories of longing, and perhaps sadness (of course we Irish are partial to sadness), but also stories of joy and humor.

Once, when a brilliant woman who had been a professor of philosophy passed away at an early age, a cousin of mine commented, "Isn't it a shame that no one with her combination of experience, study and knowledge will ever exist again." The same is true of all of us.

I'm so thankful to have had the experience of being from a stalwart working-class family in Lowell, to have had so many interesting if sometimes crazy friends, to have had Irish grandparents and great teachers, to have fallen in love with languages and literature and music, and to have had the opportunity to study and work overseas, where I saw, from a distance, that my hometown was unique and the people I knew extraordinary; that their stories were worth telling. When I returned to the city, there were new experiences: spending time with my future wife and her Colombian family; working with immigrants from all over the world; and, eventually, marriage and fatherhood. All that any of us can do is embrace our experience, learn from it, keep growing, and, if one is a writer, transform it.